'/3

The English

YIFTACH REICHER ATIR was born in 1949 on a kibbutz in the south of Israel. As a young military officer, he participated in Operation Entebbe—the hostage-rescue operation carried out by commandos of the Israel Defense Forces at Entebbe airport, Uganda, on July 4, 1976—and in other still-classified military and intelligence operations. He retired from the military in 1995, with the rank of Brigadier General. Reicher Atir is the author of four novels; his third, *The English Teacher*—based on his firsthand experience as an intelligence officer—was a bestseller in Israel, widely acclaimed by readers and critics alike.

Praise for *The English Teacher*

One of *The Washington Post*'s 10 Best Mystery Books and Thrillers of 2016

"Compelling . . . As in the works of John le Carré and Charles McCarry, here we see that in the day-to-day spy business, it's not so much countries that are in danger but individual human souls."

—*The Washington Post*

"The time is right for this astonishing thriller. . . . Though facts have been masked by censors for security reasons, the emotional and psychological elements ring true." —*Library Journal*

"Reicher Atir writes with poetic authority of the bleak isolation that pervades the life of the spy long after their active existence is over. This black yet strangely beautiful tragedy will stay with me for a long time." —Alex Marwood

"[Reicher Atir] provides an astonishing look at Middle Eastern spy-craft." —*The Denver Post*

"An extraordinary page–turner, told with clarity, insight, and compassion, *The English Teacher* offers a rare and realistic portrait of the unrelenting sacrifices of living a double life." —Gideon Raff

"[Yiftach Reicher Atir] probes how leading a double life can erode the foundations of a spy's former existence; how all of the lies are rooted in truth, and the truth, especially when it comes to love, is often coated with a patina of lies . . . Masterful." —*The Times of Israel*

"The book . . . does exactly what a novel of its kind should do: re-examine the Mossad. Throughout the book . . . doubts are cast on personal as well as national morality. . . . Reicher Atir seeks to pinpoint the fine line separating the moral actions that operatives perform for their country and their own exploitation." —*Ha'aretz*

The English Teacher

YIFTACH REICHER ATIR

TRANSLATED FROM THE HEBREW
BY PHILIP SIMPSON

PENGUIN BOOKS

PENGUIN BOOKS

An imprint of Penguin Random House LLC
375 Hudson Street
New York, New York 10014
penguin.com

Copyright © 2013 by Yiftach Reicher Atir
Translation copyright © 2016 by Yiftach Reicher Atir
Penguin supports copyright. Copyright fuels creativity, encourages diverse voices, promotes free speech, and creates a vibrant culture. Thank you for buying an authorized edition of this book and for complying with copyright laws by not reproducing, scanning, or distributing any part of it in any form without permission. You are supporting writers and allowing Penguin to continue to publish books for every reader.

Originally published in Hebrew by Keter Books, Israel.

"The Remains of Life" from *The Remains of Life* by Lea Goldberg, translated by Rachel Tzvia Back. Used by permission of the publisher, Sifriat Poalim and Rachel Tzvia Back.

LIBRARY OF CONGRESS CATALOGING-IN-PUBLICATION DATA
Names: Reicher Atir, Yiftach, author.
Title: The English teacher : a novel / Yiftach R. Atir ; translated by Philip Simpson.
Other titles: Morah le-Anglit. English
Description: New York : Penguin Books, 2016.
Identifiers: LCCN 2015049266 | ISBN 9780143129189 (paperback)
Subjects: LCSH: Women spies—Israel—Fiction. | Intelligence officers—Israel—Fiction. | Israel. Mosad le-modi°in òve-tafòkidim meyuòhadim—Fiction. | BISAC: FICTION / Espionage. | FICTION / Mystery & Detective / General. | GSAFD: Spy stories | Suspense fiction
Classification: LCC PJ5055.39.E42 M6713 2016 | DDC 892.43/7—dc23

Printed in the United States of America
3   5   7   9   10   8   6   4

Set in Dante MT   •   Designed by Elke Sigal

Already the silences are easier.
   The light is bright.
   When there's no road to travel
   there's no fear of borders.
   And there's nothing to reveal
   when there's nothing to hide.

—Lea Goldberg, *The Remains of Life*
Translated by Rachel Tzvia Back

A Note on the Text

THE BOOK YOU ARE HOLDING IN your hands is the true story of what never happened.

This is the story of a Mossad operative. She and others like her operate alone for extended periods of time, deep in enemy countries. Unlike their front-line soldier counterparts, these secret soldiers are armed with nothing but a foreign passport, a fake identity, extensive training, and inexplicable courage.

Being an IDF intelligence officer for many years, I came to know these operatives intimately. I assigned them missions; I followed their progress as they lived their strange and dangerous undercover lives; I marveled at the missions they completed; and, anxiously, I awaited their eventual safe return home.

And I wondered, What is it like to live a secret life among one's enemies for months and years? I knew what it was like to be in battle and to cross borders in the night to execute military operations; I had no idea what it would be like to live across those borders. How does one deal with the ever-present fear, and the great loneliness? And what happens to the heart?

This story is the result of those wonderings.

This book spent many months with the Israeli civilian and military censorship committees; numerous changes and omissions were imposed, until the book was approved for publication.

And so, this is a true story, of real-life operatives that are wholly made-up, and actual missions that never happened.

There is one woman, an undercover soldier in the past and a scholar in the present, to whom I owe a special thanks. I take this opportunity to thank her and all the operatives I have known, and those I don't know; *The English Teacher* is dedicated to them all.

BG (RET) YIFTACH REICHER ATIR

The English Teacher

꙳

CHAPTER ONE

London

IN A DREAM THAT SHE LOVED to remember she's standing in the kitchen of her house and preparing supper. The window faces the little garden and she watches her son, who sits on the swing and waves to her. There's no one in the house, and she doesn't mind waiting. She knows who she's waiting for. She hears the creaking of the hinges of the old swing, the roar of the cars racing down the road, and the tapping of the knife on the chopping board. The din of a world carrying on as usual.

Sitting now for the first time in her father's chair, Rachel closed her eyes to get a clearer view of the child. She wanted to know who he resembled. Every child has a father, hers included. Suddenly this became urgent, as if this was the last time.

She remembers the dream. Sometimes she wakes up with it in the morning and sometimes she returns to it in the course of the day, and her son, whom she sees clearly amid the darkness that she imposes on herself, looks like her alone, and now he's standing by the door that opens on the garden, isolated in his orphanhood. Rachel opened her eyes and wanted to get up and lead him to the swing, which was still waiting, rusty and unclaimed, in the neglected garden. But the dream disappears, and with it her son.

She leaned back, pressed against the thick wooden support, gripped the arms of the chair with both hands, ready to stand up and tackle the business that awaited her, but in the end she nestled in the chair, which was now hers, facing the photograph that the principal of the school had brought in from the faculty room and placed on the mantelpiece. The black ribbon crossed it diagonally, like a mark of distinction that someone had added to it in haste, and her father looked out at her with a severe expression, as he was and as he liked to be seen, with brows and lips tensed. Even the color photograph added no light to him. And suddenly he seemed to be smiling as he looked at her, something in his eyes telling her she was now indeed free, but a different obligation, new and more dangerous than the ones he had imposed, was unfolding for her.

The house was quiet. The shivah, the seven days of mourning, had passed, and the rabbi explained that his children couldn't do without their bedtime story, apologized, and left. She closed the door behind him and listened to his footsteps that pounded the pavement like tom-tom drums. There was no need for a codebook or for psychological insights to tell her that this time she was really alone. There was no one left in the world whose criticism might upset her, whose angry silence would make her obsess about what she was doing, or not doing, whose smile could light up her day, from whom a compliment was the thing that she longed for in vain.

She stood up and approached the artificial hearth. Her father thought it was a waste of time and money to fetch logs and light fires in the house, and he made do with an electric heater with coils disguised as flames. Rachel didn't switch on the heater despite the cold permeating the room, because it still seemed to her that she was in his sanctuary, in a place where she didn't belong, and from which at any moment she might be expelled. On the mantelpiece there was also a picture of her, standing between her parents on her eighteenth birthday; it was the last photograph of the three of them together. Beside it someone—her father, perhaps—had placed a portrait of her mother, in a black frame. Half a year later the cancer defeated her, and Rachel remembered, as if it were yesterday, how just a few days after Mother was gone she told him that she too was leaving, and going to Israel.

She studied the forced smiles, hers and her mother's, and the look in her father's eyes, ranging far beyond the photographer. He seemed to be scanning the skies, as if he were making sure that they too were in good order, they had done their homework. In the picture there was a little shadow on the wall, the fruit of a London sun that probably had put in a special appearance only for him, and Rachel thought that now that he was no more, his shadow would disappear too and she would have light and shade of her own.

֍

RACHEL RETURNED TO THE CHAIR AND ran her hands across the smooth wooden arms. She traced with a fingertip the marks left behind by his fingernails. She had the nagging feeling that she was peeping at him, like in the days when he told her not to open drawers. "Nothing here is locked," he said, "you have to believe me and I have to trust you." You know, Dad, she answers him silently now, even an open drawer can remain closed. Even something that is clear to everyone can still hide everything.

The old phone rang. As she picked up the Bakelite receiver she pictured her father sitting in the armchair glancing at an obsolete TV set. He had refused to get a cell phone. "No one ever calls me," he said, and she knew he meant her, "and I have no one to call," his words scratching her heart just as he scratched the arms of the chair. The rabbi was calling. He asked if he could do anything for her, and would she be coming to the synagogue on the Sabbath. "I knew your mother too, what a wonderful woman she was," and he regretted that her parents couldn't be buried side by side, making no reference to her father's refusal to pay for a joint cemetery plot. After the phone call, she huddled in the chair as if trying to hide there. "My father died," she said aloud. The words sounded to her sad and strange, as if someone else were saying them, and at the same time they were so familiar.

Just three words. Three words that were a wall between her and everything that had been hers. She said them for the first time fifteen years ago. Ehud was sitting beside her then, going through all the possibilities with her, and he guided her when it came to choosing the tone and the words themselves. He insisted on carrying out the exercise, and she contacted him on the internal line and said in a soft voice suffused with tears, "My father is dead." Ehud played the role of principal of the language school and he spoke English with an Arab accent that at any other time would have made her laugh. He expressed his sympathy and asked when she would be coming back. She ignored the question. Then she said she didn't know where she would be spending the next few days. He asked for a phone number, and she promised to get in touch again once she had located herself somewhere and would give him the details. She didn't give him an address either, with the excuse that she planned to travel soon and anyway she would be staying in hotels.

A few minutes later, when she was ready, it was time for the real phone call. She looked out through the window at the Milan Cathedral, took a deep breath, and dialed a number in the Arab capital. The conversation flowed. The principal wanted to know where she was and expressed his concern at her sudden disappearance. She interrupted him: "Something terrible happened. My father died." "I'm so sorry, Rachel," said the principal, and he asked if he could help. No detail was divulged beyond what had been rehearsed from the start. "There are so many things I need to do. Send them all my love, and give my last salary check to the library at the refugee camp." "Rachel, where are you speaking from?" She didn't answer him; she knew how to evade an unwanted question, and she turned to look at Ehud, who was listening to them on another extension. "My father didn't suffer at all," she said to steer the conversation back on course. She wanted to say more. To ask the principal to pass on her message to him, that she had no alternative, that if it had been up to her she would have chosen something else, that she promises to contact him soon. But Ehud's expression, and the code she was bound to, made it clear to her that this bridge too had been burnt.

RACHEL PUT HER ELBOWS ON THE table and tried to come to terms with the sense of déjà vu that enwrapped her like a fishing net. Once again she needs to contact the school and announce that her father is deceased, again they will express condolences that they don't really mean, and again she'll realize that no one expects her to return. There, in the large and yet so homey Arab capital, he was hers, and she abandoned him because she had no choice. And in Israel? In the school where she's teaching now, and in the nondescript apartment in which she's chosen to live? Who is waiting for her? Who really knows who she is and what her father was to her? She can't explain to any of them, not to any of her acquaintances, how profound grief is blending with the feeling of liberation.

And again there is only one person left with whom she can speak. She looked for Ehud's number on her cell phone and picked up the old receiver to listen to the dial tone. Once, alert to whether the phone was bugged, she used to listen for other sounds. Once, long ago, ancient history, she would walk into the apartment and immediately think of where the eavesdropping equipment could be hidden. She held on to the receiver until the sound changed from a pleasant and enticing purr to a truncated and irritating buzz, and she wondered what she would actually say to Ehud after so many years and across the sea of disappointment that separates them. Ehud will make an effort to understand her, this she knows for sure. He will also listen to her with the attentiveness that she loved so much, and he'll suggest solutions that she could have found for herself if she had only taken the trouble to think the way he did. This was another world, a world in which there were people like Ehud. For some of them in the Unit she was just a sophisticated implement nicknamed Fairy. For those who met her in the Arab countries she was Rachel Brooks or any other name that served her purposes at the time.

She replaced the receiver back in its cradle. Ehud could wait. He's used to this. "Our job," he used to tell her when she asked him how he manages to sit in a hotel room day after day, "comprises ten percent activity and ninety percent waiting." He promised her he would wait, and that she could rely on him, always.

The clock chimed. Her father wound it every evening before going to bed, and she kept it up through the days of the shivah. She isn't taking it with her. She isn't taking anything from here. In the city that once was hers and also in Tel Aviv it's already midnight. In London only ten o'clock. All that remains is to get through the night, and then . . . then what? Arrangements. Things to be done, things to be forgotten. When she sells her father's apartment nothing will be left from her past.

"You'll be set up for life," she was assured by the energetic real estate agent, who mentioned her father's death only in passing and then talked a lot about how much the house would sell for. And her mother's grave awaits her at the other end of the cemetery. She hasn't been to her mother's grave since her funeral, and she shivered when she thought of the neglect that surrounds death and its aftermath.

She climbed the narrow staircase, went into the room that was once hers, and turned on the light. The posters were still hanging on the wall, and Jim Morrison and the Doors remained as young as ever. They were the only ones. On the tidy bed was the dust of years, and she realized that her father had never been in here. Rachel went out of the room, closed the door, and approached his bedroom on tiptoe as if afraid of waking him. "Even though he was working as a volunteer, I knew Michael would never miss a day's work," the school principal told her, and described in exhaustive detail, which embarrassed her, how he telephoned her father again and again and then took a taxi at his own expense and knocked on the door, in vain, and called the police department, and they found him peacefully in bed, a young seventy-three-year-old and generally in good health. "I'd like to go the same way—a cerebral hemorrhage and passing on to a world that's all good," said the principal, and he forced a smile. The cleaning service that she called in and the neighbor from across the way had tidied the apartment, but the bed remained as it was, the depression in the pillow seeming to call out for a hand to plump it up.

She opened the drawers only with her fingertips. She glanced at the matching socks and underwear that she knew she would never find the strength to put into bags, and inspected the few suits and the bright white shirts still hanging in the wardrobe. Nothing to indicate that he wouldn't need them anymore. She opened the drawer of personal items and closed it right away, afraid she might find something that would confuse her, that would change what she thought of her father. She told herself there would yet be time for this, that eventually she must sit down and confront the memories and sort them one by one. She moved to the bathroom, but didn't open the medicine cabinet. On the sink, his toothbrush was in a cup with head uppermost. Like in her apartment, only one toothbrush.

"Goodbye, Dad, I'm going," she whispered as she closed the door of his room behind her, remembering that this was what she said then, when she was nineteen, after she packed her bag and was about to go. He told her she needed to stay and finish her studies, find a job, otherwise nothing would become of her, as it had been with her mother, of blessed memory. "So nothing became of me, Dad?" she asked now, louder, and her voice resonated around the house. "I'm not a teacher, just like you?" And as soon as the house was silent again and only the racket of a passing car rattled the windowpanes and reminded her there was life beyond the walls of the house, she thought of the questions she hadn't asked him, of the simple sentence she didn't say to him, and he didn't say to her.

Through the glass of the back door the little garden was visible, neglected since her mother died. Everything so calm, as if through the silence her father, buried just a few streets from where he was born, from the place where he lived, is trying to tell her: only here can she have a home and a garden and a little boy running around outside.

Rachel stood in her father's study, facing the mirror that he hung there to check that his tie was correct and his hair was parted right. A long face, as if not belonging to her, was reflected back to her. The tousled hair, cascading over an old nightgown that she found in one of the closets, reminded her of when she was twelve, dreaming the usual dreams of a girl that age: to be the most beautiful woman in the universe, with a prince on a white horse waiting for her to return.

Through a skylight window, the early dawn was paling and giving way to morning. She stood, arms folded on her chest, and tried to believe that this was an embrace she had long deserved. Then she dug her nails into her bare arms, tried to make it hurt, tried to open new paths for the sorrow that she could not summon. This was the time to cry, and she couldn't. This was the time to hold on to memories, and she didn't want to. Every corner of the house reminded her of something; no corner of the house reminded her of anything that she wanted to take with her. Everything too late. Even forgiveness was impossible to seek. No one left from whom to seek it.

A first ray of sunlight fell on the bookcase, and it was only then that Rachel noticed something a trained eye like hers should have seen long before. No dust. No dust on the spine of the book that he had touched recently. She turned on the desk lamp and pulled out the book, a volume of an encyclopedia, and saw the box that her father had hidden behind it.

❦

SHE READ THE LETTERS THAT EHUD had sent her father. Her mistake blew up in her face. Everything now took on a different shape. Fragments of memory, excerpts from phone conversations. His ostentatious lack of interest in her cover stories, in the lies that she recited to him as if she'd learned them by heart.

A new feeling was coming over her. Not anger. It was too late to be angry. Not sorrow either. She was too sad to let a new sorrow into her life. Even the sense of grievance, the knowledge that they had spoken to her father behind her back, she deferred for another time.

Suddenly, clearly, she knew that she wanted no more of this. No more lies, no more cover stories, no more perfectly crafted tales piled high, like fortified walls built to separate her from the world; she wanted to let the outside world *in*, to let it touch her in a real way. She longed to uncover herself at long last, expose herself, until the truth seared her.

The small fire in the garden didn't attract attention, and it may be assumed that no one on the train passing close to the fence took notice of the slim woman sitting on a swing, watching papers burn.

꧁

CHAPTER TWO

Israel, Two Days Later

THE PHONE RANG. EHUD COUNTED THREE rings and waited for the answering machine to ask the caller to leave a message. Only then would he decide whether to carry on tending the bushes that he had neglected recently or go into the house and answer whoever was daring to call him before six in the morning. The old machine kicked in but the anonymous caller didn't say anything and hung up. Ehud shrugged and resumed trimming the recalcitrant branches. His back was hurting, and he reminded himself it was time to pick up the prescriptions from the pharmacy and not neglect the exercises and the diet.

If it's important they'll try again, he thought, then turned the words over in his head and knew why he was thinking *they* and not he or she. Only *they* were in the habit of making contact at any hour and in any place, and they always expected him to follow standard procedure—lift the receiver after the third ring and hang up immediately and pick up when they call again only after the fifth ring. But all of that had come to an end many years ago, and it was only back pain and a troublesome bladder that kept him awake at night.

All the same, he came inside, to be closer, to be ready next time. He washed his hands and watched the mud submit to the water and swirl around the sink and then disappear. The clock on the wall told him it was coffee time. Rina, who rejoiced in his retirement, used to tell him to leave the plants in peace and let them enjoy a little tranquility. But Rina isn't here, and his sons are far away. His work recedes further from him, the phone no longer rings, and Ehud tries to convince himself that he's content.

Since his wife died he has made a point of going out every day to the little garden at the back of the house and working there until breakfast. The habit became a duty, the duty became a pleasure, an intermission, and a time to remember the things he loved. The flowers bloomed in their turn, the vegetation flourished, and life went on in its own way. His grandchildren used to frolic on the lawn, and Ehud loved to hear from his daughters-in-law how gifted a gardener he was, and he waited in vain for his sons to offer their help. The garden was green throughout the year. He would sit beside the bushes with the breakfast tray and watch the insects at work, the shadows that the sun pulls from one side to the other as it moves, the changing colors of the chameleon. Ehud kept quiet when he saw him lying in wait for his prey, admired the use of the long tongue, and couldn't resist admonishing him aloud whenever he was slow matching his cover to his surroundings.

Ehud began to prepare salad for one. Tomato, two cucumbers, green onion, a pinch of basil, olive oil, and a few black olives. At lunchtime he will eat soup and in the evening prepare himself something else. And so it is day after day, as retirement demands, as his older colleagues recommended, as his sons insisted. Everything was ready on the antique wooden tray that he bought with Rina in Florence: the plate of salad, a little white cheese, half a buttered roll (the other half he kept for the ten o'clock snack), and a glass of water with ice and lemon. Coffee from the machine that his children bought him for his sixtieth birthday he'll drink later, when he opens the paper. The phone rang again.

He recognized the voice right away. The soft accent, the fear that perhaps he won't remember her, the hesitant mode of speech. It was all there. All those years she had talked to him and he understood what she meant. All those years when he needed to measure every word, in case an enemy was listening, because every word is important, because her life depends on this. And then, after she returned from there, and after she left the Unit, they continued to talk from time to time. He would contact her as if on a casual basis, just to know how she was faring, and he sensed the nervousness in his voice, the anticipation and the hope that perhaps she'll tell him to come. This didn't happen—as it shouldn't have. So long as Rina was alive. So long as he needed to abide by the rules. But the rules say what they have to say, while the heart says what it wants. And when Rina fell ill it was over. And now he's standing in a corner of his house, holding the receiver with a trembling hand, and listening to her. "My father died," she said, and before he could answer she added, "He died for the second time." The broken, truncated sound told him the conversation was over. He waited another moment and tried dialing caller ID and was told the line was blocked. He looked in his old contacts book and phoned her home and her cell phone. Despite the early hour there was no response.

Ehud took the tray outside and ate slowly, as if he knew how long it would be before he could sit here again and eat breakfast in solitude. He glanced at his handiwork, as if assessing what he stood to lose, and then he phoned the Office and went to pack a small suitcase.

⚜

THE UNIT COMMANDER LEANED BACK IMPATIENTLY and his powerful body filled the chair that had been specially adapted for him after the injury. His back was definitely hurting and Ehud, who had read in the paper about the exchange of fire between unknown assailants and the bodyguards of the Iranian banker, was impressed by the commander's return to work just a month after the foiled assassination, but he didn't say a word. If the commander wants, he'll tell him about it himself. Ehud remembered the rules. The need to know is what counts. On the wall facing him hung pictures of former unit commanders, and he moved his glance from one to the other and compared them with the young man who sat before him. The commander was different from them, fruit of a different era. At the time of the Six-Day War he was a child, and Eli Cohen was for him just the name of a street and a painful chapter in the history of the Mossad.

"I need Joe," Ehud said when he saw they were all waiting for him to speak. "Which Joe?" asked the commander, and his assistant fiddled with the personal computer in front of him. "Yakov Peled," said Ehud. His eyes moved toward the photo on the wall and the Unit commander also turned to look at it, his eyes narrowing as he noted how many years ago Yakov Peled had sat at the head of the table. "And he knows her?" the commander asked, nothing in his voice showing whether he remembered anything besides the name and the nickname. "To the best of my memory he was outside the service years before she was recruited." "Correct," said Ehud, "but he knows me."

Aware that they had no choice, Ehud waited patiently. When he talked about Joe they didn't know who he was referring to. Only the real veterans, those who turn up even in wheelchairs at retirement parties, knew his nickname and had been privileged to work with him. The younger ones heard lectures from Yakov Peled on the establishment of the Unit and of those glory days, and jealously read accounts of the successes of the master spy who gave up the role of chief of the Mossad to go into business. If there's a need for it, Ehud will explain to the commander on a one-to-one basis that Joe was his mentor in the Unit, that he needed someone he could rely on. It was clear to him that the commander didn't want to broaden the circle of those who were in on the secret, and to him this whole episode was a pain in the ass. Rachel left the Unit before he arrived and he hadn't heard of her until this morning. But this was a mission like many others, and no harder than finding and bringing in Vanunu, the traitor who revealed Israeli nuclear secrets. This was what the commander said at the start of the discussion, and although Ehud was offended by the comparison he knew that it was hard to argue with.

"All right," said the commander as he noted something on the pad of yellow paper familiar to Ehud from the old days. "I agree, I'm giving you a free hand, and you'll be liaising with the war room." The commander turned to look at the head of the operations department, who nodded his assent. Ehud wondered about their working relationship, and he assumed that the veteran department chief had already submitted the plan and that the meeting was a display for Ehud's benefit, a respectful gesture to someone who was once a part of the organization and might now be indispensable.

The commander looked at him, his lips curling cynically. "I don't know what you're planning, but I trust that you want her to come back in one piece." Ehud felt a stab of pain and suppressed the impulse to respond. There would be time for that. For now, he was satisfied with how things were working out.

"I've always believed that the paved road isn't necessarily the right one to take," the commander continued, pleased with the image,

and then he told Ehud that the war room was operational and all special measures had been activated. There was an all-out search for this
one woman who threatened to become a loose cannon.

"All right," said Ehud, though he didn't know what the commander was referring to.

"And another thing," said the commander, and he pointed to a
young man wearing a blue T-shirt, in contrast to the collared and
buttoned shirts of his superiors. "Yaniv will be liaison between you
and the war room. He was her contact man in the Office." Ehud didn't
say anything. It seemed strange to him that these young people barely
out of diapers were assigned to look after operatives who had left
years ago. But times had changed and he was on the outside now;
eons had passed since he was part of the inner circle.

The commander added, "Update me directly if you find anything, and don't stay up too late working. It isn't healthy at your age."
Yaniv smiled. Ehud felt sorry for him. He still needs to curry favor
with his boss. His career depends on it.

"Since you contacted us we've had time to do some checks." The
commander opened his laptop, turned it toward Ehud, and took him
through a well-prepared PowerPoint presentation. He assumed it had
been designed for the Mossad chief and perhaps for the Prime Minister too. And all to explain to them how this ex-operative, holding
some of the most important secrets of the State of Israel close to her
heart, had simply disappeared after attending her father's funeral. Of
course, the commander isn't under any pressure, and he'll only do the
maximum, yes, the maximum, to bring her back home. "Dead or
alive," he said to Ehud, and laughed.

And why shouldn't he laugh? Why not try to stay loose even as
they were all pissing in their pants? Why not create the impression
that things are under control? This didn't happen on his watch. It isn't

his responsibility. He's just come to rescue the commanders of the past from the mess that they caused when they enabled Rachel to live her own life and paid no attention to what their operative had been doing after leaving the service. "I don't even know who she is," said the commander, as the screen showed two pictures of Rachel taken from old passports. Ehud looked and kept silent as the commander's words reverberated in his head: "Wanted: Dead or Alive."

"Of course, everything is open to you," the commander added, "the archive, operations room, communications center, everything you ask for. This operation is Priority A, and if you need additional personnel for surveillance, kidnap, or something more drastic . . ." He left a deliberate pause, and Ehud realized he had already reported to the Mossad chief and the Prime Minister and obtained the authorizations needed for any appropriate action.

⚜

AT AROUND TWELVE O'CLOCK YANIV AND Ehud entered the archive. Ehud glanced at his watch impatiently and scanned the shelves. Yaniv asked how they were going to get through all the material and what were they actually looking for. "How long has she been missing?" Ehud asked instead of answering. "A week at least," Yaniv replied. "We know she left this country with her Israeli passport, and after the shivah there's been no trace of her. We sent someone to the apartment with the estate agent. He went from room to room and found an up-to-date tourist brochure for India. Hard to draw conclusions from this, but perhaps that's the direction. We also checked the call that you received. It was on a Belgian phone card. The phone was apparently bought at the airport, with calls prepaid. Then the people we approached"—Ehud noticed that Yaniv was holding back whatever he could—"established that she used her British passport to leave England. We asked certain associates of ours to check out the airlines, where she went to, and with whom, and then it turned out she crossed the Channel by train, but they don't keep any record of onward destinations. We checked for transactions on her credit card and bank account. We're not sure how she got her bank to clear it, but she transferred close to a hundred thousand dollars to England, and the money was withdrawn from the Western Union office in Leicester Square. We sent our representative there, but needless to say they don't remember anything. That's what we have up to now." Ehud suppressed a smile. She hasn't forgotten, he told himself. She still knows the job.

They lingered beside a low shelf. Gray files filled to bursting were lined up, tied together in pairs with ancient string and covered in dust. Obviously no one had touched them in years, and only firm regulations going back to the last century had deterred some efficient clerk from sending them away for incineration. At the end of the row there was an apparently new file, noticeably slimmer than the others. Yaniv pulled it out and proudly showed Ehud how they were keeping in touch with former operatives. Ehud glanced at reports of medical exams that the department asked Rachel to undergo every year, and at letters politely declining invitations to retirement parties.

Someone had numbered the files and marked in black felt-tip the years they had been opened and closed. "Here you'll find the answer," Ehud said to Yaniv, and he pointed to the files that documented her service in the Arab country. Yaniv nodded. Despite his age and his lack of experience, he also knew these were the crucial years of her life. Fifteen years had passed since Rachel came back from there, and in the archive there were also files documenting her handling since she left, but only there, at the country of destination, were the real clues to what would later be revealed. Ehud thought of the astonishingly small number of operatives involved in that mission, of the "perfect" people, individuals capable of spending many years in a hostile country, constructing their cover stories and living them when in action and between assignments. Who knows what happens to the solitary operative, all those days and nights in a strange and tough environment? And what he will do if one day agents of the opposition's counterintelligence approach him and offer him a deal that will save his life? Betrayal? Ehud didn't dare say the word aloud, but it had haunted him since the moment he noticed the looks exchanged between the commander and Yaniv. And if she had betrayed, he thought as he looked downward to hide his now-tearful eyes from Yaniv, then she betrayed him, Ehud, who was like a father to her, the one who loved her secretly, the one who perhaps turned his back on her.

He opened one of the files and riffled through it, and a picture fell from an open envelope. Rachel bent over and stroking the back of a pigeon in St. Mark's Square. He remembered that trip to Venice. He remembered other trips too. It seemed he remembered everything. Meetings, journeys, hired cars, wayside cafés, shops, briefings, and above all the partings, the "good night" before turning to their separate rooms, the lingering look following her tall figure as she disappeared behind her door.

⚘

"WHAT DO YOU THINK HAPPENED TO her?" he asked Yaniv as they entered the modern war room and sat on the chairs marked with their names. A young clerk offered them coffee, and a technician leaned toward Ehud and offered to help him work the computer. "Don't be afraid to ask," Yaniv said when Ehud looked nervously at all the new technology and then back at the clerk, who smiled at him. "I've heard a lot about you," she said, and went on to explain that her mother used to work in the Unit. She mentioned the name, which Ehud didn't remember, but this didn't mean anything. His memory these days was letting him down often, too often.

"And what do you think happened to her?" he repeated, and let Yaniv talk about Rachel, about meetings with her, about her little apartment in Rehovot, the school, and about the private lessons she used to give here and there. "Do you think it's possible that after the funeral she went off with one of the students? A fling with someone?" Ehud asked.

"I don't think so," said Yaniv, a serious expression on his young face. "I've been monitoring her for the past five years. She's okayed every trip with us. This is something else."

"I also think there's something more dangerous here," said someone who had entered the war room by a side door, and Ehud wondered how long he had been standing behind them. Yaniv introduced Ehud to the chief security officer, and the two of them disliked each other at first sight. He was short, years younger than Ehud, but also the veteran head of a department who didn't like being contradicted. "Security trumps everything," he tended to say, and he didn't want to hear any other opinion. They all knew he did his job conscientiously, and when the day came and promotion was discussed, he would be promoted ahead of the others, ahead of those who think that a coin has two sides.

"Have you been to her flat?" Ehud asked.

The chief security officer smiled scornfully and surveyed with pleasure the group of people sitting there in the room, engrossed in the assignment they had been given only this morning. What does he know, this old man? thought the chief to himself. He had a search warrant an hour after Ehud called in. "We didn't find anything. A simple apartment, a little too orderly. One toothbrush. The place of a person who lives alone. We didn't find a safe, apparently there wasn't one. We didn't find drugs, apparently there weren't any. We found the life-signs of a normal woman who needs to work on her standards of cleanliness." He leaned back in the chair in which he sat like the lord of the manor and patted his paunch with a self-satisfied air. He didn't like outside teams being brought in, didn't like being bypassed or forced to work with people he didn't know, people who questioned his authority, who didn't rely on him and defer to him. But he had no choice. He had never met Rachel and didn't know her file, although his job description required that he meet all operatives who had spent long periods of time in Arab countries, even those who had retired. "It's essential to know the operatives of the past," was the emphatic statement. "There aren't so many of them." He himself used to say there is no substitute for personal acquaintance, but he had no time. Meetings gobbled up his time. Excursions abroad kept him busy, and his second wife was demanding her rights as well.

Ehud had no intention of trying to convince the chief security officer that there was some point in an additional visit to the apartment. He didn't want to use the authority he had been granted and the black plastic card that Yaniv gave him when they left the commander's office, but now he enjoyed pulling the card from his wallet and flaunting it before the staring eyes of the security officer. "I'm licensed for everything except killing."

"You know," said the chief security officer before they went their separate ways, "maybe her move to Rehovot is somehow connected with the Weizmann Institute. Don't forget that after she returned Rachel was assigned to the biological weapons department, and she sometimes visited the laboratories at Weizmann. Don't forget everything she learned from us, what a talented operative can get from the observation of routine actions. Who knows what she's still capable of doing?"

⚘

EHUD CLIMBED INTO JOE'S NEW MERCEDES. The soft leather seats invited him to relax, but he was too tense to give in to the small fripperies that Joe's wealth enabled him to offer. He waited patiently while his friend slowly set the car in motion and said, as if continuing a conversation that began many years before: "And perhaps she's just gone out of her mind. Perhaps everything was too much for her. The years that go by, the mirror that doesn't lie, and the glory left behind. I met her after she left and she told me she didn't want any more contact with the Unit. We sat in a café and I told her about my children and she didn't have anything to say. 'Work, work, work,' was her answer when I asked her about her life, and I saw she already wanted to go. We had nothing to talk about, because our friendship and whatever else was between us was only about her operations. Sometimes I think that's the way it should be, maybe it's wrong to develop any other kinds of relationships and there's no point taking an interest in what your operative is doing after you part company. I think of the years we were together and search my memory and I can't remember what we talked about. Maybe I don't want to remember. Memory is so selective. It chooses on its own what to ignore and what to retain."

Ehud took from his briefcase the two photographs that Yaniv supplied and studied them with Joe, who pulled up at the roadside. The Shabak, the Israeli Security Agency, required a photograph of Rachel before her visit to the Prime Minister's house sixteen years ago.

"There's no choice," the man on the phone had told him, "we need an up-to-date photograph for identification and confirmation. We too have rules that we need to comply with."

Ehud was adamant that he didn't want a photograph of his operative going to another organization. Even the Shabak could make mistakes. "I trust you," he said in a final attempt at persuasion, "and I know you're incomparable when it comes to keeping your secrets." He stressed the word *your*. "But even you don't know where this picture might end up." Ehud went on without waiting for the expected promise that everything would be kept in a secure file: "Think of the people in the archive. They travel abroad too sometimes, don't they? Imagine that one of them sees her somewhere; who can promise me that he won't point her out or approach her just for a moment, to say job well done?"

"You don't trust us?" He heard the rising resentment. But she was his responsibility and he had no intention of backing down, and the secure line enabled him to say what he wanted: "She's working undercover. She has a foreign passport."

"Without a picture there's no entry," said the voice, and the line went dead. Ehud knew he was being overprotective. The Shabak had rules of its own, and the head of the Mossad wouldn't want to become embroiled in another petty dispute with his colleague.

Rachel, sixteen years younger, looks at the camera. Her eyes were brown from the contact lenses she wears when she has to get her picture taken, and the wig flatters her face, lending it an enigmatic beauty.

Ehud started to tell Joe about her meeting with the Prime Minister, but Joe cut him off, said there would be time for that, and asked to see the other picture. The chief security officer brought it from her apartment, and Ehud wondered why she had kept it, and whether her operational skills were forgotten. Rachel stares with narrowed eyes in a mug shot inserted into a ski pass. A tag attached to the plastic card gave the name of the resort, and Ehud realized that he didn't know she had learned to ski. In training they taught her how to avoid the camera and how to leave behind her as few pictures as possible, and yet here, many years later, apparently this no longer mattered to her. Or apparently so she thought, and she was wrong. This picture would help them to track her down, would be useful to the search and surveillance teams in the field.

And there were also other pictures that had been filed in the department. There were only a few, since Rachel knew how not to appear in the center of the picture. And when photographs arrived showing her on tourist beaches or against the background of some ancient site, with a clear view of the military installation behind her, the security officer blotted out her figure with black ink. Only a very few are allowed to know the identity of the one gathering the information that will give renown to others while she remains in obscurity, in the shadows.

"We all change," said Joe, and he pointed to the differences between the pictures. Ehud nodded. He had never thought he was handsome, he battled weight gain with both determination and frequent frustration. But he too was young once. His hair, already thinning, was combed back in those days, and Rina told him that his face reflected an intriguing inner strength. And now? Now he's sixty-five, with little hair remaining on his head. He peered at Joe, who was back on the road and driving slowly and cautiously. Ehud had heard about the onset of Parkinson's, but he didn't offer to take over the driving. They had been together on more dangerous assignments than this one, and he was not about to insult the man who recruited him into the Unit.

"Give me the basic details again," Joe requested, and Ehud, who knew the importance of setting out every problem simply, explained that Rachel didn't inform the Unit she was going to her father's funeral. This was contrary to protocol and contrary to the document she had signed the day she left, normal procedure incumbent on anyone who had been party to secret information while on the staff. The chief security officer showed him the paper and said that just because of this she could cause punitive losses to her retirement pension. The phone conversation was the first and only contact with her, and it was only because he called the Office that the alarm was raised and the war room became operational. Joe asked about money and Ehud apologized for forgetting and told him about the withdrawal she had made in London. "What passport is she using?" Joe asked. "All by the book," said Ehud. "She left using her Israeli passport, entered and left England with her British passport. More than this, we don't know." He wanted to tell him that the Unit commander had already sent a team to look for her in India, but Joe was busy parking the car behind a commercial van at the end of the street, and Ehud wasn't sure that at seventy-five Joe could handle two things at once.

⚜

THE TEAM COMMANDER, BRIEFED ABOUT THEIR arrival, approached them when they finally got out of the car. He pointed out for them the white van of the cleaning company and the young men in blue overalls. They were trained, orderly, and didn't skip any detail, not even the apparently careless driver and the two middle-aged women, ideal camouflage for the job they needed to do. The team commander signaled to his men and they unpacked their cleaning equipment and prepared to set to work. Ehud watched them. They were professionals. You could sense this, but he wondered what else they were capable of beyond breaking into any place quietly and doing the job and leaving without a trace. They know how to search too, no doubt about that. They could find the needle in a haystack. You just need to tell them what to look for. He saw the commander checking his watch as he gave final instructions to the security team. "There's no need for all this," he said to the commander. "The probability that Rachel will suddenly return from a shopping trip or from a morning run is so remote, you can tell the couple sitting on the bench to go, and the moving van at the corner might as well leave too. Think of the budget."

"No one will suspect people your age," said the team commander snidely, signaling Ehud not to interfere. He gave them the number of the apartment, and one of the young men opened the door of the building. As they walked slowly up the stairs Ehud imagined the moment that Rachel answered the phone and wondered what she did afterward. What does a woman feel, hearing the ring of the phone and answering politely in English, without any trace of an accent, confirming that she is Rachel, and being told that her father is dead? We all know, he thought as he panted from climbing the steps, that at any moment someone is liable to knock on the door of our house and turn our world inside out. Few people live in constant readiness. And Rachel? She lived in the very heart of the enemy, she knew that the life she was constructing there and the links she was forging with her surroundings were for a limited time only, but you still have to live that life as if it's going to last forever. That's the secret of perfect cover, you can't overlook any detail. But this time something else has happened to her. Something that touched her deep down inside, that penetrated the shell that she created around herself.

He stood at the door and waited for Joe to join him. There are two things I need to find in the apartment, he told himself. The first relates to her life before the announcement, what she was doing and what she was hiding. The second needs to be some indication of her intentions. What she left and what she took with her once it was clear to her he wasn't around, and never would be again.

Ehud sat down at the desk, glanced at the landline phone, which already had a thin coating of dust, and tried to imagine Rachel sitting like him on a small chair or at the edge of the bed, staring at the phone before dialing his number. He didn't know why she decided to call him, and reckoned she would have no answer either. He remembered what she said to him and thought she had delayed the conversation until the shivah was behind her. Ehud counted the days on his fingers and made a note on the small pad that he kept in his pocket, a reminder to discuss with Joe the gap of two days.

And there was something else. She spoke to him in English. She, who loved to revert to Hebrew whenever possible. "That way I feel like an Israeli," she used to explain, and she wasn't ashamed of her accent, which she was unable to shake off.

He raised the receiver, listened for the dial tone, and wondered what she meant to say when she fell silent. He wanted to ask her why her last sentence sounded decisive and determined, a metallic tone with the seal of finality, what compelled her to announce that her father was dead for the second time and what accounted for the defiance in her voice, the thin shading that said to him: You're to blame.

He knew he needed to link this conversation with that time when he phoned her with the news that her father was on his deathbed and she should return at once. That was only a code phrase, Rachel, he wanted to say to her now. Your father was waiting for you. You could go to him, be with him, tell him as much as you were allowed to tell, and rebuild the connection.

Suddenly he remembered their conversation. "I'm not telling him anything," she said, and tried to convince him it was better that way.

"He'll understand," he said to her in a final attempt to persuade her that every father loves his daughter, but she was silent, and it was obvious she had nothing to add.

⚜

"WHEN I DON'T KNOW WHAT TO look for I just wait," he said to the team commander, who stood by the door, arms folded, and looked at him with a question mark. "Okay," the commander confirmed, "you have all the time in the world. Our instructions are clear; we're here to help and not to hinder. If you need anything, just ask. We can also find documents, even drugs, if you want to incriminate her. Everything is possible, and the photo lab will process the proofs. That's the way it is in the twenty-first century. There is no longer any meaning to the past or the future. Reality is imaginary. But why am I talking so much instead of letting you think in peace?" He told Ehud to let him know if he needed anything, and left the bedroom.

Ehud opened one of the drawers, looked at the folded bras and underwear, and remembered the first time he was confronted with Rachel's clothing, touching one item after another. He slid his hand under the pile and felt the delicacy of silk. There were no letters at the bottom of the drawer, just the soft underwear, smaller than Rina's, which he had packed up with all his wife's clothes once it was clear to him she wasn't coming back. Many months passed before he dared to stand and face her closets and her drawers and take her belongings out. It was like killing her memory, taking her out of his world and making space for someone else. He tried to rid himself of the feeling that this was what he wanted now, that the underwear and the other clothes and personal items laid out before him in a kind of order that was hard to fathom would move over to his house and fill the empty spaces left behind. And suddenly he had an intuition that this place was waiting for someone to gather up the objects, sort them, pack them in cardboard cartons, and take them somewhere else. That although this apartment belonged to Rachel, it would now be the property of the chief security officer, at the disposal of those who had the power to break into it, handle her personal possessions, and do with them as they pleased. That Rachel had no further interest in what was left here, in fact she never had. That like the apartment in the Arab country, this apartment was always just a place to lay one's head. That Rachel Ravid lived here on borrowed time, knowing that one day she would suddenly leave, and so she imprinted no personal stamp on the place.

He tried to remember who she was when she was the real Rachel, the one sitting in her apartment in the evening, turning off the television set, looking out through the little window, and thinking about herself, not about being an operative on a mission and not about the image that she needed to project. Ehud realized that in fact he didn't know, he'd never taken an interest, never asked her what she was reading, what she was doing, what she liked, what she was interested in. Everything relating to Rachel the operative he was well acquainted with, but about the real woman he knew nothing. A troublesome thought nagged at him—perhaps this Rachel no longer existed. Maybe he and his colleagues had destroyed her, and the one who once lived here was no more. She was stuck in an in-between state, in the limbo that he himself created for her, waiting for an assignment, waiting for time to pass, waiting for some savior like the one who came to her in the end. He remembered this wasn't the first time she left, but he was overwhelmed by the painful feeling that this was evidently the last time.

Ehud continued searching. What did she want to bring on her journey? What was missing here of all the things normally found in a house? He shifted his attention to the bookshelves. They were in order. He opened the drawer. Old pens and pencil sharpeners, all kinds of things that no one bothers to sort out. He took the drawer out from its place and bent down to see if there was anything underneath it, something that had been stuck, or some little cache that she improvised. Nothing. He emptied the drawer on the table and sorted through the few objects, until he saw a strange kind of button. "From a jacket sleeve," said Joe, suddenly standing beside him. Ehud picked up the silver object and examined it intently. There was no insignia on it, and it seemed it was there arbitrarily. But that wasn't the way it was, because she had kept it. Ehud put it in his wallet, in the compartment reserved for small change. When they meet, he'll ask her.

"Anything else?" The voice of the team commander roused him from his reverie. "The smell," said Ehud. "The smell is different." He sniffed, and the team commander did the same. "There is no smell," said the commander, disappointed. "Exactly," said Ehud. "Every place has a smell. There should be something here too, and there isn't." He moved again around the little apartment until he was sure he'd found what he was looking for: nothing. Rachel didn't take anything. She walked out of here as if she were leaving a hotel room, although the apartment of course was full of personal items. All these items belonged to a world that Rachel didn't need anymore. Rachel didn't want to come back.

⚜

THEY SAT IN A STYLISH RESTAURANT in Rehovot. In the evening it would be filled with the high-tech crowd and students who could afford it, but now it was almost empty. Joe didn't want to go to the Office and join the mob in the war room. He told Ehud that computers weren't for him and it was a waste of their time. The war room gang didn't need them there, and it wasn't for this that they had recalled Ehud to the service. "Tell me about her," he suggested, explaining that they needed to look for her in another way.

"It's been a long time since I saw her, and in spite of the picture I showed you, she's the same Rachel as she was then. A young woman with green eyes, round mouth, hair with a part, and an innocent cast of features that made you want to help her. I think her phone call to me was a cry for help. In a certain sense, she wants me to look after her as I once did, so she'll again be the little girl who came to work for us.

"After I was appointed her case officer, I sat and read everything that was written in her personal file. I searched for her motivation in wanting to join us. I knew it wasn't some epiphany she had. Such things only happen rarely and usually in movies, although in recruitment interviews some of the candidates talk about the juncture at which they chose this path. I'm a skeptic about those stories, and when I was on the interviewing panel I would ask a candidate who tried to sell me this line what it would take to make him or her change his mind again and leave us. There was nothing exceptional with Rachel, and I was satisfied. A reasonable student. A mother who died young and a stern father who it was difficult to love up close.

"The relationship with the father was never smooth. When she was already an operative I asked her to contact him every time she came off an assignment, to reassure him that all was well and promise to visit him. I pleaded with her to write to him and she refused that as well, said he wasn't interested and he didn't care. I reminded her of the checks that he was sending her, and she said the little notes he enclosed with the checks were prepared a year in advance. I had no option but to write to him myself after he went to the embassy to report that she'd disappeared. I wrote the first letter so he'd stop interfering.

I stressed how important she was to the security of the nation of Israel and insisted he not talk to anyone about this. I had to write him the second letter after she left the Unit because he asked about her as if she were still working for us. As if we needed to explain to him why she was reluctant to write letters and never got in touch. Then I wrote to him exactly what I was told to write, the truth, that she was no longer a part of our organization.

"But all of this came later. What drew my attention was her ability to get up and go to another place. She certainly studied exactly as her father wanted, but at the age of seventeen she left and came here as a volunteer for a few months. Then she went away to a university in the north of England, and after her mother died it was as if she divorced him and came to this country as an immigrant. A girl alone, nineteen years old. I saw energy in this, I saw in this a quest for something more than a profession. I also read the other reports about her, though I didn't attach much importance to them, unless I knew the assessor. What was conspicuous was her ability to adapt, to be one of the group, and also to get what she wanted. The only thing that disturbed me was the fact that she spent only about a year in each place, and I wondered how she would cope with a long stay in an Arab city, living undercover.

"I asked her why she joined. Why after finishing university and already having a job she preferred to leave everything behind, including the boyfriend, and put her life on hold with a kind of extended intermission that would put her back, years later, at square one. She said we approached her and she was curious, and she always wanted to do more to further the Zionist project, and one thing led to another. I didn't believe a word of it. I knew she only wanted to put my mind at rest and give me a standard and predictable response, the kind they give in entrance exams. That isn't what we're looking for, and you know that as well as I do. No one volunteers to go through what a solitary operative goes through only because he's a Zionist. In this country there are millions of Zionists, many among them are multilingual, but someone who's prepared to volunteer is exceptional. There's something special in him besides the ability to assume another persona and undertake operations. He needs us. That's the point. He needs us the way we need him. Sometimes he doesn't even know he's looking for us, and how well suited he is to us. Such people have difficulty identifying what it is they're looking for, they only know there's another reality that they can belong to, that it's possible to go to distant places and do what's forbidden to others, things you only dream about. There's something intoxicating in our work; suddenly it's permissible to lie, you can put on an act, and everything is sanctioned by the state. The operative is licensed to commit crimes. He steals, sometimes he even kills, and instead of going to prison he gets a commendation.

"And something else. Many of them aren't content with their lives, and they're ready for a change, and this is what happened with Rachel. We diverted her from a path that was leading her nowhere, and gave her a new world. She trusted us, trusted the respect that we felt for her, the faith we invested in her, and I daresay she saw in us an extended family. From her point of view she was an only child, as in the family she left behind. And for this reason she had a terrible crisis when it all came to an end and she was cut off all at once. In hindsight, I realize she was really just a child and we let her play some very dangerous games. We did something that wasn't right, Joe, we didn't succeed in rehabilitating her after she came back from there, and something in her life was fucked up. This is what we need to clarify."

"You're exaggerating," said Joe, and Ehud felt rebuked when he heard what was to follow: "You're giving me a lecture on operatives as if I hadn't been there when you still knew almost nothing about what goes on inside the Mossad."

"I feel this is important, to start from the beginning. To understand from where—"

But Joe interrupted him: "Okay, okay, I agree it's necessary to go back and retrace her steps." He chewed his food slowly. His hand trembled and he tried to control it. "But it seems to me you're taking this too personally. As if you're still the case officer and she's your operative. What happened to her after she left is not your problem." Ehud listened and didn't dare tell him how he felt. "The secrets that she has tucked away inside her are the problem." Joe's face was grim, and despite the years that had passed they both knew who was in charge. "You heard them in the Office just as I did. This can't be allowed to happen. These secrets, which even we are not privy to, must not be allowed to fall into their hands."

"But—" Ehud began, and wanted to say that for him it was all about Rachel, but Joe didn't let him interrupt.

"We need to find her and bring her back before there's any damage. This isn't the time to indulge in a guilt trip, and we won't win any bonus points if we admit that she meant the world to us all the time she was with us and afterwards we forgot her."

A waitress in black passed between the tables and asked if they were enjoying their meal. Her jeans were too tight, her T-shirt too short to cover a white and endearing midriff. Ehud's eyes wandered in that direction, and she noticed and pulled the hem of the T-shirt down with a bashful hand. "She's younger than my son," said Ehud, blushing, when he realized Joe had also noticed the look. "So what?" said Joe, and admitted he had been staring too. "What do you think, with age it goes away? You don't need to tell me what passed through your mind the first moment you heard from Rachel." Ehud didn't say a word. His steak was cold by now and the red fibers lacing the meat stood out like roads leading nowhere.

⚜

WHEN THEY ARRIVED AT JOE'S HOUSE, evening had already settled in. A light breeze stirred the tops of the trees and the roar of a passing train drowned their voices and helped them to hold their silence. They had known each other for many years and knew that not everything needs to be talked about. Not everything needs to be known, and knowledge, although it may be power, is also a burden. When you know, you need to do something. When you don't know, you are free.

"So what now?" Ehud asked. The traces of the long day weren't perceptible in him. Something new was happening. Energy he didn't know he had started to bubble inside him. Memories wanted to come out, and he wanted to put them in order, because left inside they were liable to fester. He wanted to talk, that was clear. Not about everything, at least not now. He used Joe like a tennis player practices against a wall. "You're my sounding board," he told him, and Joe just nodded and said that was all right, he might as well carry on. Ehud asked what was going on with the war room, and when did they need to report their findings. "What they do in the WR is not our problem, we're not their backup team," said Joe, and again he spoke in the steely and authoritative tone that Ehud thought he had lost: "Our advantage over the team in the WR consists of two things only. You know her, and I know you. That's all. Out of this we need to build the picture, and when we sense something floating up or thickening in what we're cooking, we'll pull it out and attend to it. And we're not going to construct fancy theories either, or get fixated on anything except Rachel's story. You know there are people at HQ who think maybe she's doing as Vanunu, hiding somewhere and confiding her memories to some journalist. And there are other possibilities, including the ashrams and monasteries that people run away to. There in the WR they'll take care of those issues. And we'll talk. We must observe one rule—tell the truth and be as honest as you can. You will talk, and I'll listen. I know you'll want to hide things from me. We're all ashamed of some of the things we've done. But only the truth. It's worth it. You might even enjoy it."

Joe stretched out on the deck chair in the garden and lit a cigar. He looked content, and Ehud told him he'd never heard him say so much. "Agreed," Ehud said, and waited while Joe's wife put a tray down on the little table between them. Then he yielded to temptation and added two extra spoonfuls of sugar to the teacup that he held in his hand. "This is no time to be fighting on two fronts," he said to Joe, who had noticed. "You can always start a new diet."

CHAPTER THREE

Milan

"'You'll see,' I told her, 'you'll fly there, and it will be easier than you think, and different from the training you've gone through, because the sense of danger isn't something that can be simulated. I know you're afraid, and there's nothing wrong with that. Fears are good. Don't be ashamed of them, they'll help you to be cautious and prepared. Someone who doesn't admit to being afraid—he isn't suitable. We're not looking for people like that. We need the ones who know the dangers, are afraid of them, and know how to overcome the fear. This is your baptism by fire, and the first time is always the hardest.'

"And that's the way it was, but I'm getting ahead of myself. We were at the end of one road and at the start of another." Ehud interrupted the flow of his speech for a moment and waited until Joe nodded that he was waiting for the rest. "Three months before that they sent her to me from Israel so I could prepare her for the assignment. 'She'll be your operative, and from now on she's your responsibility,' the Unit commander told me, and he showed me her file. I remember sitting with him in an empty café in a grubby little piazza in Rome at the height of a stifling summer, and I felt the setting didn't suit this kind of operation. I imagined being summoned to headquarters in Israel, going into the commander's office late at night to be told there's something only I could do; I was supposed to size up the matter carefully, solemnly, and the commander was supposed to persuade me, and then I would agree, of course. That wasn't how things worked out, but I forgave him because I was glad to have an operation of my own again, something that would be my responsibility from A to Z, the way we teach it on the operational course.

"I was a veteran case officer then and a perpetual candidate for the post of department head. 'He's better suited to work in the field,' they wrote in my file every time they bypassed me in the round of appointments, and you too said something similar when you sent me away on a three-year exile to Africa. And you know what? I adapted to it and I admit it suited me. I enjoyed being abroad and working with the operatives. There's a kind of enchantment that's hard to explain to anyone who hasn't experienced it himself. You're master of your fate and everything depends on you, and at the same time you really feel that the nation of Israel is behind you. I became used to this way of life, and I always agreed to long assignments in Europe. Rina was at home then with the children. They were young and our parents helped her. I know it was harder for her than it was for me, and telling her that the state was calling me must have seemed to her inadequate compensation.

"I asked the commander about Rachel and wondered why he decided to take me off the boring assignment I was on at the time. He told me that after two months of working on a Canadian cover with her case officer, it seemed she was falling in love with him, so they decided to replace him. Just like that, all at once. 'She'll have no problems with you,' the commander said. I was offended, of course: What kind of a man, however old he may be, doesn't want to be fancied and flirted with? I envied the case officer who left her and I admired his professionalism. He knew it wasn't healthy, and of course it was forbidden. So he separated from her, using the excuse of another urgent mission, and they passed her on to me.

"I met her in Brussels. I told her to rent a small room on a short-term basis and we would meet in cafés and museums. She told the family she rented from that she was taking a long vacation in Europe, and I devised a story about being a bachelor businessman courting an attractive young woman. No one checked us out or asked what someone like me was doing with her. Brussels is an ideal place for romances like this. The city is overflowing with diplomats wasting their time in the various international organizations, and after hours they're looking for someone on the side. I gave her a few days to get settled and then took her for dinner at a very expensive restaurant. She turned up wearing an odd outfit—some kind of overalls—and she stood out with her beauty and the sense of unease that she projected. I was disappointed that she wasn't professional enough to check what kind of a restaurant we were going to and wear appropriate clothing, and I had the impression that despite the high marks she scored in training, she was still like a plant uprooted from its garden and put in a strange place. I waited until the coffee came and then asked her if she was prepared to go there. She said yes in a tone expressing all the discipline and readiness for everything that the instructors try to inculcate. We finished the meal, I told her to carry on with her sightseeing and job-seeking, and when I escorted her to the taxi that I ordered for her, she shook my hand, as if we were parting. The next day I informed HQ that she wasn't ready yet, and we should delay her placement in the target zone for a few months; they argued with me a little, as always, and reminded me we weren't a travel agency. I told them that they should stop hassling me, that I didn't ask for their opinion.

"It turned out I was right. She was highly motivated and an outstanding pupil, but there was a big difference between a course under laboratory conditions and a long stay in Rome, playing the tourist and working as an English teacher. We were together for three months and traveled all around Europe. She established her cover and practiced again and again all the tricks she had learned in training, and I stayed in the background. At a distance, but close enough to see how she was performing, to question her afterwards and make evaluations, and then send her off for further practice until she was satisfied. She and I both knew this was her last opportunity to get feedback from someone standing right behind her and being able to see how she was coping. In the Arab country she would be alone and we would know of her only from her reports. I made a point of involving myself in everything she did. I explained to her that she didn't only need to know everything about the personality she was adopting, she had to project it too, to create a situation where some questions won't need to be asked, where someone looking at her will automatically understand who she is.

"So what did I do? I'll give you an example. I sent her to get her hair styled because I thought that with a straight cut she would look more stern and assertive, the kind of woman not many men would want to have an affair with. I told her to give up the murderous diet she had imposed on herself after all the cookies and sandwiches that they ate during the training period, and she looked at me as if I was intruding on matters that were not my concern, but she did as I asked. And once she realized I wasn't threatening her, and I realized she wasn't falling in love with me, I dared to ask about her menstrual cycle. At first she blushed, and then her face went blank and turned a new color, as if she were putting on armor. I suppose that today no one would dare to have such a conversation with a subordinate, for fear of being accused of sexual harassment, but then things were different, and I explained that her health wasn't just a personal matter; it could affect her work and her ability to function. She had a way of talking about intimate things, which gave me the impression that she was exposing the facts to me but not her feelings. This worried me, and I asked her again and again what she was feeling, and, in her particular way, she tried to reassure me while continuing to be evasive.

"And so we came to the evening before the flight. We were in Milan, in her hotel room facing the towers of the Duomo. In the morning I had sent her there to pray for the last time, which amused her. We were speaking English. I insisted on that, and of course for her it was no problem. French is my mother tongue, so speaking English was more of an effort for me. I knew the next day she would be going there for the first time, and she must not, simply must not, even think in Hebrew. She laughed at my accent, and this was good. It's important to laugh. A year later, when she was already coming and going from the Arab capital the way you fly to London, she told me all these precautions seemed stupid to her, but she wanted so much for me to be satisfied with her and to be sure she was ready, so she didn't try to stop me from struggling in English.

"Rachel sat and looked at the clothes piled on her bed. The television was switched on so we wouldn't be overheard and I checked everything she had and threw on the floor anything that looked to me too new, or too old, or not right for what she was supposed to be: a young Canadian woman who was born in England and who went back with her father to a remote place in Canada where he could spend his retirement years fishing and she could be bored to death.

And now she's twenty-six and she's on her way to the Arab capital city to teach the natives English, to save enough money to travel the world and to defer her postgraduate studies a little longer. 'Don't turn up there as if you've been out shopping,' I said to her. 'You're the one who sent me out shopping,' she said and smiled one of her tired smiles. 'You implied this was my opportunity to upgrade my wardrobe.'

"I had no choice but to give her the kind of send-off that soldiers get when they set out on operations. According to her story she didn't leave Canada until she decided she had to make changes in her life, and then she spent half a year in Europe before taking on the teaching job. But in reality, she arrived here from Israel after a vacation that I opposed. 'I have to say a final goodbye to my boyfriend,' she said, and explained in very few words that he found hard to understand why she was about to go away on such a long-term assignment to Russia. Why it will be impossible to contact her by phone, and why all this secrecy she was wrapping herself in. I tried to explain to her that she was breaking the continuity of the operation and could lose focus, but she screwed up her nose and shed a few tears and got what she wanted. I was glad they were separating. I thought she needed isolation and the awareness that no one was waiting for her in Israel. Her friends were going to be *there*, and *there* would be where she must feel at home. I didn't know then even one percent of the things I know today. It seems that age has positive aspects after all. She flew to Israel, broke up with her boyfriend, said goodbye to her few acquaintances, and came back to me after collecting her old things from the baggage repository at the railway station. It was terrible, and I wondered again whether I should postpone the flight once more. But now it was already too complicated. She had the invitation from the language school, but they wouldn't hold the job for her indefinitely, and she had a plane reservation the next morning.

"I looked at the pile of things she had scattered on the bed. Rachel was disorganized almost on purpose. I think she thought this was an asset, it was hard to suspect someone so slovenly, someone who lost things and missed appointments and forgot people's faces. But there, in the hotel, before traveling, lack of order was a hindrance, because a few moments after she arrived in the room all the items were mixed up together and I had to check that nothing from Israel had infiltrated her gear and that everything looked exactly as it should.

"And there were some who said this wasn't important, and there was no likelihood of anyone in the capital city checking every detail, and if despite this they took the trouble to do a meticulous check, they would always start with simpler things than these, like passports and the references that we prepared for her. I insisted that the preparations she was making were part of her transformation, vital for her sense of security, and they were as important as anything else. She has to feel that everything will be in order, and then everything will be in order. She mustn't hesitate to show everything she's bringing with her, she mustn't hesitate when she's explaining where she bought everything and where she was yesterday and where she's going tomorrow. Just like anyone else.

"Her eyes narrowed when I opened her toiletries bag and when I examined the labels on her bras and panties. I asked her if she was offended. She said she was embarrassed but she understood why I was doing this, and she reminded me that at Ben Gurion Airport they do exactly the same checks, and if a customs officer at an Arab airport were to examine her possessions and find something inappropriate, the problem would be a lot bigger.

"When the suitcase was packed I opened her hand luggage and saw the book on top. 'Why are you taking a book by John le Carré?' 'Why not?' she asked, and explained she was actually reading it for the second time. The first time was before we recruited her, and reading it now it's hard for her not to make comparisons between herself and the heroine. I didn't want to get into an argument with her. This wasn't the time to explain to her, again, that she's an Israeli combatant going to an Arab country undercover, whereas the eponymous little drummer girl was a British woman recruited as an agent and deceived by her handlers all along the way. I remembered the time when le Carré was going around Israel and interviewing anyone who could tell him about the working methods of the Mossad, and I almost told her about the discussions in the department whether to cooperate with him and come out of it as the invincible good guys. I felt I wanted to tell her about my own experiences in my operational past, and my ambition to write a book myself someday. There was a real temptation to sit her down facing me and say to her, Come on, listen to me, and hear about some real operations, not the fictional ones. You should listen to me not only because I've been appointed your case officer but also because I too have done things in my life, and I can be trusted. And at the same time I knew this would be too much of a distraction from the assignment facing her; she was the operative here and I was just the bag-carrier, and I forced myself back to reality. 'And what will you say when they ask why you're interested in the book?' 'No problem,' she said to me, sitting on the end of the bed and flicking through the poetry book that I hadn't commented on. 'It's about the Middle East and about the interminable war between the Israelis and the Palestinians, and it will be useful for comparative purposes when I get around to writing my postgraduate thesis.' 'And what will you feel when you give them this answer?' Rachel put the book down and looked at me. I knew what she was seeing. I was older than her and she knew I was the boss. Bosses don't ask about feelings, and bosses aren't told about feelings. You have to make an impression on them and never hesitate. 'I'll know that I'm lying,' she said, and I saw something stirring in her face. 'But I'm used to it, and besides, it's impossible to check. Perhaps I really will use my latest job as thesis material.' 'What did they tell you in training, Rachel?' I asked, and she could see I was angry. 'Why tell a lie unless you have to? Why invite trouble if it's possible to avoid it? You want to read the book? Fine, I'll keep it for you until your next vacation. You don't do things like that, just as you don't take the translated poems of Yehuda Amichai with you, even though it's allowed, even though it's possible, even though an innocent Canadian tourist can take along anything she likes.'

"A long time after this, when we were already friends, she told me at that moment I sounded exactly like her father, who used to call her to his room and check what she was reading with that critical, dismissive look, and tell her she could read what she liked but he at her age had already read . . . and he would reel off a whole list, just like the required reading list that she received when she arrived at university.

"'Are you nervous?' I asked after we finished checking the luggage. Rachel stretched out her legs in the jeans and looked at me. 'What have I to be nervous about?' she said. 'I'm going to look into prospects for work, the opportunity to earn a little money.' 'And the journey? How are you financing it? And where do your parents live? And who can be contacted if we need to ask questions about you?' She knew all the answers, but she knew something else. That I would be here when she came back. That I would wait for her to call on reaching the hotel, and I would never sit behind a desk, embalmed in a suit, far from her.

"'No, I'm not afraid,' she added, 'I just want everything to be done right. I already want to be on the way back.' I looked at her hands, clasped around her knees, at the delicate bracelet on her right arm, the thin and bony wrist. Tomorrow she'll be like a pilot flying solo for the first time, except that the pilot goes out for about twenty minutes, and she'll be there for many weeks before she sees me again. Up to this point I had been close to her in all the exercises. I waited for her on the other side of the border, played the part of her friend when she was interviewed at the language school in Rome, and it was only when she went to the enemy's embassy to apply for a visa that I stayed behind and waited for her in a nearby café.

"I felt the tension gripping me too, the feeling that I was putting her under pressure. 'Come on,' I said, and made an effort not to hold her hand. 'Let's go and eat. We'll take a break. We can talk over a meal, nothing is running away, and anyway the shops are closed. What you haven't bought you probably don't need.' Rachel put on her shoes and moved toward the door as if obeying an order. She was tall, and slim, and she knew this made the right impression on me. The short and straight coiffure framed her face and gave it the forceful look that I wanted to see, and I admit I couldn't stop my eyes wandering over her, and I hoped I wasn't annoying her. I'm twenty years older than her, and even back then I had a small paunch and a respectable bald patch.

"She stood by the door with her back to me, and I thought, Despite all the time we have spent together I know too little about her, and even with all the training and the preparations I'm not sure it will all go according to plan. Just a few months ago I told headquarters she wasn't ready, she didn't know the assignment, was incapable of telling her life history without mistakes and she would stumble the moment she arrived at enemy territory, and tomorrow she's going to board a plane, fasten her seat belt, look around her, and when the plane takes off on its way to the capital city she'll know she's alone. She'll know she's going to a place where those who are caught are hanged. If she falls, only God can lift her up.

"I led her to the corner table. Rachel sat facing the door, as she had been taught, so she could see anyone coming in, and she put on her gloomy expression, the look that says: I'm here because you asked me to come, because you told me to go out with you. I knew it, that look, she used it several times in the course of training, and it grieved me each time. I thought perhaps I was forcing myself upon her; perhaps I was deviating from what's allowed between a case officer and his operative. With a man the situation is clear. You go out with him, socialize with him, and the conversation never digresses from the subject of the operation that he's responsible for. With her it was different, and it looked that way too. There were other couples in the restaurant, and some of the men were much older than the women they were with. I was afraid that to them it was clear I was spending money on this young woman before taking her to a hotel, and I wondered what she thought of me and what I was to her besides her case officer. You know what I wanted? I wanted her to see in me a father's authority, and someone she could turn to as to a mother. I also hoped she might be secretly in love with me. Of course I wanted her, but I knew where the boundary was. I don't suppose she guessed what I was thinking about. Rachel was an operative just starting out. She had known me for several months and we had spent many hours together, but I never spoke about myself, nor did I ask her what she thought of me. I was an experienced professional, and I knew I was preparing her for her first time, her baptism of fire, solo, and she needed to be treated like a war machine.

"The waiter came over and she turned and addressed him in her deep and warm voice. I said to her, like a judge in a talent contest, that her voice, ringing out with a perfect British accent, was a weapon, something inspiring confidence and generating the sense that it is directed wholly toward the listener.

"She nodded her head with a movement that seemed to me a gesture of gratitude, and took a sip from the glass of wine that she allowed herself. It was a moment in which she seemed to condescend and to accept what was due her, like a queen responding to her subjects. And I was convinced again that for women this is easier. Easier for them to gain trust, easier to play the dependent card, ask for and receive help, and be thought of as innocent. But what good will this do her if she is caught, if she falls into their hands? For women it is also more dangerous. At the end of the day this is a man's world, and if she is jailed, she will be at the mercy of men, and men only.

"I spoke to break the tension, I spoke to infuse in her, and in me too, a bit more confidence. I went over everything we had done together, over the language school in Rome where she had worked for a month, and how easily she was accepted, and how she succeeded in convincing everyone of her Canadian identity, despite her British accent and although some of the other teachers were themselves Canadian. I reminded her of her fine achievement in obtaining the references that they were happy to provide for the language school in the Arab city, and of the trip we took together through Europe. I tried to convince her that crossing the border from Turkey into Greece was more difficult than getting into an Arab country, and I got a smile out of her when I reminded her how the joke she told the Greek customs officer, about bird food, persuaded him not to confiscate the sack of Turkish coffee that she brought with her, thereby missing the imitation plastic explosives that we had planted in the sack. Then I talked about the beautiful places we had visited, and insisted that suffering is not obligatory. On the contrary, the job should be enjoyed and done happily. She's young, beautiful, and free, and she's traveling for fun, and to earn some money. 'You'll stroll around the markets, see all the beautiful mosques, and you'll get to visit the most famous ancient sites. Everything as it was in training. Just don't make a pass at any-one, and don't let anyone make a pass at you,' I added with a smile.

"I saw the anger in her face. 'And if I were a man, would you say the same thing to me? Don't make a pass at any girls, don't smile at any women in the street? Why can a man get away with it? What are you afraid of, that I'll fall in a trap?' She took a gulp of wine and I wondered what was coming next. 'Tell me the truth,' she said, and I knew she wasn't looking for an answer. 'Have you ever asked one of your male operatives what he does when he finds he can't restrain himself any longer, or is it just me you dare ask, as if I'm made from different flesh and blood, as if with me it's allowed? In this respect too you're just like my father. He also warned me about boys, they're only after one thing.' She was incensed, and her fingers clutched the wine glass so tightly I was afraid she was going to break it. I didn't say any-thing. I had nothing to say, except to ask for her forgiveness. She went on talking and reminded me of all the things we allow ourselves to say about women. Then we were quiet. There are silences that draw people closer together, because you don't feel the need to say any-thing, and there are silences that drive people further apart, when you know that you have nothing more to say to each other.

"And then she told me not to worry. 'It's going to be all right. I'm leaving tomorrow, and you'll see, everything is going to work out the way we planned. I also know they will try their luck with me, and this time it won't be like in training, when you had men pretending to fancy me. This time it will be for real, and I'll know how to deal with them. Every girl knows that things depend on her, and you'll see that I won't mix business and pleasure. I know my business.'"

CHAPTER FOUR

᳕

Entry

"AND IN FACT, THERE WAS A good-looking man sitting next to her on
the plane, but he didn't say he knew her from somewhere, and he took
no interest in the book she was reading. Rachel was ready to respond
to him with a noncommittal nod of the head, and she told me later she
was almost disappointed when that was unnecessary. But she was
glad he understood from her body language that she wasn't interested. 'Eye contact is the name of the game,' she told me, and said she
managed to contract herself into her seat and not meet his look even
when she passed him the tray of food. She knew this was the right
thing and she shouldn't make any contact with him, as one question
leads to another and there's no knowing where it will end. Her story
was ready, down to the smallest detail. All was prepared and backed
up by paperwork and telephone contacts that we were ready to respond to at any time. And yet she had something to hide and there
was no reason to volunteer information to a stranger who she might
run into again. 'Not everyone talks to their neighbors on a flight,' I

told her before one exercise. 'They're not all sociable, charming, making contact, and exchanging business cards. You're better off keeping to yourself.'"

Ehud made sure that Joe was still listening to him. "I told her your story. I didn't tell her it was you who made that mistake, or that I was using you as an example." Joe didn't smile, and Ehud continued: "'Once upon a time, one of our operatives was flying to an Arab country, which for him was like a normal business trip, routine even. He found himself sitting beside a businessman like himself, and a conversation developed and business cards were exchanged when the plane landed. The operative went on to his hotel and forgot all about the man and the business card he left with him. The next morning the police arrived and interrogated him for hours. It turned out that the other guy was smuggling cigarettes, and when they arrested him they found the card in his pocket.'" Joe admitted that this was one of the mistakes he had made, and Ehud told him that Rachel had absorbed this lesson with ease, with ease that perhaps even disappointed her, because she too would have wanted to be friendly and liked.

"I think Rachel had a painful sense that people who were not in the Office felt that she could be doing more, that she wasn't striving hard enough and did not assert herself enough. She was talented and gifted, but she was too adept at concealing these qualities. She had a lovely face with fine features but she was somehow hard to remember, to inscribe in the memory and say: This is a woman I want to see again. She wasn't pleased when the instructors in the course told her they considered her looks an asset. 'Please don't be offended,' the Unit commander said in the final briefing. 'We see you as a weapon, and it's better for us and better for you that it's a concealed weapon. Under your facade of normality, and behind the pretty face, one among thousands like it, an operative is hiding, an operative who has completed her course with distinction and is capable of fulfilling whatever assignment is entrusted to her.' She also thought we were happy she had broken up with Oren, and didn't say he was the one who initiated the separation. To console her I told her that most operatives abandon their girlfriends after training, and she at once, in her typical way, told me it pained her to find herself in a group she didn't want to be a part of.

"'That's what you need,' she told me, 'someone like me, who doesn't have a boyfriend, who takes the world seriously.'

"'Actually, not just that . . .' I responded, and was trying to say something that would balance the picture, but she continued: 'I know I'm not funny and not charming, and perhaps that's what makes me suitable, because men don't start up with me.'

"She was right, of course. And there was something else, something I said to the Unit commander before I fell in love with her, and after he said goodbye to her and wished her success. I said to him, 'Rachel will be a good operative, but she can't be coddled. She needs to be like a wrestler climbing into the ring—lean and hungry.' And that is exactly what she was."

⚜

EHUD DIDN'T SIT IN THE ROW behind her on the plane, nor did he peer at her through the mostly opaque window of one of the vehicles waiting on the tarmac. The Unit's war room was unmanned the day she went deep into enemy territory, bearing a new identity, the image of a carefree young English teacher starting out on her way. There was no point holding a squadron of helicopters on alert for a rescue mission, because Rachel's commanders knew that if something went wrong, not even a military intervention would help. They had told Rachel this, and it was clear to her that now everything depended on her. It was her decision, when she could go ahead with the operation and when it was better to stop and say: This is too dangerous.

There was no turning back. The plane landed and she needed to get up from her seat and move toward her destination. Around her there was a strange and menacing silence. Her neighbor in the next seat said something that sounded like goodbye, and someone standing in front of her in the queue for the exit chattered with his friend in Arabic. The flight attendant said something to her, and outside was the din of jet engines, but it all sounded far away, and she was alone in the world, in her own almost-silent movie. "Enough," she said to herself aloud, and walked to the door of the plane.

Rachel shielded her eyes with her free hand and held her handbag firmly, as if someone might snatch it. The sun beat down fiercely despite the early hour of the morning, and the heat outside wrapped around her like an extra layer of clothing. She walked slowly down the steps and inadvertently exposed her thigh. "Everything has to be planned," Ehud told her in one of the briefings. "Just as you don't go out on a date in clothes you've yanked out of the closet, that's the way it has to be over the border, at the first encounter with your adversary, the one who's looking for a reason to take you aside and ask a few more questions." They chose a simple blouse with a high collar, to emphasize her long neck and focus attention on her face, and a skirt with pockets, to accommodate passport and purse. But it's impossible to think of everything, because now the light breeze forced her to use her hand to keep her skirt in place, and she drew the attention of the mechanic, who was looking up.

To her left the porters were already at work unloading baggage, and she resisted the impulse to check that her suitcase was there. There was nothing in it to incriminate her and even its loss wouldn't jeopardize the operation. But a suitcase that disappeared would cause unnecessary complications, and another encounter with the airport authorities, who would want to see her flight ticket and know which hotel she was going to. She bought the suitcase with Ehud and he helped her twist the hinges. "From now on you can open the case in two ways, the normal way and your way. You'll be able to tell if anyone has opened it. And even that doesn't mean they suspect you," he said, and went on to explain, although he saw her patience wearing thin. "The case can be opened accidentally, or by airport security, and the porters may simply do some pilfering, but better to know this and be alert."

Up to now everything has gone all right, she told herself, exactly the same as at any other airport. And yet everything felt different. The fear was real, and the price of failure would be terrible. This wasn't a case of another exercise, or crossing a border in Europe. Her teeth chattered despite the heat and she clenched her jaws to hide the tremor. Rachel took the last step and set foot on the searing tarmac to what seemed to her like a trap she was about to fall into, and she was sure that at any moment she would be approached by a tough-looking man in a safari suit who would ask her to enter one of the vehicles that were parked beside the bus, as in the exercise at Ben Gurion Airport.

A few more paces. She restrained the impulse to look around her, avoiding eye contact with the armed police and security men who stood and scrutinized the passengers. Someone touched her elbow, and she ignored him. If it's a cop, by now he would have told her to come with him; if it's a passenger walking behind her, this isn't the time to look at him angrily. When she almost reached the door of the shuttle bus to the terminal, which seemed to her a point of refuge, it closed and the full vehicle moved off and left her to wait for the next one, exposed to the inquisitive looks around her. She stood with the others and didn't dare wipe the sweat from her brow. A middle-aged lady who stood beside her said to her in English this was the way things were here, and they needed to wait until the bus had unloaded its passengers, and then it would return for the rest of them. Rachel nodded, didn't answer, and was glad that in training they acted out a similar scenario in which a passenger latched on to her before passport control, engaged her in conversation, and eventually asked her to help drag her heavy bag through customs. Her refusal earned high marks from the instructors, who were watching her through peepholes. Even the "passenger," an experienced reservist operative, praised her, and told her she was the first candidate to show herself both affable and determined, not falling into the trap that awaited her, when the bag was opened and found to be full of drugs.

The bus returned in a cloud of dust and they boarded. A policeman stood near them, and to Rachel it seemed he was looking at her with a quizzical eye. Except for her and a middle-aged passenger, all the others were talking among themselves, and most of them were Arabs. She was aware of being looked at and pressed her legs together under her skirt. The cop took one step forward. The woman who stood behind her whispered a few words but Rachel didn't hear what she said. A drop of sweat sparkled on her upper lip and she wondered if the cop thought this was suspicious. The bus set off with a jolt. The cop raised his hand and clutched the metal bar above him, and she saw the stain of sweat under his armpit and the fat and hairy midriff that was exposed. Her apprehension eased.

⚬

THE WOMAN WHO GOT ON THE bus with her stood behind her in the line for passport control. "How long will you be here?" she asked. "For a few days," said Rachel, not turning around, thereby indicating to the stranger that there was no point in asking more questions. The line moved on one pace and she heard the woman huffing. Maybe she isn't satisfied with my response. Fuck her. It isn't my problem. She stood on the yellow line and waited until the tall man standing in front of her moved ahead. She kept the passport in her pocket. No point in getting it out too soon. Why should this woman know that despite the British accent she's a Canadian citizen? Why should she see her new and empty passport?

Her turn came. She walked the three ominous paces to the passport control booth, peered at the pleasant-looking official, and handed over her passport. "Nothing happens, it's exactly like the exercises, and you need to be ready and believe in yourself," Ehud said to her last evening, in an attempt to instill a little more confidence in her. "There's no one who isn't a bit anxious at passport control. That's how it is when somebody offers his identity papers for inspection. When the officer looks up at you, look back at him and remember you have nothing to hide. This is your passport. This is your trip. This is the work you're looking for. For every question you have an answer." "True," she said to him, and added what Ehud also knew was the difference—the knowledge of the real reason for her coming, and at the end of the day the capital city isn't Jerusalem, and it's no longer a test.

The official looked up. She saw his black eyes behind thick-frame spectacles, and his tie, which was carelessly knotted, and she had time to think of what her father would have said about somebody going to work like that. "Where did you come here from?" he asked her, and she misunderstood him because of his accent and said she'd arrived just now. "No! Not when, from where?" She blushed. In training they had told her there was nothing worse than offending people in authority, the ones who think they know. All she needs is someone having a go at her now. "Sorry," she said, "I didn't understand you. I'm coming from Italy." He flipped through her passport.

"First time here?"

"Yes."

"Ever been to Israel?"

If Rachel had been a regular tourist, or a businesswoman concealing a visit to the Holy Land, perhaps she would have been confused. Nothing wrong with being confused, so long as there's nothing to hide. She was ready for this question, since Ehud trained her to answer it when they rehearsed the questions to be asked on entry to the destination country. "Not yet. It isn't far from here, is it?" she responded. The official smiled back at her and wanted to know what hotel she was staying at. Rachel didn't tell him to look at the document she had handed over with the passport. She repeated the name of the hotel twice and saw him checking that the details matched what she'd written. The official extended his hand to the heavy stamps, put a finger in the middle of the page, and stamped the page alongside the entry visa. She took the passport that was handed to her and began moving toward the baggage area. This is only the first hurdle, she told herself. Too soon to feel relieved. As if to prove to her that something unexpected can always happen, a male voice was heard behind her: "Lady, lady!" She carried on walking as if the call weren't addressed to her, and was alarmed when she saw the official who checked her passport overtaking her in an ungainly run and stopping in front of her. "Sorry, sorry," he said, and handed her the customs declaration that she had left on the counter. Rachel thanked him and cursed herself.

The suitcase was already awaiting her on the conveyor belt, and Rachel gave due credit to the host country, and to what would for the next few years be her home port. Some of the passengers who arrived with her on the flight had already collected their belongings and were gathered in three ragged lines leading to the customs counters. She walked slowly and tried to take in more and more of her surroundings before choosing the customs officer who would check her out. She had nothing that could incriminate her, but she wanted to locate a friendly and cooperative person. The young and pleasant-looking customs man proved that it's a bad bet to anticipate behavior according to outward appearance. He took the document, studied it, and asked her to bring her suitcase forward. She took it in both hands and lifted it onto the bench between them. The customs man looked at the suitcase and then at Rachel, who stood facing him. "Open it," he said, and he checked all the contents meticulously, especially the toiletries, packed in a trendy pouch that she bought herself as a leaving present. "This is yours?" he asked, and held up the emptied pouch. "Yes," she said, and realized that it might seem too chic compared with the student clothes she was wearing. "Have you brought anything else?" She showed him her handbag. He signaled to her she was free to go.

Rachel took the case and headed to the automatic door to exit the terminal. She felt the sweat in her armpits and figured a thousand eyes were fixed on her back. And then she stood outside, under an awning, and all around her there was commotion. The sun was high above the buildings surrounding the airport, and the Arabic signs, which she couldn't yet read, seemed to be speaking to her.

A new sense of power overwhelmed her. She resisted the temptation to laugh uproariously, to tell casual passersby she had done it. She was taking her first steps in a place where, as far as she knew, no Israeli had been before her. Uniformed drivers tried to persuade her to travel with them, a sweating porter offered his services, and the tourist who arrived with her invited her to share the cost of a limo. Rachel rebuffed them politely and stood in the long queue at the taxi station and enjoyed the quiet moments granted to her as she waited.

⟡

She sat down on the double bed, kicked off her shoes, and lay down on her back. The phone on the table came to life, and she counted the number of rings before answering, exactly as she had been taught. A woman asked her in English if she needed anything, and suggested she try the newly opened sauna. "A few steps and two floors in the lift, and you'll enjoy an experience like no other. Why don't you try it?" the pleasant voice pressed her, and promised lockers, total privacy, and all chargeable to the room. She promised to think about it, and when she put the receiver down she stayed sitting by the phone. It was crucial to think clearly and stick to basic logic. She repeated to herself the words that Ehud had drummed into her again and again. This is not an attempt to tempt her into leaving her room with her passport and cash stowed in one of the drawers, nor a tactic designed to make it possible to steal them from the room safe. They could have photographed the passport at the border crossing, or at the reception desk. If they want, they'll find a way of stealing it and blackmailing her. The hotel is marketing its new services, that's all. This isn't surveillance, they're not stalking her. But suddenly it seems to her the walls are closing in, and whoever is pacing around in the hall by the door of her room might as well come inside. She took a deep breath and began to unpack. Later she told Ehud that the situation reminded her of the interrogation that she went through at the end of the course, but at the time she did not know why.

⟡

THE "OPERATION" THAT SHE UNDERTOOK ON that occasion wasn't a simple one, and her second visit to the Haifa Port Authority didn't go well. She was supposed to make contact with the public relations department, and con her way into a guided tour of the bay and the docks. The instructor who prepared her for the exercise asked her to gather information about the naval base and security provisions against potential seaborne assault. Rachel studied the documentation given to her and wondered how a young Canadian who came to Israel just for one week was supposed to gain access to secure installations. The instructor said that was her problem, that was what the training was for, and he left her in the modest hotel room that she'd been assigned for the duration of the course to prepare her cover story. She decided to pose as a zoology student making a comparative survey of marine pollution levels in different ports, and after a few days spent in the university library researching the subject she printed up an ornate business card and letters of recommendation from some institutions in Canada and told the instructor she was ready. It soon became clear to her that obtaining authorization for a guided tour was going to be a lengthy process and her explanation of the urgency, the need to send the results to her tutor in Montreal, made no impression on the clerk, who gave her a hostile look and said to her colleague in Hebrew, This tourist thinks she's entitled to everything just because she's young and beautiful.

Rachel returned to the small hotel; from its window the port was visible. She took a few pictures and made a point of including the Bahai Temple in the frame. From this room a lookout could make contact with an assault team out at sea, she thought, and wondered why this hadn't been included in the critical information she was meant to bring from this exercise. Then she checked again that the door was locked and the chain in place and sat down to write the coded telegram summarizing the fifth day of the operation. And then there was a knock at the door. Through the peephole she saw a workman in hotel uniform, and it was only when she opened the door that she noticed two men standing in the corridor, a policeman in uniform and beside him a muscular young man who showed her a document and asked in Hebrew if he could come in. Rachel put a hand to the collar of her blouse with an instinctive movement and asked in English what they wanted. In halting English the policeman asked her name. For a moment a list of names flashed through her head, the names she had used in various exercises and also her real name, but she gave the name on her passport. Again, the young man asked politely, in English this time, if they could come in. She made space for them and saw they were looking at the table, which was laden with the tourist brochures and publicity she had gathered in the course of the days spent in Haifa. There was nothing about the exercise that could incriminate her, no hidden gun or secret cache of explosives. Her papers were perfectly in order, and she was prepared to explain to anyone who asked what flight she had arrived on and how she had been careless and lost her ticket. "We want you to come with us to the police station. We have some questions to ask you," said the young man, who was obviously the one running the show. "Ask your questions here," she said to them, and wondered if the women in the Port Authority had suspected her. The crumpled bed and scattered clothes testified to what she was, a young student staying in a two-star hotel on the Carmel. "It's for your own good," he insisted, and at her request he took from his pocket a short document written in English. She read slowly, recognized the stamps of the police department and the high court, and knew she had no choice. "Bring your things with you," he told her. "If we let you go, we'll send you to a better hotel." They stood beside her, and while she packed her things they checked every item. They seemed to be looking for something in particular. When she said she needed to go to the bathroom, they told her to leave the door open and promised not to peek. As far as she remembers, she wasn't afraid. She had a number abroad she could contact and leave a message, and also a local one, which was ostensibly of a friend who lived in Israel. They didn't suggest she call someone and she didn't ask. As they were about to leave, the police officer surprised her—he took handcuffs from his belt and signaled to her to hold out her hands. She refused and said she had rights, but the young man told her not to cause problems and not to make them use force. When they got into the vehicle they sat her between them, and their thighs pressed against hers. The long minutes of the car ride she spent reviewing her actions since she allegedly arrived in the country, and preparing for the questions she'd be asked. The car stopped outside a dark and menacing gate, and when it opened with a loud creak, the taciturn driver drove on and stopped by another door. Pale floodlights illuminated the police station, adjacent to an old British building, and Rachel couldn't rid herself of the feeling that this was a genuine arrest, although at any moment she could tell her jailers to phone her course instructor. The two of them helped her out of the car and walked beside her along a dark and desolate corridor. Only the sounds of their footsteps and the wheels of her suitcase, which the policeman was dragging, broke the hostile silence that pervaded the building.

A fat policewoman handed her a gray blouse and trousers and a pair of shabby plastic flip-flops and told her to change her clothes. Rachel thought perhaps it was worth arguing, and telling the female cop that detainees don't wear prison clothing, but at once she realized there was no way a Canadian tourist would know what was and what wasn't correct procedure in Israel. She held the clothes in her fingers as if they were unclean and it seemed her face expressed the outrage that the policewoman expected to see. The woman pointed silently to a dirty curtain. She went with Rachel to the other side of the curtain and turned away while Rachel quickly undressed and put on the clothes she'd been given. The clothes were too big for her and were smelly, and she tried to fight against the feeling of powerlessness that the tattered jail uniform was imposing on her. "How long will I be here?" she asked in a high and indignant voice, and tried to express all the anger of someone sure she is in the right. The policewoman held her silence and the young man who arrested her said it all depended on her. "You know I have a flight tomorrow?" Rachel said to him, and tried to look angry. He shrugged his shoulders and said this wasn't his concern.

When she was put into the cell and the heavy door closed behind her, her stress level rose. The bare walls, the hole in the floor that was the toilet, and the stained tap and basin above the concrete slab with a thin mattress on it all induced the dejection they were designed to create. The thought of having to spend the night in this cell, more than one day, perhaps, was extremely unappealing, and the idea of hammering on the door and speaking Hebrew and explaining to the astounded cops that she was just a Mossad trainee suddenly seemed reasonable to her. All the same, she knew that if she broke and blew her cover, she could say goodbye to the career that awaited her.

Rachel folded the blanket that was spread over the mattress, made it into a kind of pillow, lay on the bed, and linked her hands behind her head. Just wait it out and see what happens, she told herself, and tried to locate the camera watching her. There was no window in the cell and since her watch had been taken from her she could only guess how much time passed between her arrest and when she was taken to the interrogation room.

The first slap took her by surprise and she cried out in anger more than in pain. "You can't do that!" she barked at the interrogator, a woman, who looked at her with indifference and told her to tell the truth. "Why did you come here? And what were you looking for in the Port of Haifa?" she kept repeating, like a mantra. Rachel told the cover story she had prepared, but they didn't believe her and threatened that she'd be left rotting in her cell. From an envelope on the table the interrogator took all the photographs that Rachel had taken and claimed that the picture of the radar installation on Stella Maris would be enough to keep her in jail. Rachel said she didn't believe her, and Mount Carmel is famous throughout the Christian world and anyone can take a picture of it. The interrogator was unimpressed; she left the room and returned with another colleague. They spread out all the papers on the table and asked for the meaning of every scrap. She was afraid they might decide to contact one of the fictitious addresses in Canada. Then they focused on the passport. They asked about the stamps in it, and especially about her visit to Sudan the previous summer. Before setting out on the exercise, Rachel went through the passport with the instructor and told him she had never been to Sudan. "Neither have I," the instructor said with a smile. "We don't have the resources to adapt our training passports according to the requirements of every novice. Open an atlas, buy a tourist guide book to Khartoum, and hope they don't ask you too many questions about it."

"Where were you in Sudan?" asked the interrogator, and whispered something in Hebrew to the young man sitting beside her. "In Khartoum," said Rachel, and then she got the second slap. Her teeth clashed together and she felt blood in her mouth, and again she resisted the temptation to speak Hebrew and tell them this was all a mistake. The interrogator spread out a map of the city and asked her to show them where she went and where she walked, and Rachel began to cry and said she couldn't remember. She was in Khartoum with a friend who knew the city well and she followed around after her. Most of the time they were working as volunteers in an orphanage on the outskirts of the city and they slept in the house of one of the staff members. "It isn't my fault if staff members have no phones," she said when they wanted phone numbers and names, and she explained that it's hard to remember Sudanese names. She cried more and tried to stanch the bleeding with a handkerchief, and demanded they release her. She knew she could ask for permission to call the Canadian consul, but of course if he came and looked at her passport, he could easily tell that it was bogus.

Rachel realized that as long as she was sobbing and whimpering, they would leave her alone and wait for her to calm down. A new feeling was aroused in her, like the sensation she felt during the exams for entry to the course. She wanted to prove she was capable of withstanding pressure. That it was impossible to break her, not with tough questions, not with slaps. She licked at a tooth that had been loosened and no longer wiped away the tears and the blood. Playing the pitiful card might persuade them she's on the level.

"We have no choice," the interrogator told her. "We're sending you back to the cell. Tomorrow or the next day we'll talk to you again, and in the meantime we suggest you think about it and get ready to tell us everything, not just the crap you've been feeding us so far." Rachel started to object, mentioning the law of detention and the right of appeal to a judge, but she was silenced with a crude gesture and led away.

The concrete floor of the cell was now covered in water, the mattress and the blanket had been taken away, the cell stank. Rachel tried to tell the guard that this was no way to treat a Canadian citizen, wait and see how the press will handle a story like this. But the jailer pushed her into the cell, closed the door, and locked it.

Again she was alone. She tried to organize her thoughts. I should have been better prepared for this exercise, I shouldn't have agreed to go out with a passport showing the stamps of places I've never been, she scolded herself.

"Do you want to talk to me?" The pleasant-sounding voice emerged from a concealed speaker, and she retreated to a corner of the cell. She almost answered but held her tongue. He spoke Hebrew. She waited until the voice addressed her again, and when he asked in English if she wanted to talk, she said she had told them everything and she wanted to leave. "I'm giving you another chance," said the voice. "The clerk at the Port Authority said you know nothing about zoology and she doesn't believe you. Nor do I. Tell me why you came and I'll get you out of here." A stream of water gushed from a crack in the corner and flooded the floor again. She said nothing and was disappointed by her failure to hold back the tears. This was the time to show that she was hurt and angry, not to give them the idea she was liable to break anytime soon. The voice promised her a long stay in detention until she told the truth. Then there was silence.

She dozed; suddenly she felt a gentle hand shaking her. The policewoman escorted her to a dry and warm room. She was given a towel, handed back her clothes, and asked to sign a document written in faulty English. Rachel signed, declaring everything had been done according to the rules and she was waiving any future claim. They left the police station and walked to a nearby building. The officer knocked on an unmarked door, and when someone said, "Come in," she opened the door and almost pushed Rachel inside. Then Rachel heard the sound of applause.

She tried to smile, focused her gaze on her instructor, and it took her a moment to recognize the young man who arrested her at the hotel and the woman who interrogated her. They were all there, happy and smiling and holding glasses of wine. The instructor approached her, apologized on behalf of the team for the injury to her lip, and put a glass in her hand. "Congratulations, Rachel, you passed the final test. From now on, you're a fully fledged combatant." "But . . ." she began, and felt the anger bubbling in her. She remembered the blows, the filthy, stinking cell, the threats, and wanted to ask him if all this was necessary. The smiling faces told her that the question would spoil the party, they all looked so overjoyed, so when they wanted to tell her how they felt watching her through the two-way mirror, she gave in.

⚜

EHUD TOLD JOE WHAT HE KNEW about her entry into the enemy country and about the exercise. The things that Rachel told him mingled in his mind with other memories. Again he wasn't sure he was giving Joe an accurate report of the results of debriefings and the things they said in their long conversations. Joe encouraged him to continue and told him he didn't need to be precise: "Facts and figures are for balance sheets, and I'm telling you there are more important things to know to understand the real state of a company."

"Our operatives," Ehud continued, "pass on to us the intelligence reports that we ask for and report on the operations they have carried out. The rest we don't know. We don't ask for, and it would be impossible to get, a detailed daily report, something like a ship's log. Come to think of it, we don't know everything about our own children and what they're doing, even when they're living with us they can spring all kinds of surprises, and you can multiply the problem many times over when it's our man or woman in the field. So what is left for us? To imagine, to think what we would have done in his or her place, to try to get our heads around the sensation that they were feeling, the reality they experienced. That way maybe we could understand what motivated her, how she overcame the fears, and what she did in all the days and weeks when she was just hanging around, living there like a normal person.

"I wondered too why she told me about that interrogation, why did it even occur to her, with all the operational issues and the important things we had to talk about, to hark back to an exercise that belonged to another period. I think she couldn't let go of this memory because she experienced it as a breach of trust. She trusted us. She could not believe that we would lie to her, and collude with the police, and that Shabak would arrest her and physically abuse her and ask her questions that we had planted. Something deep inside her was broken. She told me that after the exercise was over she thought of the passport she had been given and the paperwork she had printed out for herself, and she couldn't get rid of the idea that all this time the instructor knew the cops were going to arrest her, and that he stood behind the two-way mirror and watched his protégée dirty, wet, and weeping, and that he allowed the interrogators to go on applying their pressure to test just how much she could take.

"But being there, alone, she knew she could rely only on herself. Just as she was alone in the detention cell and couldn't consult with anyone or depend on HQ to send someone to extricate her, so it would be in the field. She's on her own and she has to function as if she's the only one in the world who knows what she's doing. Although this is strange and sometimes incomprehensible, exercises and operations get mixed up together, and memory has its own ways of processing them. It isn't chronological order that decides but something else, which is usually out of our control and beyond our understanding. That was the way she associated events, and I myself see the similarity between the experience of the detention cell in the interrogation exercise and sitting in a hotel room, knowing that the world outside is an unfamiliar and hostile place.

"I tried to prepare her for this feeling. For the first night in enemy territory, for the anxiety that they're watching her and listening to her. That at any moment there could be a knock on the door and a man will be standing there, someone who will take her away just like in the exercise in Haifa. I told her that with time people get used to it—the seaman cannot sail thinking about the depth of water underneath him. You learn to live with the danger as if it's a given that can't be changed. But all the explanations and the preparations and the training, even the interrogation exercise, bear no resemblance to reality, because the danger is real and definite and because you are absolutely alone. I remember this. The entry into the room, the silence that falls after the door closes, and the sudden feeling that overwhelms you that someone is watching you. I told her you must get through this the first time and understand that this is it, that's the way you operate, as if they can see you and as if you don't care. I told her the days will come when she will have to hide the things she does, and we'll worry about it when the time comes.

"Then she told me what happened, as if this verbal disrobing would fortify her against fear. Of course nothing happened. Rachel was a young tourist who arrived in the capital city intending to find work. The prospect of counterintelligence anticipating her arrival and taking the trouble to put her in a room fitted with cameras and two-way mirrors was remote. It was unlikely that they would follow her from the moment she arrived in the city or put listening devices in her room. But logic doesn't dissolve fear.

"RACHEL FINISHED PUTTING AWAY HER FEW possessions in the battered wall closet and looked around her. It was the time to report her arrival and give a coded version of the room number. She knew I was waiting by the phone but decided to wait awhile, take a shower, and try to calm down. 'Relaxation is important,' I told her. 'Problems will come soon enough and you don't need to reproach yourself in advance. Eat well, get as much sleep as you need, and behave like any other young woman like you. The assignments you carry out and the information you collect have to be integrated into your normal life. That's the way you have to work, without standing out.' Even the series of reports that we demanded of her on arrival at her destination were prepared with this in mind. Everything had an appropriate cover, and no phone conversation or postcard that she sent deviated from what would be considered reasonable.

"She finished showering and wrapped herself in a towel. The light of the smoke detector winked at her. When she was in training the security officer explained there were hotels with rooms fitted out with peepholes, cameras, and listening gear, so anything going on in there could be observed. But she reminded herself there was no reason to think hers was like that. Why would they bother? It's expensive, it consumes resources. There would need to be some suspicion.

"Rachel released the towel, placed her leg on the bed, and rubbed herself with a fragrant body cream. She knew this was absurd, but all the same she turned her back to the flashing light. Why give them any freebies? she was thinking. She got dressed and sat by the phone and took a deep breath. She knew no one was going to answer at the number she was dialing. And after hearing the voice-mail message we had devised together, she left a short and reassuring message for her friend in Paris. She knew I would check the recording from another machine, and she also knew by heart the emergency hotline number. It was all in the manual. We had gone through everything, there was no reason to use any of the emergency measures we had devised, and she left the room and went for a walk in the streets around the hotel.

"And in the night, exhausted from her tour of the city and saturated with the smells and the tastes that were all new and exciting, she heard the footsteps. By the small light she had left on in the bathroom she could make out the time. Three in the morning, and she hears them clearly, passing by the door of her room and disappearing at the other end of the corridor. The smoke detector in the corner of the room continued to wink at her, and for a moment she wanted to believe that whoever was watching her with a hidden camera was there for her protection. And again she heard them coming back, heavy and rhythmic like the pacing of the guardsmen at Buckingham Palace. They sounded loud, as if the thin door would be no barrier to them. And then they receded and faded away, and came back again.

"She pulled the blanket over her head and huddled down in the bed, as if she could find refuge in the darkness. The unknown walker continued his pacing, and she wondered whether to call reception and report a stalker outside her room. The thought that they were coming for her did not subside.

"They know about me. They know about me and they're coming to get me. Any moment now there will be a light knock on the door, and then a squeeze of the handle. The heavy key was in the lock. They couldn't open the door without breaking it down, but the chain and the flimsy woodwork wouldn't stop them. Rachel peered at the window, which was covered by a curtain, and remembered how earlier that evening, before going down to the dreary dining room, having showered and put on a simple dress, she checked the window and found it couldn't be opened, and she looked for something heavy, to break the glass in case of need. This won't work either, she thought. She tried to calm herself down by concentrating on the rules that I repeated over and over again: 'Not everything is related to you. Always ask yourself: Did I do anything wrong? What reason have I given them to look for me? Whatever happens, always look for the simple answer.'

"I'm not made for all of this—the thought passed through her head and refused to move on. Logic told her everything was okay, her papers were in order and her story was good, and crossing the border and registering at the hotel had gone smoothly. Tomorrow she goes to the school for an interview and then she'll walk the streets of the city again, like any tourist. Everything's fine. But for the fear, it was business as usual. What did they do with the passport if they photographed it? Can they check it and find out what's wrong with it? What if they contact Canada to verify my identity? And if tomorrow, in the heart of the city, I meet someone who knows me, an innocent tourist, who was in Tel Aviv before and is now on the next leg of a Middle Eastern tour? And what happens if I fail?

"She tried to ignore the sounds she heard from the air-conditioning, the clicking of the smoke detector, and what seemed to her like footsteps in the corridor, and to concentrate on the mission ahead of her. What happens if I don't get the job and I can't obtain a residence permit or rent an apartment in the area assigned to me? How will I feel if I go back empty-handed and Ehud debriefs me and says in his quiet way that I could have done more? And then the Unit commander will send for me, and shake his head and tell me how much my operation has cost the State of Israel so far, and he'll talk about all the months of training that they invested in me and all the people who fussed over me, and I'm not even capable of landing a job in a crappy school? I expected more of you, Rachel, he'll say, and I'll be thinking, My father would say the same thing. My father who is so remote from me, Ehud who is so close, and I'm in the middle, wanting to prove to both of them that I can do it, I can fly.

"Again she heard footsteps. Passing in the corridor, heavy and rhythmic, stopping from time to time, and continuing. If they were coming to take me, like in the exercise in Haifa, they would already be stopping and knocking on the door. They would have posted someone outside the emergency exit, cutting off my escape. But I don't need to escape, because I have nothing to hide, and there are no secrets they can uncover. It's all with me, and it depends on me. Slowly, feeling a strange blend of diffidence and bravado, she lowered the sheet that covered her eyes and looked at the small red light flashing on and off. This flickering now gave a little boost to her confidence, as if the light were winking at her, telling her it would be all right. She got up and tiptoed to the door.

"Rachel put her eye to the peephole and waited. She heard her heart beating so hard she was afraid the person on the other side must be hearing it too. A moment passed, and she saw the old hotel security man moving at a steady pace along the corridor and passing by her, and then she remembered the chair. She had wondered why it was there at the end of the corridor, and now she wanted to open the door and thank him for watching over her."

⚜

"AND YOU'RE ASKING ME IF SHE was suitable for the job? If someone who's so scared can ignore the thought that any moment they might come and arrest her? Then I have to tell you that I don't know. I don't know how they do this. How they can live the identity that we've designed for them, lead an apparently normal life, even fall in love with someone, and at the same time think about the job that has to be done, about the real reason they are there, about the dangers that surround them and what is forbidden and what is permitted. In the movies they go on dangerous missions, fall into the traps set by beautiful women, and come home crowned in glory. In books we read about their spectacular adventures, and in the autobiographies that we allow them to publish, they write only what they want us to know. No one tells us what happens in hotel rooms and in the chambers of the heart in the days and nights that they spend there, and about the effects that remain when they return home after years of assuming that the world revolved around them.

"They don't tell us what they really feel. From their point of view they are always on duty. This is what they were found suitable for, what they were trained for. Just as they know how to project their identity in the field, so they learn over time to show us only the angle that they choose. They believe we have their interests at heart, but they know very well what we want, and they try to deliver the goods.

"And Rachel? She was openhearted, especially with me. She trusted me and she had a logical grasp of the world. She said that whenever she's afraid to tell, or afraid she may be harmed by the things she's going to say, she speaks out and copes with the consequences. 'If I dare not expose my feelings, it means that I'm ashamed of them,' she said. And there was something else. She shared things with me because I was no threat to her. Because she knew I was in love with her, because she didn't love me. You don't need to make an impression on people you don't love.

"When she came back from her first time out there, I was as pleased as she was that everything had gone smoothly and she was accepted for the job. After the fact I learned that she didn't say anything then about the first night, and I didn't ask, though I knew how hard it must have been. There were other things we had to go through together. It's just as well she didn't tell me straightaway about the knocking of the knees and standing at the peephole. I admit, I'd have thought she wasn't ready and needed to go back into training.

"And you know what? There's no harm in fear. Fear sharpens the senses; it makes you more careful and helps prevent foolish mistakes. The question isn't the fear but the ability to control it and continue to function. Although it wraps around you and ties you to the ground, fear also nourishes strength. Just as pain after an injury forces you to pay attention to the wound and treat it, so fear makes you more alert to danger. Not being able to be afraid is a kind of mental illness, and we need people with healthy minds. Not disturbed, not suicidal. We're looking for well-adjusted operatives who can feel the fear and know how to cope with it rationally."

In the neighboring house the lights had gone out hours ago. He looked at his watch and was astonished when he realized how long they had been sitting together, since he decided to tell all that he knew, all that was needed to bring her home. Joe got up and went to the bathroom. Ehud was left with his thoughts. What else is there to tell? What else is there to hide? Joe apparently isn't going to make it to eighty, and I'm a widower retiree and my grandchildren are far away. Rachel was right. What have I to be afraid of? Shame is our enemy in this business. Pretending that everything is fine and that we're working like a well-oiled machine is a perversion of reality. Hence the problems begin, the way is open to self-deception and the cracks that it brings with it.

He saw Joe approaching. His body, clearly racked by disease, moved cautiously on the rough paving stones that someone laid there in the days when they could all walk nimbly and didn't need to pay attention to each step.

CHAPTER FIVE

⤞⤝

The Operation

"Carry on," said Joe after lowering himself cautiously into the armchair. "I've spoken to the war room. They're checking every airport in Europe, and soon they'll start searching in hospitals. It's a Herculean task, but there is a point to it. But I'm also thinking about something else, something that might have to do with the gulf between living under a borrowed identity and the real life she knew after she came back."

Ehud listened to him and sipped his tea. Rachel had been embedded in enemy territory for nearly four years, he reflected. There are people who marry and have children in that span of time, people start and finish their studies, others build up their careers. Those people are not working undercover, living two parallel lives. He tried to remember what he knew about the daily purchases she made, about her work in the school, about the tiresome days between special operations, and realized that he remembered very little.

"We'll start with the operations," he told Joe. "We'll talk about the mundane side of her life later, maybe, after we've touched on the flash points that nearly burnt her out along the way."

He paused for a moment as if checking a diary, and continued: "It started in North Africa. We canceled her assignment at that time and put her on a liquidation operation. We teamed her up with someone, because we assumed she was the only one capable of doing what the operational plan demanded. It was hard persuading the intelligence community that was dependent on her reports to suspend her surveillance activities for a few weeks, but we had no choice.

"When she arrived at the safe house that we'd rented for the operation, I called her out to the balcony and told her she would need to share a room with Stefan. She glanced at me, and it seemed she was looking for something that hadn't been said. 'You're supposed to act like a couple,' I explained, and felt myself blushing. My voice shook and I was glad she didn't say anything. I knew there was no choice, and this was the way it was done. A requirement of the mission, an operational necessity. We don't have married couples for jobs like this, and what they do behind closed doors is their business. I envied Stefan the opportunity he had been given, and wanted to think this was no big deal, and the operation was the only thing that mattered to me. This wasn't true, because I knew Stefan and all the stories about him. I'd worked with him too on a joint assignment, and I knew how hard it is, waiting together for days and hours, waiting for the moment of climax.

"We went back to the sitting room and I showed them the passports chosen for the mission. Angie and Stephen Brown. We decided on Kenyan passports and identified them as British expats with dual nationality. Their mission, in a sentence: check into the hotel, identify the target, liquidate him, come home safely. When it was all over, Rachel Brooks would return to the flat in her adopted city, and Stefan to his kibbutz. Stefan lounged in an armchair. He looked very cool and he inspected Rachel as if assessing her both as a colleague and as a woman. Perhaps he was already wondering if sleeping with her was part of the deal.

"Stefan was our 'liquidator' at that time. The 'operator' is what this function was called when you headed the Unit. There were some who said his courage bordered on the psychotic; others said he had no feelings, no blood, with only ice flowing in his veins. He was the one who fired his weapon at point-blank range, two shots in rapid succession, straight into the heart. No chance of missing. Behind his back they said he killed a lot of blacks in South Africa before he came to this country. That's what he was like. The cowboy from the kibbutz who could doze in the saddle, sleep in a gully between rocks, tend his herd like a devoted nanny, and handle weapons as if nursing a baby.

"I once accompanied him on an expedition to Europe. He knew how to shoot, but had no idea how to behave like a tourist or a businessman. 'I'm not an actor,' he used to say, and every time they tried to teach him how to pretend, he lost his temper and threatened to leave. We needed him, and so he was always paired up with an experienced operative who took him in hand and spoke on his behalf and transported him from place to place like a ticking bomb. I traveled with him by train to Sofia and we slipped into an apartment overlooking the square. The guy who had rented the place handed me the keys and left Bulgaria. We knew that even if they went after him, they'd come up with a fake passport that would lead them nowhere. We stayed in the apartment for a week before the target arrived. We hardly exchanged a word between us. Stefan slept and ate and did his exercises, and it seemed that if he had to stay there till the end of time, that would be fine with him. He tended to sit by the window, watching the square and estimating wind strength, then go back to the bed and lie on his back and stare at the ceiling. I tried to read a book, I cooked for both of us, and the waiting was driving me crazy. When the alert came through, he got up calmly, took the rifle out of its case, fitted the silencer, and took up his position by the window with the chair-back in front of him.

"He sat there for three hours. I watched him. Sitting calmly and looking out as if he had all the time in the world, and if the victim didn't show up and we had to wait another day, it wouldn't bother him in the slightest. As if he were on his horse out on the prairie, watching his herd with a bored look but not missing a detail. When the lookout told us the car was arriving, Stefan raised the rifle and checked the telescopic sights. He was breathing like an artificial lung in open-heart surgery: slow and measured. Besides this, he was like a statue. The Angel of Death. We knew this would be difficult, and there was room for only one shot because the terrorist tended not to leave the car until his bodyguards had scoured the terrain. It was hard to identify him, and in the run-through we found it would take him five seconds to reach the door of the office building. Someone suggested blowing up the car along with its occupants, but we couldn't find a way of planting explosives at the entrance to the building. Someone else suggested the assassin should go on foot and arrive alongside the target, but we couldn't synchronize this to the degree required, and we knew the chances of getting our man out of there alive were slim. A drive-by with a couple on a motorbike was normal practice, and therefore too predictable. Only sniping was left, and it was clear we had to bring Stefan in. The Unit commander went to the kibbutz in person, to persuade the powers that be that he needed their cowboy in the middle of the calving season. They were skeptical about his made-up reason, but even if he had told them Stefan was his number one hit man, they would have stared in disbelief. Stefan? they would say. He sheds a tear when a calf dies. A sentimental song makes him cry.

"'Tell me what's happening,' said Stefan softly, and he went on staring at the front of the building through the telescopic sights. The narrow field of vision meant that he couldn't see the car approaching, or the reception committee waiting for it. This was my job. I held the binoculars close to my eyes, straining with the effort not to miss a single movement. The car stopped and the bodyguards stepped down to check the surroundings. 'Get ready,' I said to Stefan, who didn't respond. Another minute passed, and I thought my heart was going to burst. This was the moment I was supposed to freeze and avoid any movement that might distract him. The door of the car opened and nothing happened. I felt myself breathing heavily, and my hands shook. Then I heard the shot and saw the target fall. When he got out of the car, and how Stefan had time to aim and fire, to this day I don't know."

⚜

"RACHEL EXAMINED THE PASSPORT. I KNEW she didn't like it. Every operative has a particular angle, a sensitive and personal point that he'll argue over as if it's the most important detail in the world. I knew operatives who refused to be parted from their watches, from their medallions, from things that brought them luck. For her it was the name. She wanted to be Rachel and she hated the fictitious names. She wanted her own name; as if it allowed her to be herself in spite of the image she needed to project.

"When I told Stefan about the passport he shrugged and said it suited him, and he would introduce himself as a Kenyan farmer. I didn't ask him if he'd visited that country before. He didn't seem worried, and I knew that if something went wrong, no passport would help him. 'They'll check your passports and take them away for at least two days. Don't object and don't protest. You won't need them after the shooting in any event, and in the getaway car there will be new passports waiting for you,' I said.

"Stefan reviewed again what Rachel already knew from the briefing. 'You must make sure he shows me all of him,' he said. 'Make sure no one gets between us, and give me at least three seconds. I need all of him, the head isn't enough. Putting a bullet between the eyes only works in the movies.' Then he spoke to the armorer, who spread a cloth on the polished dining table and assembled the handgun, which had been fully dismantled. 'This is what there is, and you'll make it work,' said the armorer, and he explained that only a small plastic pistol could get through the hotel's metal detector. 'We checked this with the firm that supplied the hotel with the appliance—it's Israeli.' He suppressed a smile, inserted a loaded magazine, and turned the television up to maximum volume, then fired a single bullet into the mattress in the bedroom. 'That's it—except for putting on the silencer, the pistol is ready for firing,' he said. 'You don't need to adjust anything. It's firing now and it will fire again. Don't dismantle and don't reassemble.' Stefan didn't respond, and I admired his ability to let the boy do his job, although he had already forgotten what this young man had yet to learn. The weapon was packed in the pouch specially prepared for it, in Rachel's makeup case, and they were ready to set out."

⚘

ANGIE BROWN CHECKED INTO THE HOTEL, and when the clerk at the reception desk asked Mr. Brown for his passport, she answered on his behalf and kissed him and wrapped him in an impenetrable long embrace. The clerk smiled knowingly, said a bellboy would be there shortly, and apologized for the commotion in the lobby. "That's the way it is when there's a conference," he said, and pointed to the metal detector placed alongside the revolving door. "It ruins the atmosphere," he added, and Mrs. Brown smiled and said it was nice to feel protected.

The bellboy opened the door for them and invited her to go in first. Tall and broad-shouldered, Stefan followed her inside, and his body nearly filled the too-small room. A young couple should have a bigger room for a honeymoon, she was thinking, but it didn't stop her from thanking the bellboy with a smile for the bowl of fruit and the bottle of wine. She specifically asked for this room, and she had to lavish all the charm she could muster on the hotel's reservation clerk, via a transatlantic phone call, to be sure of getting it. The room was at the end of the hall and the window gave direct access to the fire escape. It was another part of the detailed operation plan. An operative checked the hotel right after the Mossad received the information about the upcoming conference and located the security camera and the alarm sensor that was connected to the emergency exit doors at the end of the hall, so using those doors to get to the fire escape was ruled out. Rachel left her case on the double bed and went to the bathroom. Another operative who checked out the room for them two weeks before noted the shower wasn't working well but the bathroom was clean, and it turned out he was right. Stefan stood at the window and peered out, saying nothing and paying no attention to the bellboy, who was explaining how to operate the air-conditioning.

Rachel walked up to Stefan and hugged him from behind, kissed the back of his neck, gave the bellboy five dollars, and watched him leave the room. Stefan freed himself from her embrace the moment the door was closed and sat down on the bed. The springs groaned under his weight, his outstretched legs almost reached the end of the room, and he looked at her like a hunter watching a rabbit caught in the headlights of his car.

⚜

TOWARD EVENING THEY STROLLED IN THE city. The trail from one tourist site to the next enabled them to check the escape route and the local traffic intersections. She marked the traffic lights and the one-way streets on the tourist map, and dropped the map behind a low wall before entering the hotel. Ehud wanted mapping for the benefit of the evacuation team due to arrive the next day, and another operative, waiting in a nearby hotel, retrieved the map and took it to the command yacht. Ehud was proud of the clean job executed by his young protégée. "Rachel's performance was exemplary," the other operative reported. She had hung on Stefan's arm, given him adoring looks and kisses, and anyone observing them, whether casually or professionally, would've taken her for a young bride in love. "Stefan succumbed to her charms too," the operative said, and described how Stefan's big arm had wrapped around her waist as if she were his prisoner. Ehud took care to keep a professional expression on his face and didn't reveal his feelings. "You must behave like newlyweds, they're the only ones allowed to do silly things," he told them at the preliminary briefing, and now they're doing their job.

They ate dinner in the hotel restaurant and walked up the stairs back up to their room, kissing after every landing. With this the preparations were complete, and all that remained was to wait and stare at CNN, the only channel in English. The Unit commander didn't want them moving around outside any more than was necessary: "You're a married couple. You can stay in the room and do what young people do."

☙

SHE REMOVED THE COVERLET FROM THE bed and saw, as she expected, there was only one blanket, the normal arrangement for a double bed, and she contacted reception. The clerk told her there were no extra blankets. "Sorry, Mrs. Brown, they are all in the laundry, perhaps tomorrow." Rachel laid the suitcase down by her side of the bed and pulled out her nightgown. "Only tarts sleep in T-shirts," she said, and told him this was what her father said when he saw her going to the bathroom in the night. Stefan pretended not to hear, but afterward he mentioned this in his report. "A strange thing for her to say," he wrote, and didn't elaborate.

The moment of truth arrived. It was clear that everything depended on her. Stefan sat on the single chair in the room and looked at her as she stood holding the nightdress up to her chest, like the last line of defense. She was silent and he was silent, and the noise of the street beyond the curtain and the double-glazed window was hushed too, waiting for their next move. She thought of Oren, left behind in another world, the world of Rachel Ravid from Israel. She stood in the alien hotel room and thought of the apartment in the capital city that belonged to Rachel Brooks, and she knew that now she must do what Angie Brown would do in her place. She asked Stefan what he expected to happen. "Nothing," was his brief answer. "We'll go to bed, get as much fun out of it as we can, and go to sleep." "And is there another way?" she asked in a tone that sounded strange to her. "Like, you sleep on your side and I on mine, end of story." "If you want to give me a hand job, or use your mouth, whatever suits you best, that's fine by me too," he replied. She refrained from asking if that was how things were on the farm. Before turning in, does he pick out a heifer from the herd, or a mare from the stable, and that's the only way he can sleep?

"No," she said, and felt so small in comparison to him, like a novice taking a test that's beyond her. "That isn't going to happen. I don't want you and this wasn't part of the deal. You'll wait until I go to bed and then you can go and masturbate in the shower to your heart's content. Then come back and sleep beside me and don't touch me." It seemed to her he was enjoying the conversation, he liked being crude and arrogant and sure of himself. As it was on the kibbutz, where all the female volunteers wanted to go with him out into the countryside, to ride a horse, feel close to nature, and be screwed by him on the hard ground in the shack that he built for himself next to the barn. "You'll see," he said to her indifferently. "Better to do it and be done with it. It's only sex between consenting adults. This isn't an affair—there's no beginning and no end, just the middle. It's better that way, it releases the tension. But I'll do whatever you want, and I'll lie down beside you, and we'll both lie awake until you decide for yourself you're going to touch me, and everything will be fine."

Then she knew he was right and she was even angrier at herself. She lay beside him tense and frozen and listened to his breathing and felt the warmth of his body and smelled his smell, till she realized if she didn't give in to what was burning in her, she wouldn't be capable of thinking about anything else, and then she touched him. Afterward, she hated him for the lifelessness of the experience, for the condom that he put on with such proficiency, for the way he loomed over her and the way he turned his back on her afterward. "We have a hard day ahead of us tomorrow," he said before he fell asleep, and she lay on her back, put on the panties she had left on the bedside table, and pulled down her rumpled nightgown.

☙

TOWARD MORNING HE WANTED HER AGAIN. This time it was enjoyable. His heavy body covered her and she felt safe under his bulk. She didn't come and didn't even try to come. She gave him what he wanted and he gave her the confidence she was looking for. He won't betray her. He won't leave her behind if something goes wrong. Not after he slept with her and kissed her and caressed her with such tenderness. He dozed again, like a baby satisfied after a feed. A few hours from now they will have half a minute to carry out an operation that has been put together during the long weeks that elapsed since she was called away from the school and from the tranquil life she created for herself there. It seemed strange to her to think of the excursions and the lookouts as something easy and normal, but life has rhythms of its own and after some time she got used to the routine, and the sense of danger diminished. She actually enjoyed the teaching, enjoyed exploring the markets, and enjoyed the independence she felt within the parameters laid down by Ehud. She no longer thought that someone was listening to her, that the Mukhabarat was on her trail, she understood the environment in which she was working, and felt confident of her ability. And she knew this evening would be different. She'll have to wait in the lobby until the target arrives with his bodyguard beside him, follow them into the lift, flashing her most winsome of smiles, and tap in the number of the lift on the transmitter concealed in her purse. She'll apologize and press the button for her floor, and she'll make sure, as only a woman knows how, to have the bodyguard backed into the corner of the lift, behind her. When the door opens Stefan will be there, ready to do his job. She must not fail, and she must not move. Stefan will shoot the target and then the bodyguard. It won't be easy, and there's a chance she'll be hit. Now, lying in bed, she felt more confident. She played with his fingers and stroked his nails, with the traces of the farm embedded deeply beneath them.

When the dawn lit up one of the corners of the room she carefully extricated herself from the bed, picked up the makeup case, which she made a point of keeping close at hand, and padded naked to the bathroom. She felt him watching her, quickened her pace, and closed the door behind her. When she came out, a towel was wrapped around her and she asked him to look away while she dressed.

Stefan held out a hand and touched her. She didn't think it was going to happen again, but until the evening they would have time on their hands. In her case there was a book, and she knew she'd be incapable of reading anything. She wanted to talk. She wanted him to look at her, touch her, assure her that his bullets won't miss their mark—he owes her that much. Once the two targets are dead, they'll go to their room at the end of the corridor, Stefan will break the glass window, and they'll go down the fire escape to a vehicle waiting for them. If there are people in the corridor, Stefan will scare them away, and the security staff will be held up for some time by the door, which will be locked from inside. And despite all the planning and the training, of course things could still go horribly wrong. Stefan is a big and strong man, experienced and armed and coolheaded, and for her this is the first operation. "You're not to move," Stefan told her in the briefings. "I can take out the bodyguard as long as you don't move. One moving target is enough." But she knew the silencer would muffle only part of the sound and the bodyguard might grab her and use her as a shield, and from the moment the door opened it all depended on Stefan, who was now lying in the bed barely covered by a sheet and fiddling with the remote control.

"How can you?" She sat down beside him in her clothes, as he put a hand on her knee. She tried to choose her words with care. They were both professionals and they knew it was forbidden to discuss operational matters in the room, and they had also learned how to conceal what they meant to say. "How can you lie here as if you're bored, having screwed me twice, and look for an interesting program on the TV, when you know what's at stake for us this evening, and it's a deal that might not come off?" Stefan wanted to tell her you get used to it, with time it gets easier, and anyway there's nothing he needs to be doing now, but he restrained himself.

&

"She's too young and she has no experience," Stefan said to Ehud, back in the holiday apartment in Sicily, rented for the time when they were preparing for the operation. Rachel had gone into her room to change her clothes for the final dress rehearsal, and he took the last opportunity to try and change the decision to use her.

Ehud had seen the way Stefan was watching and sizing her up, and he now realized just how much Stefan liked her, and he told him she'd be fine.

"Also, we have no one else," said the Unit commander, overhearing the conversation. "Besides, you've seen how she conducts herself, like a lady. You can go anywhere with her and you don't need to open your mouth."

Stefan ignored the allusion to his shortcomings as an operative. "She's too sensitive," he said. He started to say more but the Unit commander cut him off. "There's no alternative. There's always a first time, and I'm trusting you to bring her up to speed."

He winked at Stefan, and Ehud felt the anger and jealousy welling up in him. He hated this kind of fraternity talk and was uncomfortable having to be a part of it. Rachel was an operative. She had risked her life and spent time in a foreign location that none of the men sitting in this room would have been capable of reaching. She didn't have as much experience as Stefan, and her only exposure to guns had been on the practice range, where all operatives were required to take firearms training, but in this operation she was risking her life like Stefan, perhaps more so, and yet they were talking about her as if she were an object, an appliance with only one purpose, to set up the target in the line of fire.

Stefan wasn't giving up, and he told the Unit commander how scared she was every time the door of the lift opened and he burst in with the drawn pistol.

"Calm her down. Take the role of the father. You're the responsible adult."

"Am I?" said Stefan. He didn't smile.

"Listen to her and be patient with her," said the commander. "According to her psychological profile, she has a father-complex, and she's looking for a substitute for the father she had issues with. Try for once not to seduce your partner."

The commander laughed and Ehud held his silence, because the operation was more important than Rachel, more important than her intimate secrets.

⚜

STEFAN PLAYED WITH THE REMOTE UNTIL he found some raucous rock music and turned up the volume. He sat up and pulled Rachel closer to him "We have no choice," he said. "We can sit here all day and let the pressure grind us down until we can't move. I've seen this happen before. He looked away from the singer gyrating on the screen and turned to face her. "We won't improve our efficiency by thinking about all the bad things. We need to rest and just wait patiently."

"Rest? Patiently?" she asked, and the tone of her voice told him that was unlikely.

"I see you've brought a book," he said, and pointed to the slim volume of poetry.

"Yes," she said. He had obviously never heard of Emily Dickinson, and she realized now that she would open this book only if she had to wait too long in the lobby.

"So how about it? Are you going to sit and read by the window, like in some movie? You could even read me something, if the mood takes you."

"No!" she said firmly. "We need to talk."

The room service arrived and she got up to take the tray. Stefan poured her a cup of coffee and she said now they really were acting like a couple. Stefan smiled at her. His smile pleased her and she didn't want to lose it. She was afraid of something happening to him. He was the one who would hold the gun, the one who must shoot without hesitation and then disappear with her. They ate in silence, and she spread jam on a slice of bread and gave it to him and said that her father used to eat beans in the morning. Stefan was surprised, and she explained to him there are Englishmen who eat hot beans on toast for their breakfast.

And then they talked, or rather she did, and Stefan, who was used to sitting alone on a horse, with only the dog to shout at from time to time, listened to her and recorded the words in his memory, and afterward wrote them up in a report that he marked for Ehud's attention only, which needless to say didn't work, because a report is a report, and it went into the debriefing file.

"This is strange," she said, "but I'm thinking about my father," and she told him that when she was frightened in the night her father wouldn't let her into her parents' bedroom, and for as long as she could remember her parents had slept in separate beds. She wondered if they had ever shared a bed, but her mother died before she asked her.

"And if it had been allowed, which of the beds would you have chosen to get into?"

She was amazed that he was capable of asking such a question, amazed that he was listening to her at all. Something soft, which she didn't recognize, crept into his voice, and his English, usually so stiff and formal, suddenly sounded accessible and melodious. "My mother's, I think. But I would have liked it to be my father's."

Stefan held out a hand and touched her. She was surprised. The hand was warm and soft to the touch. She wanted to tell him more. She wanted to tell him about arriving in Israel, her days of loneliness until *they* approached her, until *they* offered her something else to do, but she knew this was off-limits. Even just between them, in this closed room.

"I was twelve years old, not a woman and not a girl." She didn't know why she was telling him this. "Our house was always dark. My father was a miser and my mother didn't dare argue with him. When I'd come home from school, Mom was usually in the kitchen and Dad was sitting at his desk. I loved running to Mom and hugging her. There was such a feeling of safety about it. Mama, in the kitchen, preparing supper, which was served at ten to six precisely, so Dad would have time to watch the news. Then to the pub for one drink, then back home and into the bathroom, and no one dared disturb him there. Then to bed, and listening to the BBC news and then a concert, every night, until he fell asleep. A man of fixed habits.

"I had my habits too. After hugging my Mom, I used to go into his study. He'd look up from his papers, turning his chair in my direction, and I'd sit on his knees and look at what he was doing.

"I loved sitting on his lap or leaning against him and I liked the feel of his jacket. All this before I began maturing, all this before I thought about anything at all.

"Then one day he said, 'That's enough,' and pushed me off. I remember this as if it were happening now. He just pushed me off. 'That's enough,' he said, 'girls of your age don't do things like this.' I didn't understand him. I only knew that he didn't want me. Something about me wasn't right. I didn't try anymore. I'd go to his study and stand beside him and he'd take a sweet from the drawer. I'd stand there and eat it, and it seemed he didn't care about crumbs falling on the desk. That was the compensation he chose for me."

⚜

A FEW HOURS LATER SHE WAS still stunned by the shooting in the lift and utterly absorbed in the rapid action afterward. Things had gone according to plan, except for the part with the bodyguard. Instead of reaching for his gun he grabbed her from behind and held her tight with both arms. After shooting the terrorist, Stefan walked into the elevator, and before Rachel realized what he intended to do he jammed the end of the silencer between the bodyguard's eyes and fired a single shot. They got out before the doors closed and made it to their room without anyone seeing them. Stefan said there was no time, but he waited a minute while Rachel changed her trousers, which were wet. He didn't mention this in his report, and Ehud, who questioned her at length and had all the details from her, didn't reveal it to anyone. The car that was waiting for them behind the hotel took them to the yacht, which was ready to set sail, and by the time a popular TV program was interrupted to announce the murder of one of the chief freedom fighters, they were already at sea.

⚜

"AND THAT'S IT?" ASKED JOE. "THAT'S everything you've learned from the report and from the conversations you had with her after the operation? From your story it seems like there really was some chemistry between them. They had a reason to continue with each other."

"There was no chance of that," said Ehud. "It seemed strange to me too, but the Unit commander wouldn't let them come back here together, or receive the plaudits due to them. He insisted that Rachel must return to her covert life right away, and she'd have other opportunities to celebrate. She just did as she was told. I spoke to him from the yacht on an old radiophone and we knew the line wasn't secure, and I couldn't argue with him without revealing details that shouldn't be disclosed, so I let it go. In hindsight, I think he was right. This operation was routine for Stefan, it was the way he worked, and he was ready to go back to the farm. For Rachel this was a one-off experience that could have done her some damage and distracted her from her central objective. We were on the yacht for a few days. It was crowded and noisy, and I made sure she shared a cabin with the girl who drove the getaway car. Stefan had a roommate too, and he and Rachel had no opportunity to talk, at least not as far as I know. When we got to Sicily we sent the rest of the team on its way and Rachel and I flew to France to buy her a car and prepare her for the next assignment. She was no longer Angie Brown, or even Rachel Goldschmitt. Rachel Brooks didn't know anyone called Stefan and had never even visited North Africa. Rachel Brooks was on her way to Paris, after her holiday in Sicily, to buy an old Volvo in reasonable condition. She intended to park it in the reserved space at her apartment building belonging to her flat and use it for travel and recreation."

༄

CHAPTER SIX

Out There

"'You know I have no reason to go there,' she said to me after I outlined the next mission we had planned for her. I knew she was right. Why would a foreign national just happen to be on a side road leading to a string of military bases? What is she looking for? How would she know about a road that is marked on the map as a dust track? There were other things I knew but didn't tell her: If she falls into their hands and reveals everything she knows, other networks will be compromised, and that must never happen. Keeping things compartmentalized is what it's all about, and this is for her protection too. No one other than us knows she's in the field, and all the information she transmits we camouflage before passing it on to the analysts. I explained to her once how we obscured her image in photographs, and I saw a trace of disappointment in her eyes, as if I were taking away something that belonged to her and denying her existence. When I showed her the blurred pictures she winced as if feeling it physically. 'You're erasing me,' she said. 'If one day I really disappear, no one will notice.'

"The operation was dangerous, but she was a combatant, and this is what combatants do. It isn't just rhetorical to say they're working in the service of the state in times of peace and in times of war. Soldiers go into battle and risk their lives in pursuit of the objective, and there was no reason why her case should be different. Why wouldn't we endanger one person to get the information that could save many lives?

"We all knew her. We knew where she was born and who her friends were, and it was hard to imagine a situation of her being captured, suddenly not being there anymore. But that didn't make her blood any redder than the blood of the soldiers on patrol in Nablus, in action in the Gaza Strip, preparing for war.

"'This is a risk we can take,' I said. 'Oh, we can, can we?' was her sardonic response, and I knew she was right. We'll devise a reason for her to go there, and rehearse it with her beforehand, but when all is said and done she'll be out there on her own, while the rest of us sit at home, drink coffee, and wait for her to report.

"I can see you're dying to ask what actually happened there, and what she did, and all I can tell you is that I don't know. How is it possible to know exactly what's happening when the facts are so few and simple? She stopped the car outside the gate and did the job, and more than that. A whole lot more. 'A few pictures, and as much as you can remember,' the operations officer told her in the briefing, and that's what we were training her for. We didn't ask for more, and she didn't tell us what she understood from the training and the ops officer's remarks. I saw the results in the pictures and heard them in the conversations we held during debrief. I saw a picture of her hugging the sentry and some shots of the entrance to the base, and in another, the climax of the operation—she's shaking hands with the base commander, in front of the sentry's booth. 'That's what you wanted, isn't it?' she said to me, and I saw in her eyes the anger that was germinating, as if she wanted me to praise her and reprimand her at the same time, tell her she'd brought back premium information but she shouldn't have taken such a risk. But there was something else in this remark of hers and in her posture, sitting bolt upright in the chair. You're to blame, she was telling me silently. You're pushing me to the limit. You're always drumming it into me that I'm not made of sugar and I won't melt and I have to take risks too, not just sit in a nice apartment at the state's expense, counting my pension credits. So there you have it.

"The debriefing after the operation shocked me. I wasn't prepared for it. The report was full of details. There were no pictures taken inside the base, but we compared the report with other fragments of information that we had and we knew it was accurate. The ops officer was licking his chops, in the Intelligence Corps they were singing the Mossad's praises, but I gave her a black mark and wrote a memo to the Unit commander: this wasn't a good sign; she threw off the yoke and acted outside of what she was supposed to be doing. More than we asked for and way beyond the instructions she received. We agreed beforehand that she would stop the car by the main gate to check the rear tires. We also said she should get out of the car so she could see more and memorize the details. We didn't ask her to approach the sentry, or point to her stomach and explain to him in her rudimentary Arabic that she needed the bathroom urgently. Until the face-to-face debriefing I didn't know she spoke to the sentry and memorized the entry procedures for access to the camp before he handed her the phone to talk to his boss. Imagine it, our Rachel sitting there on the john in the middle of a missile base, doing her thing and all the time thinking about what's missing, about opportunities that won't be repeated. Then she drank coffee with the commander in his office, memorized the map on the wall behind him, complimented him on his excellent English, and found out where he studied chemistry and who his classmates had been at Moscow University.

"I listened to her report and wondered what was going through her head when she took such colossal risks. Did she think about her car, parked outside the base? The danger that an agent of the Mukhabarat might want to know what a car with foreign license plates was doing there? I wanted to know more than that, but she didn't tell me how she felt when she was talking to the base commander, and if she was afraid he would notice how inquisitive she was about him, and how shy when asked about herself."

❧

FROM A DISTANCE, EVEN BEFORE SHE passed the last bend, Rachel felt the tension constricting her stomach and tightening her grip on the wheel. She reviewed once more the details of the plan: identify the base, pass by it, take a look, and continue driving. Verify that this is the base, if it's like the picture that I was shown. Where did they get it from? Why are they sending me if they already have a picture? Then I continue on to my tourist destination. I go for a walk around the church. I come out, buy an exorbitantly priced souvenir, chat with the vendor so he'll remember me and confirm that I was there, I'm a nice person, there's nothing bad about me. That's the way I look to him, at least. And then I wait until the sun is behind me. I check the camera, put in new film, take a few pictures. Put the camera in my handbag, align it with the small hole in the bag, check the mechanism to operate the shutter. Here is where it starts.

Rachel passed the bend and slowed down. From a distance she saw fences and buildings. Must be "her" base. She went on a kilometer farther and saw there was more than one base. There were several bases. She slowed down again, and a truck behind her tooted. She stepped on the gas pedal but the truck stayed close behind. The road was crowded and she couldn't pass the car in front or get rid of the truck behind her. Besides, if she overtakes she's liable to miss the gate. Now she needed to find the right base and also pay attention to the truck that seemed stuck to the rear of her car. For a moment she thought of dispensing with accurate measuring and precise identification, but she knew this was a mistake. For the purposes of the mission she had to stop, as if by chance, close by the gate, located on the other side of the narrow road, and to do this she needed to identify it now and measure the precise distance to the filling station. Having recorded this detail she will turn the trip odometer back to zero, so she won't be caught measuring distances to and from the base. A lot of details to deal with, and she needs to drive and watch both sides of the road, with the truck pushing her from behind. She was coming close to the first base and knew that if she stopped now and let the truck overtake her, she risked having the truck stop beside her, and somebody else might also stop and later recall the car that stopped twice in this area. A light nudge from behind, just a touch. He's playing with me, fancies his chances because I'm a woman alone in a Volvo and my hair is loose; he thinks I'm fair game. Rachel accelerated slightly and moved away from the truck, which hooted at her as if saying farewell. She was approaching the camp. The picture they showed her had been taken from the side and there was no way of knowing if this was the base she was supposed to be heading for. The gauge showed that the distance from the last intersection was approximately what the ops officer had told her. He said it wasn't exact, and the difference could be two hundred meters—the margin of error in taking measurements from the maps at their disposal and from aerial photographs. Also the mechanic they brought especially from Israel in order to prepare the car she "bought" from an operative who brought it to France said that's all there is and with that she has to just do it.

"From the bend in the road onward you'll need to rely on the photograph and on your own judgment," the ops officer said, and in training this had seemed simple. She came closer to the base, but behind it there was another, and behind that another, and the truck was closing in on her again. It was too late to stop, and impossible to pick up speed; she needed to keep watching both sides of the road and turn the trip odometer back to zero in time. She took a deep breath and let it out slowly, imagining herself squeezing the trigger of a sniper's rifle, and inhaled again. Tall fences, barbed wire, sentry booth, pull-off area. It didn't match what she remembered from the photograph the ops officer showed her, but it was a month since she saw it, and he wouldn't let her make a sketch of it. "You have to commit it to memory," he said. She obviously didn't want to get caught with a sketch of a secure location. She passed by the gate and looked to her right. No, this wasn't the base she was looking for. Go on. The second base. Floodlights around the perimeter. A low wall topped by a wire fence. Another guard post. Again she turned her head to the right, and hoped the driver of the truck behind her would think she was checking her rearview mirror. That's it, that's the base. She pressed the distance gauge and stole a glance at the sentry beside the yellow barrier. The truck tooted at her again and she resisted the temptation to show the driver the finger. Instead she laughed and thumped the steering wheel and kept on driving. When she passed the third base she checked it out carefully to be sure she hadn't made a mistake. This time there was no one from headquarters following her, as in the exercise on a side road outside Rome. She was alone now. Only she could do this for them ("for us, Rachel, for us"—Ehud never tired of stressing that she wasn't a hired hand, they were working together, a team). She accelerated and pulled away from the truck, but was careful not to get too far ahead, so the pattern of her driving wouldn't arouse suspicion, and thought about the operation. Why do they need to know the width of the gate and what it's made of? Are there obstacles in the roadway? Is there a telephone link between the sentry and the command center, and where is the command center? "Look for a nice house flying a flag," the ops officer briefed her. Rachel started to tell him it would be useful to have the purpose of all this information explained to her, so she could look for other things that hadn't been specifically mentioned, but the ops officer invoked the need-to-know principle and she let it go.

When she reached the filling station she jotted down the distance to the base on a piece of paper and put a dot between the figures. Ehud had wanted her to memorize the numbers and she agreed, but she thought that she might forget, and she decided that if asked about the note she'll say it's the price of a statuette that she saw in an antique shop in the market. No, I don't remember which shop, she'll say. No one will ask, and yet there needs to be an answer ready, as with everything that she's planned to do, with the exception of the photography. "The photograph we have is blurred and no use at all. Impossible to see the gate and the security post. That's why you need to stop the car and get out. Activate the camera in the handbag, the way they showed you, and take pictures while you're moving from one side of the car to the other," said the ops officer, and added that he thought this was a risk worth taking. "Why would I get out of the car with my handbag if I'm just checking one of the tires?" she asked, and saw all eyes turning to her. "We'll need to find an answer to that," said Ehud, and he suggested discussing it later. "We simply can't do without these photographs."

⟡

To her surprise, the tour of the local church was interesting. Rachel gave credit to the priest who taught her in training how to act like a devout Christian, and she remembered the church she found in Montreal when she went there to work on her new identity. She had no difficulty presenting herself to the parish priest as the daughter of strictly secular parents and asking him to teach her all that was required for a baptism. The priest was very kind and also curious, but his kindness prevailed over his curiosity, and he stopped asking questions about her past, which remained wrapped in silence. Rachel was an avid pupil, joined in all the prayers and rituals, and they were both genuinely sorry when she had to leave sometime before the scheduled ceremony, as she was offered a job in another town. The case officer who accompanied her in Canada had been opposed to the idea of her going through with it, on the grounds that she couldn't possibly give the priest her real name, and therefore it wouldn't be valid anyway. Rachel yielded, and afterward told Ehud she assumed the skullcap that the case officer made a point of removing before every meeting with her might be the real reason. "Don't worry," Ehud reassured her when she told him there was no substitute for imbibing other religious traditions along with mother's milk. "No one's going to test you. No one strips you to check you're a woman, and casual acquaintances don't insist on seeing your passport. People believe what they see and what they hear until they're given a reason to think otherwise. Just wear a small crucifix, inherited from your grandma, and make sure you mumble something about Christian holidays from time to time. Be grateful you don't need to explain away a circumcision."

Rachel didn't forget to light a candle and cross herself, and she took photographs of the ancient building from every angle. The ops officer will be glad to have these pictures too, she thought. Then she bought a small rug in a souvenir shop, and it was only when she came out that she remembered she should have gotten a receipt. The accountants always groaned when they saw the expenses she submitted, and they didn't like declarations instead of receipts. "I don't see why I should collect receipts from the supermarket," she told them, and Ehud signed off on all of it for her; there was no arguing with his signature. But things like souvenirs were different, and any addition to the apartment needed clearance from the start.

Okay, I'm ready, she decided after leaving the grimy toilets of the big empty café opened opposite the church in better times. There was no one to notify that she was on her way. Ehud didn't even know she was planning to travel that day. She looked around her. They all seemed to sense she was up to something. Men stared at her, children asked for coins. One man tried to sell her fruit and then offered her hashish. She refused, although that might have been worth considering at another time. She looked at her watch again. Time to move. She got into the car and started it up. A Volvo in good condition. A bit conspicuous around here, but so is she, a young foreign woman traveling alone. It isn't against the law. On the Sabbath there's no teaching and this is her day off, she can go anywhere.

There was no need to unfold the note with the recorded distance on it. She stopped for fuel as planned, then went to the air pump to check the pressure in the tires. Then she slipped the camera into her handbag, attached the cord to it, and fixed it to the buckle of the carrying-strap. She secured the camera in place with the special strap provided by the technical department. She was ready. She had rehearsed this many times, and now it took less than a minute. If someone disturbs her she knows how to pull the cord and detach it from the camera, and release the camera from the strap so it looks completely innocent.

A glance in the mirror. Her hair is combed and parted. Her face clean of makeup, blouse buttoned, and sandals buckled. On the way.

And again her heart is pounding. She turns the distance gauge to zero. She has an explanation for this too, it's her way of monitoring fuel consumption. She sees the base in the distance. The sun is at a good angle. She approaches the gate, checks that the distance is right, and uses the gap between two cars to cross to the other side of the road and stop as close as possible. If she's challenged she'll point to the narrow shoulder and comment on how dangerous it is. No one challenges her. She sees the sentry and gets out of the car, her handbag slung on her shoulder, and immediately starts photographing on her way to the back wheel. After removing the plastic bag that she wrapped around the axle in the filling station, she knows she has an excuse for washing her hands, and the sentry, who has walked over, is standing beside her, sees her bending over the wheel. His attention is focused on the young woman, not on her intentions, not on her handbag or on what she's doing. "No stop," says the scruffy young soldier. "One moment," she says, and smiles at him, glad that he's younger than her and his eyes are studying her body. "Problem?" he asks, and points to the car. "No, no. Okay, okay," she says while scrutinizing the gate and the barrier and the wire fence that could be opened out quickly to block the entrance, and the well-camouflaged watchtower. The soldier smiles at her and she smiles at him. Nice day today, she wants to say to him, and knows he won't understand. Everything seems to have been too easy, and after weeks of preparation she's collected in half a minute all the information that Ehud authorized her to look for. She knows the ops officer wants more. They always want more, and before her departure the ops officer made a point of telling her that if he had more confidence in her experience he would be asking for more.

One gesture. For this you don't need to know Arabic. This was enough to convey her particular problem to the sentry. He smiled and said, "No problem," and she walked with him to the guard post, taking more photographs on the way. He rang someone and then someone else and when his back was turned she detached the cord from the camera and released it. Everything in order. Even if he checks her handbag and finds the camera he'll have no reason to suspect anything. It was only when she finally made it to the john and sat down that she realized just how tense she was.

The commander of the base was pleasant and affable. Rachel was glad he was making an effort to speak English and she told him it was excellent. The conversation flowed and she memorized every detail she could take in from the map on the wall behind him. When the coffee was late in arriving he went out and shouted at someone and she resisted the impulse to reach out for one of the documents on the desk. He returned with the tray and poured for her himself, and she felt she could even tempt him to reveal his own secrets. "Sorry," she said, and pointed to her watch. He apologized for taking up her time and said he was busy too, because of the big exercise starting tomorrow, and he walked with her to the gate of the base.

♣

RACHEL PARKED THE VOLVO IN THE enclosed parking lot, went up to the apartment, hid the film, and then realized her legs were shaking. She made it to the bathroom just in time and sat on the toilet, regaining some of the freedom that had been stolen from her during the day. She was sweating, she had a bad case of the runs, and was in tears, and, still sitting there, she reached out for the sink and splashed water on her face. She stayed where she was, half naked, her elbows on her knees, head between her hands, and tried to relax. It isn't over yet, she told herself. I still have to write the report and pass it on, I must get the film to the drop-off, there are still a lot of things to do. She isn't a pilot who returns from a sortie and gets home an hour later—she's in enemy territory.

The phone rang, she didn't answer it, and waited to hear the message on the answering machine. "Hi, it's me. I know you're there, you can't get away from me. The Sheraton, as usual? Contact me. 'Bye." She liked Barbara, and Barbara loved her. Rachel recovered some composure and took a hot shower, washing her hair slowly and carefully, combing it out under the water.

"Barbara is all right," she reported to Ehud during her first vacation. "A bit inquisitive, as a girl has to be, but all right. I have to invite her. I have no choice."

"Why?" Ehud asked, although he knew the answer.

"She's my friend. All strangers are regarded as friends, that's the way it is there."

"And the equipment?" He wasn't reassured. With men it's different. They don't pry into the business of others.

"It'll be all right. She wouldn't understand anything."

Ehud asked again and again, and didn't rest until he was sure Rachel was prepared for any eventuality, Barbara switching on the radio or the cassette player, for example. He asked her to send him more information about Barbara. Rachel went to the school administration office and offered to help with the personnel files of the teaching staff and got him her passport number and national insurance number, and succeeded in persuading Barbara to tell her all her secrets.

"And you have other friends?" he asked her delicately, and she, knowing what he was driving at, told him about the other teachers, about poetry evenings and field trips with the students. When he asked who they were, she mentioned *his* name too and left it at that.

She got out of the shower, wrapped herself in a towel, and switched on the answering machine. Her aunt in Provence asked how she was and reported on the health of the uncle. This was a signal from Ehud, telling her to get in touch, report if everything was okay and if the mission had been accomplished. "This will only complicate things for me," she told him before they parted in Milan. "Why do you need this? I'll report everything by coded telegram, all together." But Ehud insisted, and she knew if she didn't call him and report the operation using the code words they agreed upon before, he would inform the Unit commander and perhaps even phone her according to the set emergency plan.

She wondered if she really wanted him to look for her. Although she knew it was childish and irresponsible, she wanted him to worry, to fret about her. She was postoperational, and hungry, and emotional, and wanted someone to confide in, someone who understood what she was doing, and instead she was going to call Barbara and arrange to meet her in the lobby of the Sheraton, think of what she was going to say, decide what to write in her report, and carry on alone, living, alone, with all that she had seen and done.

"Pity you didn't tell me you were going out," said Barbara over the tall glasses of lemonade. "I'd have been glad to join you."

And this is the price of friendship, Rachel was thinking, the price of deceit, the need to prepare for this too, and have a story to tell about everything. "Okay, maybe next time," she replied, and put on a sour expression. Don't be too sympathetic. It isn't good. Barbara could become a good friend, but the more she knows, the more trouble she's going to be. Rachel tried to focus.

"And how was it?" Barbara was genuinely interested, and Rachel figured she could tell her about driving on the narrow road, the truck that tailgated her on the approach to the army bases. "How did you come to be there?" Barbara asked, and was amazed when she heard Rachel had chosen such a winding switchback road for her journey. And Rachel knew she had no choice, she couldn't pretend she'd opted for a different route, that was against the rules. It was only the purpose of the journey that had to be concealed. That's the way it is. She couldn't sit down with Barbara, or with *him*, and pour out her heart. She'll always need to choose her words carefully and think about what she's saying. But Barbara could be a true friend in the other world, and Rachel didn't want to lie to her more than she really had to. So she told her about the early morning rising she forced on herself and the excitement she felt when she stopped to photograph the exotic blooms that proliferated only in the mountainous terrain. "Bring back any nice posies with you? Any chance of getting something to decorate my boring flat?" Then, "Something not all right?" Barbara asked when their salad arrived. The swarthy handsome young waiter, wearing the traditional costume that the hotel required him to wear, hovered close and waited for them to order drinks. "My stomach hurts," said Rachel, who suspected he was listening to their conversation. She wasn't lying. It still felt like there was a metal ball in her gut, impeding her breathing. The film, cached in the perfume box, was in her handbag, and she was supposed to go and "lose" it under a bench in the public park. Ehud didn't tell her who would be picking it up, and she knew it was better that way. But still she felt uneasy, knowing that anyone following her was likely to see the film drop-off. Ehud too thought that the film could wait until she came home on leave, but the intelligence branch was hungry for information and they insisted, as usual, and stressed the urgency, and Ehud agreed to modify his stance and relax the security guidelines. "Make sure you're not followed," he said to Rachel, though he knew if they were doing their job, she probably wouldn't know that she was being tailed.

And Barbara carried on talking about their weekend recreations and the little traditions they had invented. Rachel agreed with her. Routine is a curse, and in training they taught her not to slip into the fixed habits that will make life easier for those who want to follow her and intercept her. But no one can do without routine. There have to be some regular patterns, like getting up in the morning, going to work, resting on the weekend. "I can't go out there in the middle of the week," she told Ehud. "I'm a working girl, don't forget." And in the evening when her friends went out to have a good time, she sat in her room and watched the lights in the Defense Ministry building that were never extinguished, and the cars constantly moving. I have no strength left, she thought, and she explained to Barbara that pills wouldn't help and she just needed to rest. "A pity we came," said Barbara, and that wasn't what she meant.

⚜

BARBARA WAS SHORTER, AND PLUMP AND cheerful, and she claimed to be absolutely without morals. "Morality won't get me anywhere. Morality has no part in what I'm doing."

"And what are you doing?" Rachel asked after getting to know her.

"I'm looking for a rich Arab. I want a big house, cars, servants, the whole lot."

"And for this you're prepared to marry someone you don't love?"

"If there's no other choice, that's what I'll do. There are other things besides love."

Maybe she was right, Rachel reflected.

"I want economic security," Barbara said emphatically. "Life doesn't revolve around a partner. You need to know what you can do without, and I can do without love."

They became friends from the first day. Rachel was early arriving at the school and went to the bathroom to freshen up. After closing the door she heard a voice from one of the cubicles and thought for a moment she'd gone to the men's room by mistake.

"Fucking hell," said the voice. "Someone's used up all the paper again and I'm stuck in here with my pants down." And then: "Hey, SOS, Houston, Houston, we have a problem." Rachel pushed a roll of toilet paper under the door.

"You'll see, "Barbara said to her after she'd helped her with the registration procedure and sorted her out with discount coupons for the local supermarket, "to them we're strangers, the kind of creatures who can be used and exploited. This is a Middle Eastern state in all the worst senses. Not like in Israel. Things are different there."

"You've been to Israel?"

"Yes, certainly, I taught there for a year. And you?"

"No, I haven't had the chance yet," said Rachel, thoroughly alarmed and wondering how Ehud would react to this.

Barbara showed her around the city, took her to the market, helped her to learn to shop, familiarized her with the strange names, and took her into her heart. Rachel loved walking the streets with

Barbara, going with her to the few tourist attractions that they were both bored with after one visit, and spending time with her in cafés. Rachel invited her to her apartment and went to parties organized by Barbara. It wasn't hard rejecting Barbara's idea that they should live together and save on the rent, on the grounds that with a bit of luck she might find herself a boyfriend soon, although she didn't respond to the discreet advances of one of the teachers, or to the unsubtle hints dropped by Barbara whenever some foreign tourist met them on one of their strolls. And so she went on lying to her and using her and enjoying her company, and she wondered what would happen if all this suddenly came to an end, and Barbara found out who she was and how she had been deceived.

⚜

BARBARA CAME BACK FROM THE BATHROOM and Rachel saw how she'd adjusted her makeup and added eye shadow.

"Somebody new?" Rachel asked.

"You won't believe it. Blind date with a rich Arab. Exactly what I wanted." Barbara put a hand in her blouse and adjusted her bra, and asked Rachel to inspect her cleavage and advise on buttons. "You think I should leave one button closed? At least for the first meeting?" she asked. She told Rachel that Mustafa would be arriving soon and she had no idea what he looked like. She asked her to stay with her at least for a few minutes.

"Exploiting me a bit, aren't you?"

Barbara didn't hide her smile and said she had no choice.

"You wanted backup for your assignation and you sold me a cover story. That's why you suddenly started taking an interest in dried flowers," Rachel said, and realized how the professional jargon suited this situation too.

"You wouldn't have come if I'd told you."

Rachel felt relieved. Everyone lies a little or a lot in the subjects most important to them, she reflected, and wondered what Barbara would say if she told her about Rashid, and what Ehud will say when she finally reports to him about what she should have for quite some time by now.

CHAPTER SEVEN

⁂

Rashid

"In hindsight I understand her," said Ehud, as if to himself. "She wanted to camouflage the story of Rashid in the report. That's the rule. Every contact has to be logged.

"'I've made another friend at school,' she told me.

"'He or she?' 'He,' she answered, and I noticed a slight tension in her voice.

"'Foreign or local?' I asked, and I hadn't started taking an interest yet.

"'Local,' she said, as if he were one of many.

"'Student?' I asked, and when she said yes I just advised her to be careful. Obviously she couldn't be expected to live there without making some friends, and I already knew about Barbara.

"She looked at me as if she hoped this would be the end of the conversation—she'd done what was required of her, and the subject was closed. And then I felt that something strange was happening to her. Even her posture, her body language, was different. Usually she sat forward, on the edge of the chair, like someone needing to make an impression, and she had the manners of an upper-crust boarding-school girl in a British movie. I remember asking her where she got that; as far as I knew she came from a simple home.

"'My father made me do it, the way he learned from his parents,' she said, and I heard the pain in her voice when she explained that he never ceased to remind her there was nothing to be learned from her mother's parents. 'They were primitive, from a neighborhood on the periphery of Berlin, he repeated even in front of my mother, and the only good thing her parents had done was to send her away at the last moment, before they and all the others went to the incinerators.'

"I just listened to her. This was another subject I didn't want to get into. I hoped the departmental shrink had dealt with this when the time was right and that the wound had healed. Sometimes scar tissue is stronger than the original skin.

"'So I owe these manners to him and they help me to think calmly,' she told me, and I thought that perhaps in spite of everything she was saying something good about her father, and of course I agreed with her that he'd presented her with an efficient and effective skill. Manners were like armor, a defense mechanism. Anyone trying to make contact with her had to get through the *don't-touch-me* force field that she radiated; she could listen calmly and politely to the other person, indulge in a short silence, take a deep breath, and only then come up with a suitably equivocal answer. This was her standard procedure, and I feared the day she would use it against us.

"We were in the safe apartment that was leased for her, and we went over the usual things. Accounts, reports to be completed, introduction to the new communications system. She was on "family leave," which was easily explained in her workplace. The school agreed she could take a vacation, and Barbara volunteered to come into the apartment now and then and water the plants. Of course we had a problem with this, because the old communications system would still be there. But clearly she had no choice, she couldn't explain why the apartment was locked up and the plants had been left to die. I remember it was during this vacation that I raised the issue of the dog. I thought it would be useful if she had an excuse to go for walks up the road and get close to the gate of the Defense Ministry. 'Spies don't have dogs!' was her immediate response. 'It's completely impractical. Who would take care of it when I travel, and what if I fall in love with it?' 'That's the very reason you should have one. A dog will add to your domestic image, allow you to do things only those in love can get away with.' She smiled, not convinced, but I was pleased that I could finally allude to this subject. I carried on processing the fresh information, and we discussed the pros and cons of keeping a dog in a house, in a Muslim society where dogs are considered impure. I asked her where she knows him from. She chuckled and said she still did not know the dog, and it was clear she was being evasive. I again asked her about the man. 'He's a student in our school. Rather a good one,' she said.

"'And what's his line of work?'

"She didn't answer right away. 'I'm not sure I understood, but as far as I can tell from the business English he's trying to learn it's something to do with importing chemicals. He purchases them for the Defense Ministry. At least that's what he says when he practices with me. I play the vendor and he comes to me and says Ministry of Defense and names several other government departments.'

"You can imagine my surprise, and the adrenaline that started to flow. I admit I was thinking of myself. At once I started fantasizing over penetrating chemical weapons projects, and the plaudits that would accompany that success. And the fears started kicking in too. All this in those few seconds before I responded. What's going to happen to her? What is she capable of? I looked at her, sprawled comfortably in the armchair, wearing a simple skirt that covered her knees, and looking back at me as if we were discussing a shopping list in the supermarket. You've seen her face in the picture. Pleasant, pretty perhaps, but not sexy. A regular girl. Not one of those temptresses you see in films who could seduce the Pope."

"We had some like that," said Joe. "All of them a great disappointment. When we were just starting out we thought we needed men who knew how to lie, including some petty criminals, and women capable of playing honey-trap schemes."

Ehud had heard all this before from Joe but he had no intention of interrupting the flow of memories.

"It didn't succeed. Someone who's good at lying will end up deceiving you, and a queen among temptresses will end up being tempted herself. We tried several times and failed, and then we constructed a different template for our operatives."

"Like Rachel," said Ehud, not sure that Joe would agree with him.

"Exactly. That's why your combatant has been so successful. A woman healthy in mind and body, a talented and loyal Zionist." Joe added that in his opinion getting a woman operative into a man's bed would be too dangerous. "Of course, I warned her to be careful, that it was not worth exposing herself and in any case she shouldn't do anything out of the ordinary. She nodded and I tried to visualize for myself the plans she was devising while listening to my lecture. I found myself explaining the security protocols again, and thinking at the same time about the potential of this new friend, and thus in my excitement I did not notice she was telling me only part of the truth. That she was testing me, listening to me, assessing me with all the means we had supplied her with in training, and thinking perhaps she had found the cure for loneliness.

"Think of her loneliness, Joe, loneliness in the middle of a crowd. The loneliness of someone leading a double life, hiding her objectives and her motives and the things most important to her. Think of the longing for warmth, love, someone to listen to you, to want you. I could see Rachel leaving the school at the end of the working day. I saw her in my mind's eye passing by cafés and being ogled by the men sitting there, and I thought of her refusing offers of friendship from other teachers, knowing it would be hard to disengage from them. I asked her once what she's eating, where she sends her clothes for dry-cleaning and when she cleans the apartment. She gave me a dismissive look and told me I could figure out those things, because there was nothing surprising. She goes shopping in the market, carries the plastic bags to the car like anyone else, generally cooks for herself, and keeps the apartment tidy even when she has no visitors. She lived as if she were a normal person. As if. And she told me she reads, listens to music, does her job, and I knew she was yearning for something but she didn't know what.

"I think that's why I got it wrong. I veered between sympathy for her and happiness that she might have found a friend, and the firm conviction that she mustn't fall in love with anyone. And I wanted to get some operational advantage from the connection with him, and I admit that I found it hard to suppress the jealousy that was welling up in me, simple and spiteful—that she had chosen him and not me. It may have already been too late, the bud had opened, and the only way to stop it was to pull the stalk out by the root, but what could I do? The temptation to go on was overwhelming."

"Stop there," said Joe. "Tell me again, from the beginning."

⚘

"How DID SHE MEET HIM, AND what did she see in their first encounter? I'll try to repeat her words, but you know how memory works, it chooses what to erase and what to retain. And even when you remember and you try to share the words and pictures, you find yourself telling a different story from the one you intended. That is certainly my experience.

"I didn't record her, and I didn't take notes. I knew she was choosing and creating the picture she wanted to present. Her true feelings she kept to herself, and even if she'd written a diary, I don't suppose she would have been entirely honest.

"'I met Rashid in the school,' she said, and I saw she was making an effort to play down the importance of the relationship. As if, when an operative in the field meets someone and goes out with him, it's a small detail that can be overlooked. She could tell straightaway how tense I was, and asked, 'Why are you so uptight about this? Is it against the rules? I'm not allowed to drink coffee with someone? Not allowed to talk to a man? I can't go out with him?'

"And what could I say to her? That I didn't want to hear about him? That what she does with her free time is her business? She and I knew that wasn't correct. An undercover operative has no free time, and there's nothing that's of no significance. With male operatives we already had a convention: Ask no questions and hear no lies. We knew they were fucking, they were finding relief that way. But we don't ask, don't want to know. Because the moment you know, you have to do something. Start worrying about the prostitutes they're going to, about the amount of alcohol they're consuming in solitude. So we don't ask and only want to know how things are going, and we're glad when we're told everything is in order. And we wait for the periodic polygraph test and hide behind it instead of having a heart-to-heart talk. If you're having an open conversation you have to reveal something of yourself too. You have to show your operative there are other sides to you, the humane side, the good friend side, to let him feel that he is sitting with someone who is taking care of him, someone he can trust. And then he'll talk, because he knows you're listening and he can rely on you. You might criticize him, but you're doing your job as a handler, as the one responsible for his safety and the success of the mission, and you're his friend too. But I couldn't be Rachel's friend. I simply couldn't.

"I kept quiet and let her go on. She looked at me, tugged the hem of her skirt down, and shifted her gaze to a corner of the room. I closed the notebook, put it aside, and waited. She wiped her face with a handkerchief that she held in a clenched fist. After a few moments of silence, she turned to me. 'You want to know what we did together?' I could tell she wanted to be angry, she knew she had done something wrong. Everyone makes connections. It's almost inhuman to forbid them, unnecessary too. So what if you tell a child to be careful? Maybe the very declaration that something is forbidden is an important way to emphasize it. So it will be in their head all the time. Who doesn't lie? Who doesn't sin?

"When she started I was hoping for something light, a cup of coffee in the school canteen, something that would enable us to continue to manage the situation until we decided what to do. As if it would make any difference, as if we could force her to do something with him on our behalf. 'What is there to tell?' she said, and described the school to me, the unprepossessing lobby and the Arab receptionist whose main asset was her ability to order take-away meals from restaurants where there were no English speakers. I imagine how this receptionist looked at him when he came in. A good-looking man in a smart European suit, accompanied by a burly driver jangling a bundle of keys, right out of a gangster film. Mafia or secret service, she was probably thinking, and she stood up to meet him, smoothing down her dress and adjusting the scarf on her head.

"The receptionist greeted them politely, and later, after they had gone, she told Rachel that the bodyguard, or perhaps he was the driver, or perhaps both, looked at her as if she were for sale. Rashid acknowledged her with a nod and said he had an appointment with the headmaster. She said there was nothing in the diary and asked them to wait. The driver, or bodyguard, wiped one of the chairs with his handkerchief, and it was only then that the guest sat down. His aide stood beside him with arms folded and watched the main entrance, and both waited in a menacing silence.

"Rachel arrived in jeans and a T-shirt under a loose open blouse. She told me, in her particular way, exactly what she was wearing and what impression she wanted to make in the school—the proverbial girl next door, not someone you could expect anything from. Still, she was wearing a backpack and the straps stretched the T-shirt in a cheeky way that only young women can get away with. The bodyguard tensed when she opened the door and came hurrying in, and he put a hand under his jacket. Rashid didn't turn his head, but it was obvious he had noticed her, and Rachel had a moment of dread, the moment feared by someone who has something to hide, the feeling they had come for her. She was used to seeing only the receptionist at this time, and although she had a reason for arriving an hour before the start of the school day, she didn't talk about the regular route that she followed in the early morning hours, that passed by the Defense Ministry. In those days before satellites it was important for us to know that the routine was kept. At night she observed the Defense Ministry from her apartment, and in the day she passed it going to work and on her way home. A routine can be a dangerous thing, unless it's part of something that's easily explained, like the way you go from your apartment to your workplace. Rachel tended to arrive a few minutes after the receptionist and enjoyed chatting with her briefly, practicing her Arabic.

"'And this was the first time I saw him,' she said. 'He sat upright like a teacher but he was relaxed, and the strange thing is I remember the glass vase and the bunch of grubby plastic flowers on the table. It seemed he was looking at them, and although I was afraid he was from the Mukhabarat and had come for me, I felt embarrassed that the reception area looked so shabby. And I also thought, in that split second before I turned to the receptionist, if I'd known that today they were going to take me in for questioning, I'd have worn more comfortable clothing and had a change of underwear with me.

"'I ignored them as best I could, though I had no doubt they were looking only at me. She gave me the day's class schedule. "Nothing special today," she said, in English. This was the rule in the school—speak English—and she signaled to me that this was no time to be careless; the working day had begun and I needed to watch out. I heard a soft sound behind me and guessed the important-looking one had stood up. My body stiffened in anticipation and I went on talking to the receptionist as if the two men approaching me didn't exist. Needless to say, the receptionist would not stand by me if anything happened.

"'He said, "Excuse me"—in an accented English and waited for me to turn around and face him. I didn't respond. I don't owe him anything, and I can use every extra second to prepare for what's coming. Again: "Excuse me," and this time in a firmer tone, the voice of someone who knows what he wants and knows how to give orders politely. Something touched my elbow, and I thought, Here it comes, now he'll put his hand on my shoulder and tell me I'm under arrest. Hard to explain to you what I was thinking at that moment. I didn't even have time to feel afraid. I figured that even if they stripped me and saw me naked they would never know what I was thinking and what I had to hide, and this was some consolation. I couldn't ignore him any longer. I turned around. I saw a smiling face, thick pink lips beneath the black mustache, and brown reassuring eyes.

"'Without introducing himself he asked me my name. As if the suit, the polished shoes, and the bodyguard were his ID card. I said, "Rachel," and already I felt different. In the movies the cop knows the name of his quarry. He repeated the name twice and then said it again with a more pronounced Arab pronunciation. I waited for him to say why he came. "I want you to teach me English," he said simply, and then asked me, in a tone that sounded almost like a command, to tell him about the school and the method we used, instead of wasting his time waiting for the headmaster.

"'I glanced in the direction of the muscleman, still standing motionless in the corner. "He's just my assistant," he said, and still he didn't introduce himself. His English was simple and deliberate. I assumed that he had studied at the local school, and what he wanted from me was to become fluent, to use idioms, to become more confident in English. There wasn't much chance of getting rid of the accent, he was too old and I had no expertise in this area. Strange, to be thinking about my professional competence at a time like this. He radiated an air of pride and self-assurance: his poise, his clothes, the bodyguard at his service. And so I wanted to show him I wasn't just a young woman in jeans who knows English. "All right," I said, "you want to join the advanced class? So let's go, see what you make of this, and I started speaking fast in a London accent, like some kind of a cockney bimbo. He looked disconcerted for a moment. "I'm sure you're a good teacher," he said, as his right-hand man went on counting prayer beads in one hand and holding the Mercedes keys in the other, his eyes on the door.

"'He finally held out his hand and said, "Rashid." "Rachel," I answered, and I'm sure I blushed.'

"'And that's all?' I asked her when she finished. 'Yes,' she said, and blushed."

⚜

Joe lit a cigar and blew a perfect smoke ring into the darkening sky. Logic told him he should give up smoking, but he had decided to allow himself this one forbidden pleasure, and he invited Ehud to join him. Ehud declined and asked Joe what he thought. Joe didn't answer and went on smoking placidly. Ehud's story reminded him of operatives who had been under his command, and the special relationship that evolved every time between the case officer sitting in Europe and the operative embedded in enemy territory. He believed Ehud and thought he was doing his best to clarify Rachel's image, but he wasn't sure that Ehud knew what was really happening in the field, or if things were really going as they should. A long life had taught Joe that in romantic matters there is no logic, and there are a lot of lies.

Ehud wasn't deceiving himself either. Not now and not then, when he sat facing her and heard the reports about Rashid. He listened to her and felt that although she trusted his discretion and his judgment, she was still keeping something to herself. She hadn't told him everything. No one tells everything, not even to a lover, especially not to a lover. Ehud was Rachel's case officer and her connection with headquarters staff. No one met her without his approval and with one word he could veto any project or request for information directed at her. The memory of the Eli Cohen debacle and the hanging of the operatives in Egypt had faded over the years, but the feeling that those operatives had fallen into the hands of the enemy because there had been too many demands made on them was always there, and if Ehud said that was enough, she could do no more, no one would put pressure on him or on her to go on. This responsibility had two sides to it: there was the appetite to do more and more, and it was his job when to say enough, when things were getting out of control.

He closed the debrief meeting, sent Rachel to buy some essentials and meet a few people to back up her cover story in Milan, and then he tried to take stock of things. He believed that although he didn't know all the details, he knew the essentials: Rachel is loyal to the organization, and she won't do anything to jeopardize her assignments or endanger herself. So he decided not to ask what else was happening besides the friendship with Rashid, and ostensibly he took no interest in the minute details of what and how, even when she brought him the photograph that gave the go-ahead for her next mission.

Rachel too, he knew, didn't want to tell him how she felt, or what she thought of him, or about her life behind the mask. When she was out there, Ehud was in the distance. Reporting from the field was hazardous and she needed to be brief and precise, and she knew Ehud wasn't the only one reading her cables. In Europe it was different. They sat face-to-face, and Ehud asked not only what she had done but also what she was feeling. He asked and waited for her to tell him, and she, like anyone wanting to keep her beloved to herself, decided to conceal broad swaths of information.

⚜

RASHID WAS ALREADY SITTING AT THE table, which was set for three, and she spotted the bodyguard, standing in the corner of the restaurant and watching the guests enter. Rashid stood up and came to meet her, shook her outstretched hand, pulled a chair out for her, and waited until she sat down. Rachel pulled her knees back. He wasn't a big man, but she wanted to avoid contact between their legs under the table. "Are there three of us?" she asked, and smiled when he explained, "You can tell anyone who asks that your girlfriend is on the way, and I'll be spared unnecessary explanations." She put her hand-bag down on the vacant seat and decided not to ask which number was she in the procession of foreign girls who sat with him in restaurants.

"Let's speak English," he said, as if there were an alternative, and pointed out that he was counting this meal as a lesson. "And which official in your department clears your expenses?" she asked, and waited for him to tell her who he was working for. He grimaced and she repeated the question in a simpler form. "You see? It's a lesson," he said, and he wanted to know the name of every utensil on the table, and how to order food. It was all so simple.

And all this time, while the conversation flowed and moved from place to place, she was thinking too of the things that must be kept hidden, and she was glad that English was a struggle for him and his questions were simple and asked slowly. "Tell me something about yourself," he said, and she talked about her father, who left a hectic life in London behind and was growing old by himself in a remote corner of Canada, and she knew that she was telling him a truth.

"He doesn't care much about me. When I told him I was going traveling in Europe he just said, 'Oh,' and when I got the job here I called him and he wasn't even interested in meeting me before I left. I'm paying him back in the same currency."

"With us it's different," Rashid said, and in his eyes she saw what she was looking for. "There's nothing more important than family."

She thought about her cover-story family, and how she missed the father she once had.

Rashid seemed to notice the difference in her tone; he changed the subject and she was pleased by his sensitivity and admitted to herself that she liked him. She liked talking to him, although she had to stay on guard and not let his curiosity and his sympathy penetrate her armor. She too wanted to gather information from him, exactly as other couples do on a first date. She tried to ask him something personal. Rashid said he was paying her for this lesson and so he had the right to choose the topic. She shook off the jab and struggled over whether it was the mission entrusted to her that kept her here at the table, or whether there was also something else. "Tell me what business you're in and something about your family," she persisted. "This is what you'll need to do in any business encounter. Everyone wants to know about the guy sitting in front of him." "Okay," he said, "on condition that for every detail I give you about myself, you give me something in return." Now she was ready and she responded to the challenge, and since she was lying most of the time she wondered if Rashid was telling the truth.

She enjoyed his company. She wanted the evening to go on, wanted Rashid to keep up the shared pretense that this was just an English lesson. The situation was new and confusing. With Barbara it had been easier. Rachel liked her but her attitude toward Barbara was professional and cool, and although Barbara was curious it was easy to deflect her inquiries and not expose any detail she didn't want to reveal. Whereas in this restaurant, in the heart of the foreign capital, she wanted to tell him about herself and behave like a young woman with an attentive and attractive man.

When the coffee arrived she asked to be excused and went to the bathroom. Get a grip, she told herself while touching up her makeup and brushing her hair. Rashid is an information target, a local friend, and a potential enemy. You mustn't fall into any traps that he sets for you. Remember what Ehud is going to ask you about him, and be ready to report everything to him. But this didn't help either, and when she walked back to the table she noticed the eyes of the men following her and was glad to see him sitting and waiting for her, his hands folded on the table, as if holding her heart between them. They drank the coffee in silence, and a pleasant frisson passed through her when her knees brushed his.

Rashid signaled to the waiter to bring the bill, and the bodyguard went out to bring the car around to the main entrance. "Will you let me take you home?" he asked. She tried to resist the influence of the extra glasses of wine she had drunk ("I'm an enlightened Muslim," he told her, but still refrained from drinking) and to decide if there was any harm in this. Rashid knows her address from work, and if he's as important as he says he is, he'll have no problem finding out the rest of her personal details. And besides that, the apartment suits her circumstances, other foreigners live in the district, and only she knows the real purpose that the apartment is serving. The bodyguard will drive them and he'll drop her at her door, and she'll say goodbye to him. The wine fogged her head and she felt her knees weaken. It was only an English lesson, she told herself. She had a good time and he paid for the meal, but it was only an English lesson.

He sat beside her in the back, and Rachel made sure to keep her distance from him. The scent that wafted from him was pleasant and soft. His hands were on his knees, and he leaned back in the seat and waited. They were both silent. The bodyguard didn't ask where to drive to, and the black Mercedes set out on its way. She tried to summarize the restaurant scenario in her mind. He already knew about her work and about her apartment, and now he knows about her father too and about the Open University in Italy. What else does he know? That her boyfriend jilted her? That she's not allowed to form emotional relationships here? Impossible. As far as he's concerned, she's an English teacher. Not the most beautiful woman in the world, but good-looking enough. Not blessed with a great sense of humor, but with a talent for listening and a curiosity. She hoped he didn't just see her as easy prey, a casual adventure.

And what is he to her? What can the man sitting beside her be other than something taboo? It's forbidden to do anything that could expose her to danger. Mustn't even dream of it. But she did dream of it. She was dreaming about precisely this when they arrived at her home and she said "Goodbye" and "Thank you" and "See you tomorrow in class," and stepped down and walked the few paces to the door of the building and went inside before Rashid had the chance to follow her. Through the frosted glass she saw him standing a moment longer before going back to the waiting car and getting in the front seat.

The creak of the old key in the door. The check she always does to be sure no one has been there. A familiar routine. She's glad to be in a safe place. To feel confident that now no one is watching her and no one is listening to her. She can be herself, if only for a short time, in the little soundproofed cubicle that a local handyman built for her, so her music practice wouldn't disturb the neighbors. This too was Ehud's idea. He pressed her to develop hobbies and have this room added to accommodate them, and he vetoed the suggestion it should serve as a photography studio—too great a risk. Rachel chose an electric guitar, took lessons, even though it was boring, discovered to her surprise that she had some aptitude for it, but played very little. She kicked off the flat shoes she had worn in deference to Rashid's short stature and stretched out on the bed. The newscast in English celebrated the tireless efforts of the President for his people and described the opening ceremony of a new orphanage, paid for by the President's family and greeted by a surge of popular joy. If I were a foreign citizen, a casual tourist, I'd think everything here was idyllic. No one hosting the representatives of terror organizations, no one planning to go to war against Israel, no one torturing prisoners in secret jails. No poor and no rich, just the ruler and his subjects. And Rashid.

At eleven she must listen to the transmission from headquarters. An everyday matter. And then it will be her turn to send a radio message, always a different time on a different day. That's the way the system works. The chances that she's being bugged are remote, but routine is an enemy that has to be resisted. What will they want now, she asks herself, as she prepares to receive the message and decode it. What do they want to know? She opened the window and watered the plants in the pots. The lights around the Defense Ministry were burning, as usual. Nothing to report. Really? And what about Rashid? Is there anything to report about Rashid?

The silence that she loved so much now was sad and boring, and she found herself longing for his warm voice, his heavy accent, wanting to hear him stumble as he tried to use the expressions she's taught him. She thought of the attention he paid her, and realized she wanted to think he was interested in her and not in the English she was teaching him.

Rachel closed the heavy curtains and went into the little music compartment. The sophisticated radio set, a present from her favorite aunt, was tuned to a rap music station in the USA. She switched it on for a few moments at high volume and then put on headphones and turned the needle to another station. She turned the dial until she found her frequency, and heard an announcer telling tourists in Europe that the weather would be normal for the time of year. This was all she needed to know before sending the coded broadcast. Her guardian angels, intelligence personnel checking she wasn't under surveillance, staffers at departmental HQ working to guarantee her security, all had reported in turn to the operations room that all was in order and she could go ahead and transmit.

She took a pad of paper, tore off a sheet, took care to lay it out on a smooth metal plate to avoid leaving traces on the table, and started to compose the summary: "Rashid Kanafani, Muslim. Old and wealthy merchant family. Father is exclusive agent for the import of chemical products for the Defense Ministry, and Rashid is replacing him now. A great deal of low-level technical activity, including lists of materials that need to be compiled in the correct format and written in very clear terms. But there are also other items that I'm following up. He's been studying at the school for some months, and now he's having private lessons as well." She was content with that, although she knew that if they hitched her up to a polygraph, the needle would jump.

When the time came she spread the communication system out in front of her and quickly keyed in the message. The apparatus concealed in the amplifier that she "bought" on her last visit to France accumulated the material and then transmitted it in a short burst. What do they do with this back there? What would Ehud, who sometimes seemed more aware of her than she was herself, think after reading the decoded statement? Will he hear the beating of her heart, her expectations of tomorrow, her desire to see Rashid again? Will he know this is the first time she has thought of anything not connected with the mission? She packed away the apparatus and was startled when she realized how carelessly she was doing it, neglecting the obligatory checks. Her thoughts had strayed to other places. When she finished tidying up she stripped off her clothes and curled up in the big double bed left by the previous tenants, a couple with a little boy.

In the middle of the night she woke up. She dreamed someone was hugging her and whispering something in Hebrew, and she thought of Rashid. She pulled the blanket over her head, cupped her breasts in her hands, and thought of his big hands playing with the glass of lemonade. "Muslims don't drink," he said, "at least not in public," and he laughed, exposing his white teeth.

When she got out of bed, at five-thirty, she was sure she hadn't slept all night. She pulled open the curtains. The sun hadn't risen yet but the sky was paling in the east. The lights were still on in the Defense Ministry, and the early morning traffic was the same as always. Trucks full of vegetables from the fields, pickups laden with chickens for the market, a milk truck, early-rising commuters setting out for work.

She looked around her, taking in the apartment and the furnishings. Is this home? She sighed. I volunteered. I want this mission. I'm doing something only I am capable of doing.

At eight she arrived at the school, as usual, and was glad when she was told Rashid would not be attending the lesson that day.

And when he didn't show up the following week she began to suspect something wasn't right.

⚜

WHEN HE RETURNED THREE WEEKS LATER, tanned and looking thinner, she smiled at him and felt her stomach constricting as he responded with a cold greeting and turned away.

Perhaps he suspects me? Perhaps he's not allowed to fraternize with foreigners? Perhaps he doesn't like me? Where has he been? Too many questions, she told herself, and she made a point of not addressing him and was pleased when the class ended. She packed her books slowly, dragging out the time, and watched through narrowed eyes as the students left the room one after another. He was still sitting there.

"Miss Rachel," he began when they were alone.

She knew they had only a few seconds, after which his driver would poke his head around the door and signal to him they were running late. "I'm glad to see you back," she said, and her voice cracked. "You've missed quite a few sessions."

He too answered as if the two of them were making a language-training film. "That's right. I'm sorry. I'd like to have some private lessons with you in school so I can catch up."

"It isn't that simple. Talk to the secretary."

"About what?"

"About private lessons. I can't promise you it will be with me. Barbara's a very good teacher."

And then he smiled at her and she breathed easier. She turned to the board and wiped it carefully, still aware of his scrutiny, which continued until she went out. Before leaving the room she looked in the little mirror she kept in her handbag and checked that the normal color had returned to her face. The office manager handed her the schedule and told her with a smile that Rashid was intent on studying only with her.

"Where were you?" she dared to ask him a few days later, when they sat face-to-face for the private lesson he had imposed upon her. She saw him hesitate, looking for an answer that would reassure her, while using halting English as an excuse for stalling, and then she got it. Afterward she asked herself again and again why it took her so long to realize she was supposed to be uncovering the clandestine and finding out the purpose of his journey, and she came to the gloomy conclusion she was so besotted with him she wanted to protect him.

"Did you miss me?" he asked.

"Yes."

"I went away," he said. "I went and I came back. You're not satisfied?"

He took a bottle of perfume and a simple string of beads from his case, gave them to her, and mentioned the name of an exotic location. Rachel said she was very well satisfied, thanked him, and thought about her next transmission, how to word it so she would be authorized to see him again, and then again. Back in the apartment she consulted the atlas and identified the place.

"Rashid Kanafani," she wrote, "said he spent three weeks in Russia and returned with a suntan. Continuing the relationship with him." She didn't hang around and wait for the veto to come through. She didn't think that was likely. She was carrying out the mission she was sent here for.

⁂

RACHEL SAT ON THE GREEN SOFA that she bought with Barbara and looked around her. The checkered cushions were plumped up against the chair-backs, the coffee table was spotless, and the album of pictures by local artists was placed in the middle beside a small vase of flowers. The door to the bedroom was closed, and she wondered if he would carry her there in his arms or lead her in, or if nothing at all would happen.

"I don't want it to be like this anymore," she said after they made love for hours in his car on the side of the road, on the hill, wherever they felt like stopping. "Nor do I," he agreed. And now it's happening, any moment now she'll hear his car stopping on the open ground outside the house, the sound of the door closing, the sound of the beeper confirming that everything is locked, and the erratic beating of her heart. She wore a dress to make it easier for him to touch her and was barefoot to give him a sense of domesticity.

Of course she remembered the security rules. Of course she made sure her equipment was in a safe place, the music room was locked, and the books on display testified to no unusual interests. But there's no way of controlling the pulse and no way of slowing the flow of the blood.

And then she heard the sound she had been waiting for, stood up and smoothed down her dress, looked at her face in the mirror again, and saw in it anticipation and excitement and longing for his embrace. There was a knock on the door. She turned the key and saw him standing there, holding a bouquet of flowers and a bottle of wine. She wanted to hug him, she wanted to fall on his neck, but instead led him inside and signaled to him to sit in the armchair beside the table.

Her voice sounded hollow when she offered him a drink, and she was glad when he answered her with a joke. Why did you come? Why don't you take me in your arms? she wanted to ask, but she put the wine on the table that was set for supper and arranged the flowers in a colorful vase, bought on one of her trips to the south. Then she stood with her back to him and made him tea, as he requested, and asked him about ordinary things, as if she didn't know his father had a different woman in mind for him. And he talked to her about the weather (as if she cared), and about the visit of the American Secretary of State (as if she didn't know), and a planned concert featuring a well-known rock band whose arrival had been delayed pending presidential approval, because the band had played in Israel. Occupied Palestine, he called it.

She didn't quite remember how they ended up in her bed, and she knew she wouldn't be telling Ehud about this. Rachel clung to Rashid. His body was warm and hairy, and she adored it. He sighed when he came and she remembered Oren, who always laughed.

Rashid slept on his back, close to her, his hand in hers. The candle on the dining table lit up the plates, which remained unused. She lay awake, thinking about all the things she wanted. She wanted him for herself and daydreamed about a little house and a child playing in the garden; it wasn't impossible. But there was a price to be paid for this. She wanted to love him the way an English teacher can love a favorite pupil, but she also wanted to complete her operation, to obtain information in accordance with the directives sent to her, find out from him what he was doing, look at his papers, and use him. This was possible too, but this also came at a price. Impossible to do it all—you have to choose a route and follow it, and anyone who doesn't do this and tries to be in two places and hold both ends of the stick, needs to lie. And this is what she did.

⚜

EHUD SIGHS AS IF HE'S CARRYING a heavy burden. "I don't know when this happened, but from the first day she slept with him she knew she wasn't prepared to give him up, and that was the day she started lying to us too. I too wanted the best of all worlds, I wanted to think she was in control of the situation; she was exploiting him, blowing his mind. She could, of course, have told me she loved him. I would have shaken my head and told her that human frailties were nothing new to me, made her swear not to endanger herself, and then I would go straight to the Unit commander and make him pull her out. Love and secret service are like oil and water. But she said something about companionship and a casual fling, what it is to be young and frivolous, and I wanted to believe her.

"A few months passed before she was able to do anything really big. Till then she used him as a way of getting access to all kinds of places, and she sent us some interesting scraps of information. We assumed we had a new routine in place.

"When we received the photographs of the documents, we called her to Milan urgently. I asked her to tell me exactly how this happened and what she did. I explained to her there had to be serious analysis of the risks she had taken and the likelihood of exposure. I promised her this would stay between us because I wanted to hear all the details. And because I was jealous. Of course I reported that she exploited the fact he was asleep, but I didn't elaborate.

"She told me she passed a hand over his face. If he'd woken up, she'd have changed it to a caress. Rashid slept and she got up quickly. If he opened his eyes she would carry on to the bathroom. She had no time to spare, and if he caught her she would confess that she needed money. This was the first time he brought his briefcase with him when sleeping with her, and she was afraid the opportunity wouldn't be repeated. She couldn't read Arabic or Russian, so she photographed the documents quickly by the light of the bathroom. This was very dangerous, I reprimanded her, and told her stunts like this are pulled only in movies and she must not do such a thing ever again, but secretly I was elated. The reactions we had from the research department were excellent, and the data on chemical warheads was seen as vitally important. The operations officer sent me a private cable, encoded of course, congratulating me for a small victory in the endless turf war between the information-gatherers of the Mossad and Army Intelligence, and pressing me to ask her for more. And the jewel of the collection? The photograph of the German scientist was the last piece in the jigsaw that our operations department had been trying to complete for years."

CHAPTER EIGHT

⌘

Strauss

"It was some time until I met her again. It was only when we'd completed the preparations that we sent her a coded message saying she was needed in Florence for a briefing. 'Busy. No one else?' was her initial response. 'No choice,' we replied, and I almost felt the need to remind her why she was there. She came back to us with 'Rashid, Barbara, questions,' and I had the feeling, although I had no real evidence for it, that she was answerable to him as well, and not just to us.

"I thought about the life she had set up for herself there and wondered if there was something else I didn't know. She carried out the regular tasks and toured various parts of the country in accordance with the coded instructions sent to her electronically. By now this was a relatively easy assignment for her, since she could rely on Rashid to help her get into places normally inaccessible to foreigners. I went through the file of cables, dispatches, and reports, to see if anything had changed since I last saw her, and it seemed to me she was growing impatient as well as more self-confident. Some would say this is a familiar symptom with veteran operatives, and I suspected perhaps that her life was too good and she was slipping into a dangerous routine.

"Then there was a long and exhaustive debate in headquarters. Some said the time had come to pull her out, things get dangerous when the operative in the field starts to dictate policy to the case officers, and naturally there were some who said the opposite. They asked me what I thought. I was ambivalent: if the opinion of the hardliners was accepted, she would be on her way home, and me too. No more comfortable life in Rome and American School for the boys. I hoped my judgment wasn't influenced by this fact, or by my other thoughts about her, but there's no way of knowing.

"I looked at them. They were depending on me. They came to the department every morning, they felt important, they read the dispatches, and held long conversations with their cronies in the intelligence branch. I was in the field. Not in the operational zone, but as close as I could get to Rachel, and I was the last barrier between her and the demands that were constantly being issued by someone sitting behind a desk in an air-conditioned office in Tel Aviv. I recognized this feeling, and the difference between us. A staffer at headquarters can issue requests, give instructions, offer advice, but he isn't the one who does it, he isn't the executor. Rachel was like a crane with a very long arm, long enough to reach all objectives, and I was the operator of this crane. Without me, nothing could happen. I felt the power in me, and I convinced myself I was making proper use of it.

"I said it was just as well I had arrived in the country in time for this discussion, and bearing in mind the fact that Strauss knew we were on to him and was unlikely to leave the Middle East, we had no option but to use her. I hated having to put it that way, like she was just an implement, but that was the truth. She was our weapons system, and that was how they saw her, all those sitting at the table.

There was no doubting this would be dangerous and complicated, and it could also be her last operation, but we were all in agreement on the need to terminate the activities of this scientist; no one objected to the idea of a former Nazi departing this world under mysterious circumstances."

⚜

"SHE ARRIVED IN FLORENCE AFTER A few days of touring and shopping in Milan, giving her a chance to relax and also to frustrate anyone taking the trouble to follow her. I remember she opened the door to me and retreated at once to the armchair by the window. I could see she was tense, as if she had something to tell me. I didn't ask her what had happened. I hoped she would tell me herself.

"Usually she would give me a big smile, hug, and start speaking Hebrew; it was a treat for her to come out from under her rigid cover and be an operative on leave. I approached her and held out my hand, and I sensed there was something new in her handshake and her body language, as if she had not been waiting impatiently to see me before spending a few days of debriefing and briefing.

"And there was something else. I sensed something was burning inside her and she was keeping it to herself. I repeated what I had told her at the very beginning. I said I needed to know everything about her, and this was to her advantage, there could be no secrets between us, and she denied there were any. I wanted to know how she felt about Rashid, and she replied without so much as a blink that Rashid was an information source and she understood her job. But I heard the way she spoke his name, and I didn't believe her.

"I decided that instead of going through a detailed survey of her recent activities in the field and then moving on to the accounts and all the other technical details that shape the lives of those living undercover, I would start straightaway with the mission. Perhaps this would bring her back to me and release the Rachel that I knew from the start. I spoke very slowly and cautiously before getting to the central point. I wanted to be sure she wasn't afraid, that she wouldn't tell me she was incapable of the mission. As I talked I saw her eyes narrowing and her fingers twitching. We had returned once more to the situation I was used to, the situation I wanted. I was in control, and she was an operative accepting instructions. 'And what are you asking me to do?' she said. Something about the way she said *you* suggested it was meant to be singular rather than plural, as if all this was between the two of us, the two of us and no one else.

"I showed her the picture that she copied from Rashid's briefcase and told her about Strauss. 'At the end of every month he goes away for a two-day break and stays in the same hotel. A German is a German and routine can kill,' I said, and showed her a number of pictures of him in the hotel lobby and in other places. Then she asked me why we didn't give the job to the man who took these pictures, and I had no choice but to admit he was scared of getting too close to him, and not everyone is capable of taking on an operation like this.

"It was evening. Outside, through the double-glazed windows, there was the roar of traffic, and the rumbling of a heavy truck shook the wall and the picture of the Madonna and Child, obligatory room decoration in every Florentine hotel. She examined the equipment I'd brought. It was obvious what she needed to do; it was less obvious how she was going to do it. How would it be possible to get so close to Strauss and also disappear after the operation without leaving any traces?

"'I know this isn't your private operation,' she said suddenly, 'but it sounds to me like an exercise in irrelevance. Forgotten history.'

"'There are some who remember.'

"'I thought they didn't do things like this anymore,' she said. 'Even Eichmann they put on trial before they executed him. You're asking me to commit murder.'

"'This isn't murder,' I said, 'this is an executive action, something like the liquidation you carried out with Stefan.' But she wasn't convinced.

"'Why don't they snatch him when he's on vacation in Europe and bring him to justice? Who knows, maybe he's not guilty, who knows? Maybe it's a case of mistaken identity.' She wrapped herself in a thin sweater that she took from her case, and it seemed to me she was defending herself against me. She sank into the armchair, leaned back, and closed her eyes. I waited. I knew she needed time."

⚜

"I ONCE DID THIS TOO," SAID Joe, "but it was immediately after the war. That was different. I wouldn't envy her. Interesting to know what she was thinking."

"I don't know," said Ehud. "She didn't tell me. She just kept on asking questions, and although I wasn't planning to disclose that he was supervising a biological warfare facility, designing toxic warheads for missiles that would ultimately be aimed at us, I did eventually tell her. I wanted her to be sure the operation was justified; we weren't just eliminating an old Nazi scientist. So I violated the sacred principle of need-to-know and wrecked the cover story they'd prepared in Israel. The chief security officer never forgave me for this. He said, 'If she falls into their hands and reveals this information, the source we've been cultivating in the missile project will be blown as well.' I couldn't convince him it was necessary to tell her; fortunately, the Unit commander stood by me. He had been an operative before he moved to headquarters and he understood the needs and the problems, not only as seen from the control desk but from the sharp end as well.

"The next day we traveled to Zurich and moved into a room rented by one of the other staffers. No one checked our papers on the train between Italy and Switzerland, and as far as the authorities knew, Rachel wasn't there. 'You're sure this will work?' she asked our scientist, who was explaining to her how to use the materials, and I sensed that privately she was comparing him with Strauss, and thinking they weren't so different: both of them understanding toxins, both of them wanting to kill their enemies, but now she has a side to support, and that makes all the difference.

"'Yes, but pay attention,' he said.

"'To what?'

"'The three substances are completely innocuous by themselves, and as long as they're in their "original" packaging it will be very hard to figure out their real purpose. Only experts could do that, and they would need to suspect something wasn't right before investigating. Only after mixing does this stuff become lethal. Don't forget the material dissolves four hours after mixing. That's to erase any traces and protect you if you discard it instead of using it, but this is also the window of time available for you to get the job done.' He waited a moment, she nodded, and he continued, 'Don't worry, the gloves that you'll smear the poison on can be kept at home if you don't manage to dispose of them. But'—and here I saw him swallow a smile—'don't push your luck. Don't go kissing them the morning after. Everyone reacts slightly differently.'

"Rachel took the three medicine bottles and read the labels. We went through it all with her. She knew where she bought them and how much she paid for them. She had a prescription that we prepared for her, and the labels were correct. She examined the gloves that the technical department had stitched according to the latest style and reminded me that German men don't always kiss women's hands.

"It was her idea to travel to Berlin. I saw the instructor we brought in from Israel looking bemused. She had been hired to train her in German manners and mannerisms, and Rachel commented that if her grandparents were still alive she could have learned from them. We were in Berlin for a week and she didn't ask to see the apartment they left behind or the antique shop that had changed hands. I didn't encourage her to take time out and revisit her family's past. It could have affected her judgment at the crucial moment. It was likely that there wouldn't be another opportunity to meet Strauss without risking recognition, and she needed to be focused, precise, and confident.

"And after that there will be the operation. She would pack her belongings and fly back to her adopted country and her apartment. From there she would drive across the border and arrive in the other country. There was no longer any need to check her clothes and go to a restaurant the night before to reassure her. She seemed to know what she was doing, and there was no point in giving her pep talks. At the age of twenty-nine she was already an experienced operative and knew the countries surrounding us better than any of the staffers who stayed behind in Israel. She packed the substances in her toiletries bag, and when I asked her if she was afraid, she smiled at me dryly and said there would be time for that yet. We returned together by train to Milan and I said goodbye to her at the door of the taxi that was taking her to the airport. I felt that in spite of all the training and the briefings and the meeting with the Unit commander, who brought her a letter signed by the Prime Minister authorizing the mission, she still had reservations about the task we had assigned her. It's not always easy to explain what's to be gained by the elimination of one individual. Harder still to impose a mission like this on someone else and not do it yourself. And hardest of all is when the one you are sending out there is the love of your life.

"I try to relive the moments before. To think how I would feel and what I would do. She packed her gear in the hotel very slowly, the way you might at the end of a vacation. Everything so normal. I did this myself innumerable times. I put my clothes in the case, wrapped the presents I'd bought in newspaper, checked under the bed, threw wrappers and envelopes in the bin, left a tip for the maid, and made sure I'd filled out the chits for the minibar. I did the trivial tasks and went on my way, but I ask myself, and I ask you too, what would you be feeling if you were in hostile territory, in a room overlooking Strauss's hotel? If it were you that goes into the bathroom, having first made sure the chain is in place on the door, putting on two pairs of disposable gloves, mixing the substances the way you were shown? The hands do the work they have been trained to do, the eyes watch as the solution is applied to the back of the glove and the fingers too. You are keyed up and ready to go, while the mind processes all kinds of thoughts at manic speed. And what if he doesn't come, and what if he doesn't come out, and what if I get nervous, and what if he doesn't kiss my hand? And on top of all this is the surreal sense that she's watching herself from the sidelines.

"And then I know she's thinking again about the exercises in Berlin, and the letter the Unit commander showed her, proving it was necessary, there was no choice, she was doing the right thing—killing an old man on his vacation. Beyond the window overlooking the street, she can see the ornate entrance doors of the hotel, the concierge standing outside in the cold wind. And she wonders, Will he remember me when they investigate the man's death? And she knows she still has the option of retreat. There's no one else around, and if she says she saw a police patrol, or Strauss arrive with an escort, or she simply took fright, we'll believe her because we have no alternative.

"The rest she summed up in a brief cable, sent after she returned to her apartment. 'I went into the hotel,' she wrote, 'I drank coffee, paid, waited for one hour. I got up. I knew he could arrive at any moment. I put my gloves on, ready to leave. He came in. I bumped into him and dropped my paper. He picked it up for me and apologized. He introduced himself, I mumbled my name, not a name he was likely to remember. He said he was glad to have been of service and kissed my hand and shook it with his own gloved hand. Everything exactly as planned, just like the last exercise.'

"I kept for her the modest obituary notice that appeared in the city of his birth. I didn't show her a transcript of the secret report we intercepted, an assessment of the damage caused by the untimely death of their eminent scientist. Nor did I tell her it was suspected he had been poisoned but that postmortem tests had revealed nothing. I couldn't resist sending her the message: 'How are you feeling?' And she replied, 'I have done the deed,' and I imagined a smile of quiet satisfaction. It's happening to her. She's playing with the grown-ups now, making a difference to the world, a difference achieved through a sudden death. 'Did he suffer?' she wrote to me a few days later. I said no, and I knew I was lying. But for the right reason, lying is permissible. Permissible to help Rachel bear the heavy burden of a human life taken."

Ehud looked at his friend and asked, "Have you ever killed anyone who wasn't a direct threat to you, who came into a hotel and wanted to help you, who smiled at you affably, who could have been your own father, whose English was ponderous and formal, who kissed your hand? In exercises it was always this part. A typical mannerism of polite Germans. When they kiss hands they lower their heads, but still manage to look directly into your eyes. That's how she saw him when they parted company.

"I collected the letters of congratulation and put them into her file, also the small feature that was run by *Haaretz* after the Reuters agency noticed the modest funeral in Germany. The correspondent was floundering in the dark and he could only report that back in the sixties Israel had targeted German scientists working in Egypt and mention other notorious poisonings. The subject was closed, and only from surveillance data and random reports from local agents could we gauge the scale of the success, also the delays and the cancellations, the desperate search for a replacement.

"And I? I enjoyed the praise on her behalf. She went back to the capital city the same day, and the day after she was in school again as usual. Another two months were to pass before her next furlough, and when we met there was already another assignment on the agenda. And in the meantime we had a successful operation, and when the Prime Minister wanted to meet who had carried it out, and it was explained to him that bringing her in on such short notice was not feasible, the chief of the Mossad asked me and the Unit commander to accompany him to the meeting and represent her."

⚜

"'HOW DID SHE DO IT?' THE Prime Minister asked, and the Unit commander was generous to me and didn't demand the right to speak for himself. I took out a map and showed the route of travel and the border she needed to cross. 'Driving was preferable to an international flight, and it also meant she could come and go at times of her own choosing,' I said, and he nodded; it seemed he understood the intricacies and the mechanics of arriving at the objective and departure from it. Then I explained the location of the hotel where the target was in residence, and also pointed out the small hotel where our operative was based, watching Strauss go through his daily routine, with the regularity that only an elderly German is capable of. I explained to him how the poison worked and showed him the formulas the scientists had provided. 'Even if they found the poison in a postmortem examination, the likelihood of working out when it was administered would be extremely remote, and there would be nothing to link her to it.' I was very sure of myself, and the Unit commander and the Mossad chief were backing me up. I haven't told you yet what happened much later, and we'll come to that too. As always, in retrospect everything seems clear now, but we were all in postoperative euphoria.

"I was prepared to go on and explain how we trained her for the operation and the precise synchronization that was needed, so she could identify Strauss in the hotel lobby and go out to meet him precisely on time, without observers to tell her when he arrived, without backup and a getaway vehicle in case either he or the bodyguard assigned to him should realize that the elegant young woman did not collide with him by chance, that she was carrying out a death sentence approved by the Prime Minister himself six months ago. I also wanted to tell him about the misgivings Rachel had before the operation, and the authorization we needed to get from his office, but the Mossad chief gave me a look and the Unit commander put a hand on my arm, and I realized as well that the Prime Minister wasn't interested and in fact he wanted to say something himself.

"He leaned back in his unpretentious armchair. His expression, which always appeared angry and harassed on TV, was calm and engaged and you could tell he was in a congenial mood. In his youth he too served in a special unit, and concepts like teamwork and strategic planning and other military codes were well known to him. On the way to Jerusalem the Unit commander told me the Prime Minister loved hobnobbing with men of action in small gatherings such as this, and he always took the stage himself as a way of indulging in his past.

"He spoke, and we all listened. My bosses listened out of politeness, having heard all these stories before, and I was fascinated. I don't remember all of it, and that isn't important, and I'll tell you only what leapt out at me straightaway, it was all so different from what she was going through out there. The Prime Minister talked of his days in the army and described in particular the return from operations, the last few paces before crossing the fence and his commander standing there and shaking hands with every soldier individually, and then to the canteen, which was open whatever the hour, where a feast had been prepared.

"I was sure he meant to go on and on, but there was a knock at the door and the Military Secretary looked in and gestured to the Prime Minister, pointing to the clock, to tell him time was pressing and there were other things to be done besides telling heroic tales. The Prime Minister nodded impatiently and signaled to the chagrined secretary to go away and close the door behind him. I had insisted the man be kept out of the room.

⚜

"'HE KNOWS RACHEL. SHE GAVE HIS son private lessons before we recruited her,' I told the Unit commander on our way to Jerusalem.

"'So what? You don't trust him?'

"'I don't know. And I don't want to put him to the test. He doesn't need to know that the teacher who came to his house is living in a place he's only seen in newsreels.'"

"'You're exaggerating,' the commander said, but he knew I was right. In the Prime Minister's inner sanctum there are no secrets, but the Military Secretary does his job and moves on elsewhere when the next PM is voted into office. Better he doesn't know.'"

⚘

"'AND FAIRY?' THE PRIME MINISTER ASKED. 'Is she there now? Going on living there after poisoning that lowlife? Unbelievable. It takes a lot of character to do something like that and carry on as if nothing has happened. I want to meet her when she comes to Israel and, in the meantime, find some way of passing on my appreciation to her.' I felt he meant more than this. He admired her because she did something that he himself, and the former officers who made up his personal staff, would be incapable of doing.

"He apparently pressed a hidden button, and a fan on the ceiling began to circulate the air in the room. Cigars were handed out and the Prime Minister made a point of telling us these had been bought at his personal expense. I knew this was the ritual that followed a successful operation, but I had never been a participant before. The four of us sat around a low coffee table that I remembered from television news stories. Just imagine it, there I was, Ehud, who grew up in some hole in Morocco, sent from there straight to the transit camp, worked for the Mossad all my life, and now I'm sitting beside the Prime Minister and he's offering me a cigar. Of course, I refused.

"'How does she feel? What does she do with the knowledge that every moment she has to be in control? That the danger never diminishes? That operations will never be behind her?' The Prime Minister shot the questions out in sync with the perfect smoke rings he was blowing toward the fan, and it wasn't clear if he was waiting for an answer. 'Ask Ehud,' said the Unit commander. 'He's her handler, he knows her better than anyone else.'

"'Isolation,' I said, 'that's what you feel, and the need to trust, to know that what you're doing is important. That someone is thinking about you all the time. That although you're far away, you're not forgotten. Like an artist in a garret—you sit and work and sleep and eat and move, all by yourself, and just occasionally you meet one of your friends, someone who gives you the chance to speak your language, who gives you the chance to reveal your true identity, your real problems and real joys. And then you want everything from him, as from a lover or a parent. You want him to listen to you, make sympathetic noises in the right places, show empathy and solidarity. And you pay attention to every nuance, every hint of impatience, and you forget, as a child forgets, that your handler has problems too, that he has a family and a timetable and a function that he needs to fulfill. You don't care about any of this and you feel deprived if he doesn't satisfy all your needs.'

"I could have gone further and expanded on this theme, but the Mossad chief glanced at his watch and the Prime Minister, who was listening to me with rapt attention, noticed this and said that regretfully he must ask us to excuse him, since party business was calling him. We left the building, and I knew that what I really wanted to tell him was how she obtained the first picture of Strauss. Believe me, it would take nerves of steel to do what she did to Rashid, while loving him with all her heart."

CHAPTER NINE

⚛

The Capital City

EHUD FELT GREAT WHEN THEY LEFT the Prime Minister's house. The operation had succeeded, and he hadn't been shunted aside when others were congratulated. He had no second thoughts about Strauss. The man was helping to develop the enemy's war machine and he knew the risks. About Rachel too he had no doubts. This was what she was recruited for. She did her job like a true professional, and she would receive her certificate of merit at a drink-fueled celebration in her honor the next time she came back on vacation. Meanwhile, there's more work to be done, no time to wonder what's happening between her and Rashid, who was the source of the picture and the key to the start of the operation. Ehud thought of Rashid as an instrument, and privately he admitted this made it easier for him to accept their relationship. She doesn't love him, he told himself again and again, and in his reports to Unit Headquarters he made a point of stressing that Rachel was exploiting Rashid, and was apparently sleeping with him for the same purpose. Nothing more than that.

And if Ehud wanted to know more about what was going on between them, he wouldn't get far, because Rachel didn't inform him about what she was thinking on the way back and what she was preoccupied with instead of focusing on the operation that wasn't yet over. She did report that the journey had gone smoothly, but she said nothing at all about what she had gone through on that journey. "There were no hitches," she reported tersely.

And indeed there were not. She was supposed to drive carefully and cautiously toward the border crossing. If she succeeds in crossing it without checks, as on the way to the operation, it's likely no one will know she was there. True, she was registered at the hotel, but the ops officer said that to the best of his knowledge, hotels don't submit lists of their guests to the security services on a regular basis, and anyway, cross-checking would be very difficult. In the school she didn't tell them about the trip, and even Barbara didn't know. But Rashid knew. She had to tell him, her friend, her lover.

So instead of looking in the mirror to see if anyone was following her, and instead of opening a button of her blouse as she approached the barrier—usually a useful ploy—she was thinking about him. She thought about their conversation before the journey, and the disappointment she heard in his voice when she told him she was going alone, she needed time to herself to review what was going on between them, everything was so stifling and so new and so intense, she needed a short break away from it all.

"Take your time," he said. It was obvious he was hurt, but there was something else. The expression in English made it sound as if she really were the mistress of her time and as though she didn't have to turn up for a final observation of Strauss's hotel a few hours from now.

She felt her stomach tightening and the tears threatening to break out. Why did I choose this terrible cover story? She resisted the urge to hug him. Why didn't I invent something else? And then the thought occurred to her that perhaps this was right after all. Perhaps she really was feeling that everything was becoming too loaded and too confusing, and sacrosanct rules were being broken, and the reason for the journey loomed up before her like an iceberg—threatening to sink everything around it. It's thanks to you I'm going, Rashid, she wanted to tell him. You made it possible for me to copy the documents and the picture of Strauss. You were careless and you trusted me and you don't know who I really am. And I'm exploiting you and I'm going to kill the man you were embracing at the factory gate.

Rashid opposed the unexpected journey, also her intention to drive to a strange city in the middle of winter and find herself a hotel at the last moment, because she didn't tell him the hotel was booked and she even knew the number of the room, overlooking Strauss's hotel. He wanted to contact his friends and ask them to look after her. It took all her powers of persuasion, and a tsunami of kisses, to reassure him and make him tell her that he loves her, in the accent of a Levantine Lothario out of central casting. In fact his English had improved a great deal and they both loved to remind each other that when it came to learning a language, there was no substitute for time shared in bed. She liked to hear his deep voice, the mistakes he was unable to get rid of, and the heavy accent, which always made her feel he belonged only to her.

I really love him, she told herself. It's true that I need to lie to him, true that I'm using him, but I love him, and that is no lie. I want him, and I won't do anything to harm him. Her fingers played with his curly hair. He mumbled something she didn't understand, and she knew she must not fool herself or be led astray by dreams. She's risking her heart's greatest love for the sake of the mission she's been sent on. She cried, and Rashid woke up when she reached out for the tissues on the shelf beside her. Still drowsy, he licked her tears and told her everything would be all right, he loves her and he'll wait for her.

I need to talk to him, she told herself on the winding road from the border crossing to the city. Her mind was made up, she's going to spend a whole night with him. He won't be going back to his parents' house, as he always does, and she'll get up with him in the morning, hair mussed and the smell of sleep in her mouth, and she'll kiss him before brushing her teeth. She'll curl up with him and indulge with him in delights, a picture of their future life together, before she even thinks about the next step.

So instead of checking out the army camps alongside the road and making sure she wasn't being followed, she was busy making plans for their night's reunion, and she tried, in vain, to convince herself that even a woman who doesn't have to hide the fact that she's a spy has to tread carefully where love is concerned.

⚜

SHE REACHED HER APARTMENT EARLY THAT evening and called his office before even taking off her shoes. The driver answered her and said Rashid was busy. She didn't like the driver and the driver didn't like her from the beginning, and she guessed he disapproved that the young Muslim who employed him was spending time with a Christian infidel. Sometimes it occurred to her he might be informing on her to the security services, but there was nothing she could do about this and she remembered the ops officer saying, "Half the population are informers and the other half are intelligence targets who have to be watched."

She asked the driver to tell Rashid she was home, and after checking that no one had tampered with her cache of communications gear, she went out to retrieve her pets. The little old lady in the impoverished neighborhood opened the door, and with difficulty restrained Gracie from leaping on Rachel and licking her joyfully. "It's hard for me to part from them," said the woman, a Christian like Rachel and every inch an Arab. And Rachel was thinking, What would you say if you knew that for me they were just tools, backing up my cover story? and yet she wouldn't deny she was touched by the emotional reception. She put a small envelope on the table and said it was a present from her, as if the widow who barely survived on her pension was doing her a favor and not getting money in return for her service. Mango the cat was put in the traveling cage, Gracie leapt into the backseat, the old woman waved goodbye to her, and Rachel drove back to her apartment with her operational accessories.

The red light of the answering machine was flashing, and when she played the message she was disappointed to hear the voice of Ehud, pretending to be the director of the course she had attended at the Open University in Florence, congratulating her on her success on the examination. She wanted to hear Rashid's voice. This is because of me, she concluded, I sold him the story about needing a break and he took it seriously, and now he's wondering about the connection between us.

Rachel gave Mango a saucer of milk and let Gracie off the lead, and the bitch sniffed her way around the apartment. She needed to write and encode an operation report and send it at the stipulated time, but her thoughts were somewhere else. She showered quickly, sat beside the phone, and called his office. Again the driver answered, and again he said in basic English that his boss was busy. She had to struggle to explain to him why she needed to talk to Rashid urgently, shouted at him in the loudest voice she could muster, and he, not used to hearing such high-pitched and insistent tones from her, said, "One moment," and left the receiver on the desk. She could hear the babble of voices, a door opening, someone talking loudly, and someone she assumed was Rashid answering him curtly. Then there was silence, and she heard the sound of footsteps approaching, also the sound of her heartbeat, which had speeded up and was now beyond her control.

The "Yes" with which he opened told her everything and her stomach turned over. "Rashid," she said, and inserted in his name all the pathos she was capable of expressing. "Yes"—he repeated the word as if he didn't understand. "I'm back," she said, and knew this sounded stupid. "Yes," he said for the third time, like a switchboard operator taking a report. "I want to see you," she said, and felt she was mustering her last strength: the poisoning at the hotel, the slow walk to Strauss's hotel, the tense wait, the moment of action, and the return to the city—all paled in comparison to what her lover was going to say to her.

After he'd finished the short sermon that he probably rehearsed during the two days of her absence, she told him she understood and put the telephone down. She didn't understand anything. She wanted to take a sheet of paper and record from memory everything he said to her just now and everything she said to him before the mission. She was the one who told him she wanted to think. He was the one who said he would wait for her. And now she hears the hesitation in his voice, leading her to the unequivocal conclusion that he too wants a break. It's important for him too to examine their relationship from a distance. Because of his English and the quality of the line, it all sounded to her so dismal and unreal, and when he told her he would make it easy for her and from now on take only private lessons in his office, she knew it was over.

Not a word of all this appeared in the cable she sent that evening, and even Ehud, who thought he knew how to read her between the lines, didn't notice the storm that was brewing. And why should he notice? This belonged to another world, a world the sophisticated operational apparatus wanted to ignore. The Unit commander said that male operatives should keep their pricks in their pants, and more than that he didn't want to know, and as for female operatives, no one dared say anything; they were just warned of the dangers.

In the coming weeks too she didn't write about Rashid, nor was there any need, because the reports dealt only with operational and intelligence issues, and her moods she could keep to herself. Rashid didn't call and didn't turn up at school. She heard from the secretary that one of the veteran teachers was going to his office to give him lessons once a week, and she didn't dare go to the teacher and ask after the student.

Rachel arrived at the school on time and taught her assigned classes. She drove past the government offices at the times prescribed, took walks with Gracie on the familiar paths, and transmitted reports on schedule. She heard and didn't hear what they said to her, she saw and didn't see who was coming toward her. It seemed to her that she needed to chart a course through this murky environment and make an effort to breathe. After a few weeks she invited Barbara for a heart-to-heart and told her best friend it was over, she had ruined everything. Barbara wasn't letting her give up that easily. She asked Rachel what happened, how could it be that after all she told her, Rashid had left her just like that. Rachel didn't tell Barbara about the trip that started it all, and she was prepared to explain that lie, if it should come up, on the basis of her need not to tell everything that happened between her and Rashid. Barbara didn't ask. She was busy with her new temporary steady boyfriend, when she wasn't delving into Rachel's psyche.

"Why don't you force yourself on him?" she asked. "That's what

I'd do. I wouldn't give up. Okay, you told him you wanted to think, and he took offense and he's not coming back to you anymore. So what? This is one of those exercises that boys know how to do too. Phone him. Go to his office. Ask him what's going on. Don't let him wriggle away from standing up and facing you and talking it through. Look him in the eyes. Tell him what you think, tell him you love him, you'll marry him—he suggested that once, didn't he? Tell him you'll become a Muslim if that's what he wants, you'll stay and live here, you'll wear long dresses and listen to your mother-in-law's lectures." She wasn't laughing.

Rachel listened to her patiently as she poured sweet tea and folded her laundry and waited for Barbara to finish her homily and leave. She thought about what Barbara said, and wondered if she really wanted this, and knew it was impossible.

So she didn't do anything. She continued her routine, which was interrupted one day by an urgent summons from Ehud, telling her to meet him in Europe. She sighed with relief. Action would lift her out of the grime, help her to forget Rashid and get some flavor back into her life. She asked in her cable if this could wait till her next furlough and was glad when Ehud insisted it was urgent and offered to write the school principal a letter from the director of the Open University in Florence, explaining that her final exam had to be done *viva voce*. It felt strange to Rachel that she was going without telling Rashid; she found substitute teachers to stand in for her and flew to Europe, ready to take on the next assignment and immerse herself in work.

⚘

PREPARATIONS FOR THE BIG OPERATION WERE at hand. She returned from another trial run, driving a hundred kilometers to the provincial capital and back. The school secretary fell ill and Rachel surprised her with a visit that ensured Rachel support of her cover story for the trip and the chance to hear some news about Rashid. Rachel gave her a bouquet of wildflowers that she plucked on the hill overlooking the garage, the object of her surveillance, wished her a quick recovery, and went on her way, with no updates of Rashid.

She noted on a sheet of paper the driving schedule that would take her to the garage precisely on time, memorized it, and dropped it in the trash compactor she had installed in her kitchen. The radio was tuned to an Israeli music station and she was listening to a concert to mark Israel's Memorial Day. "I don't like this," Ehud said to her once when she told him about a concert she had heard, and she said everyone here listened to foreign stations, and she wasn't living in North Korea. Only there is it considered a crime.

Evening came, infusing her with restrained sadness; Rachel Ravid from Israel would have worn a white blouse at this time and gone with Oren on the long walk from Ramat Gan to the municipal square. Oren knew that Boaz had been killed on the first day of the Lebanon war, and in the two years they were together he respected her need to light a candle in the middle of a wreath of flowers that she arranged with great care. She told him how she arrived in Israel in the summer of 1982 as a volunteer, and how Boaz, who was king of the banana groves on the Golan Heights, told her in his crude fashion that a fortified Syrian strongpoint was a tougher proposition than she was, and he seduced her with ease. Oren said the past was the past, and he didn't ask her if she had other boyfriends after Boaz and what had happened in England before she came to this country, and she didn't ask him questions either, and made an effort to be content with what she had. Rachel Brooks from Canada didn't know any Boaz or Oren. According to her cover story she had her first sexual experience in a summer camp near Montreal. Their climbing instructor was called

Bobby, and he was killed a few months later while scaling a cliff in the Rockies. After this Rachel Brooks from Canada had a few casual relationships with boys whose names she barely remembered. She then decided to travel alone in the world.

It's just as well I know one fallen soldier, she reflected, a laughing face I can think of when they play the sad songs. Her heart lurched when she remembered how once she wanted to go to the Golan Heights and stand by Boaz's grave when the memorial siren sounded, but she was nervous about meeting his family and afraid seeing his earlier girlfriends there would hurt and embarrass her, and she let it go.

⚜

"COMMEMORATION IS VERY IMPORTANT TO US, and we remember all our combatants," one of the instructors told her during training, and insisted on taking her to visit the monument in the memorial garden dedicated to intelligence personnel. They circled the great blocks of stone and she studied the names and wondered which of them, besides the famous ones like Eli Cohen, had been combatants. The instructor followed her, allowing her to be impressed by the sequence of the years and the fact that there were casualties between the wars too. She couldn't resist asking if her name would be inscribed here as well if she fell too. He told her it would be some years before her name could be displayed, because the garden was open to the public and military attachés and other spies were always coming here and taking photographs and looking for connections with episodes that Israel was at pains to deny. "We'll keep a space for you," he said, and the smile on his face turned to a look of contrition and apology when she started to cry.

⚜

AT EIGHT IN THE EVENING THE siren will sound, and she'll be careful to turn the radio off a minute before that and light a candle, to glow in the middle of a bowl of flowers that she prepared at midday. If someone comes, she'll have an explanation. Romance is always easy to explain, especially for a young woman living alone, who's prepared to admit she's waiting for someone who probably won't come. Then the radio programs will start. She won't listen to them, there's a limit to the risks she will take. Someone is bound to talk about soldiers on the frontiers, the security forces, working night and day to defend the state, and not a word about her and the other nameless combatants, whose existence is only acknowledged, if at all, when they die.

The phone rang, and Barbara, who had just finished another futile diet, said she'd come around at eight to tell her how it went. Rachel thought of asking her to come a bit later, but no excuse occurred to her and Barbara had already hung up. Better if she came later, so I could at least be alone for a moment and remember this is one of the reasons I'm here. That I too have a part to play in Israel's struggles for existence. I don't need the department's rabbi to tell me I'm allowed not to fast on Yom Kippur. But if you were to come now, Rashid, I could endure it all. She wondered why this Memorial Day was so hard for her, and if the dull pain she felt in her stomach was emotional. It's because of him, she said to herself, it's Rashid who isn't here. He's the love of my life, who can console me without even knowing the truth. She glanced at her watch and tried to imagine what he had been doing since they parted.

Barbara knocked on the door and she let her in, not before looking to check that the apartment was ready, although this apartment was always ready for all visitors. The housekeeper had a key and came in as and when she wanted, and the agents of counterintelligence didn't need keys to get in and search. I have nothing to hide—this was her mantra.

"Wow, how nice," said Barbara, pointing to the candle burning in the basin strewn with leaves. "Are you waiting for a mystery lover? Have you found a substitute for our Rashid?" Rachel put on one of her best smiles, and said she was in training and getting ready for the next in line, but she still wanted Rashid. They sat on the balcony and she suppressed her impulse to tell her about the death of Boaz in the war, or about Bobby. She didn't want to lie to Barbara more than was necessary. And all the same, why is it impossible, just this once, to sit down with her and talk about Boaz, we'll call him Bobby, whom she slept with just once? Why not tell her about the last embrace, his promise to return and teach her everything a girl of seventeen can learn from a kibbutznik, twenty-three years old and an officer in the paratroopers? "Two pairs of socks, and the underwear I'm wearing now, that's all I need," he said when she stared in disbelief at the tiny pack he was taking with him. "We'll teach them a lesson and come back. That's what they're like. Now and then they need reminding." She figured she could tell her about Bobby, who went out on that climb although he knew the season was dangerous and the cliff face not dry enough. And about herself, how she stood beside his vehicle and watched him as he got in, and at the last moment she picked two flowers and put one in his hand and kept the other in a jam-jar vase, and urged it not to wilt before Bobby came back. But there was no point telling. The effort would be too great, and when she comes to the moment when someone knocked on the door of the room she shared with other volunteers and asked where was Rachel, she'll burst into tears that will reveal all.

Barbara stroked the dog, said proudly that Gracie loved her most of all, and agreed to take her in while Rachel was away from home. "Isn't it a shame about the money?" she said about the forthcoming trip. "You'll be using up all your savings." "My aunt is paying," she replied, "she wants me there beside her, and bad girl that I am, I'm thinking of the inheritance she's going to leave me." Then she confessed about her chronic stomach pain.

Barbara chattered nonstop. A new teacher had arrived at the school. The air-conditioning in her classroom had been repaired at last. One of her pupils invited her to go out with him. In the papers they were warning again that the situation on the border was volatile, and Rachel, politely refusing a pill that Barbara was offering, struggled to keep up. The stomach pain was constant and growing more intense, as if pincers had been inserted in her body to torment her. Barbara was insistent but she refused again with all the courtesy she could muster. She won't take anything from her, since nobody can be relied on and she needs to sort herself out by herself. Her medicine chest was well stocked, with everything a young and responsible girl could need for life in a third world country. The Mossad doctor told her how and what to buy, and from the first aid course she remembered some rules that had helped her in the past when she felt ill, but this time it was something else, much worse, and she waited for Barbara to go so she could listen to the daily bulletin and go to bed.

⚜

SHE THREW UP IN THE TOILET bowl, on her knees, and felt her strength ebbing away with the retching and the bitter fluids. She could contact Barbara and ask her to come back, but the signal from headquarters was waiting for her and she hadn't yet sent the cable with the results of the week's information-gathering. "This target won't wait for us forever," the ops officer said at the first briefing, and although Ehud told him not to put pressure on her, she understood the urgency. Rachel lay down on the sofa and probed with her fingers in search of the pain, moving down as if heading for the exit. Sensing something was wrong, Gracie licked her hand and then withdrew to her corner, curled up, and went to sleep. Rachel closed her eyes too and tried not to move, and remembered how her mother used to put a wet towel on her forehead and how her father refused to make any concessions to ill health, boasting that he never in his life had a day's sickness. A stomachache was just stomachache, not an excuse for not doing homework.

The hands on the clock beside her bed showed it was time, but she wasn't going to send the cable. They would have to wait for the next one. Her night surveillance was going to be missed as well. She couldn't even stand up. When she could bear the pain no longer and heard herself crying out for help, she called an ambulance and then phoned Barbara and asked her to come over and look after the dog. She knew Rashid's home number. He had given it to her and told her to contact him if ever she was in trouble. But that was in other times, and despite the pain and the dizziness she decided against it.

In the ambulance she was sure she was going to pass out, and she had the strange feeling that in fact she wanted to be ill, she wanted the release from responsibility that sickness allows, the dependence on others, the incomparable moments when someone else takes charge, lifting you onto the stretcher, cooling your brow with a wet towel, giving you his full attention, entirely at your service. The paramedic had a peculiar smell and his mustache frightened her, but his hands were good and warm, and when he told her everything would be all right she believed him and nodded. This is what I need to do, she thought as the last of her strength drained away, speak as little as possible, not lose consciousness, and deny, deny everything.

⚜

A MURKY LIGHT LIT THE ROOM and the beds around her. A middle-aged nurse approached her, and Rachel hardly resisted the impulse to cry and tell her she was tired and her whole body was in pain, and she wanted them to diagnose her with a genuine illness, a condition even her father would admit existed. This is no fault of hers, Ehud will repatriate her and no one will be angry with her, as illness is illness and it's not only weaklings who are sick, as her father says.

The nurse plumped the pillows under her head and smoothed the sheet that covered her, and Rachel noticed she was naked under the hospital pajamas. The contact with the starched pajamas was pleasant and the touch of the nurse's hands as she checked the intravenous drips had a calming effect. Like the paramedic, the nurse assured her that everything would be all right. This must be something they learn in the course for dealing with foreign patients, she reflected. "Okay, okay," said the nurse, and she continued her night rounds. Rachel tried to reach out for the bedside cabinet to look at her watch and was shocked by the sudden pain. She moved her hand over the area of the pain and felt the big bandage bound tightly around her stomach. An operation, she thought in panic. General anesthetic. Recuperation. What have they done to me? What did I say? She was glad she insisted on not changing her first name. "I'll get it wrong if they wake me in the middle of the night and ask me what my name is," she explained to Ehud, and he conceded the point.

"How are you feeling?" asked the nurse, returning. Rachel was gratified to note that she was devoting more time to her than to the others.

"All right," said Rachel, even though the opposite was the true.

"Who is your regular doctor?"

Rachel didn't answer. Here, in this city, she had never registered at a clinic, and in Europe it was the Mossad doctor who came to her.

"They took out your appendix, they got to it just in time."

"Really?" Rachel whispered, and asked her how soon she could leave.

"You'll need to spend a few days here. You want us to contact anyone?" She went on talking as she looked through the patient's notes attached to the bed. "Rachel. That's a nice name. I had a friend called Rachel when I was studying in London." The nurse stood over her and gave her a quizzical look while adjusting the tubes and checking the infusions. "This is your bell. Ring it if you want me to bring you a bedpan. You know that's the important thing now, we need to be sure all your systems are working. In the morning the doctors will come and then I'll try to get you a phone."

Rachel thanked her and said this could wait, that she didn't want to worry her father.

"Perhaps in the meantime you'd like to give me a local number, if there's anyone you want me to call. You know, you were saying things before I didn't understand. But that doesn't matter now. Get some rest, and I'll see you in the morning."

She was sure she wouldn't be going back to sleep. This has nothing to do with Hebrew. To her, Hebrew is a foreign language. She thought of the target she was supposed to be watching, her surveillance of his house, his schedule, which she was trying to memorize, the names of the people he socialized with, she thought of Strauss too, Strauss who picked up a paper for her when she dropped it on purpose, whose blue eyes met her eyes when he kissed her gloved hand, his lips in contact with the poison prepared especially for him.

His eyes. His kindly expression. The perfect manners of someone who spent his last days in a hospital bed, hooked up to machines just like her.

So the inevitable will happen. The nurse will bring them to her, and she'll be full of good intentions, she can't be blamed for telling what she heard. The genial interrogator will ask her how she is and then he'll want to clarify a few things. And when he goes they'll transfer her to a private room of her own, which will even have a window, also an iron door and a grille, and a guard who won't let anyone enter or leave until she's well enough to be moved somewhere else.

Near sunrise she woke from fitful sleep and saw the darkness outside giving way to a pale dawn and the new day taking shape. She thought of her father and cried when she realized that once again she couldn't contact him and tell him she was sick.

⚜

HER BED WAS IN THE CORNER of the room, close to the window and somewhat away from the rest of the patients. It was clear she was the only foreigner in the ward, perhaps in the entire hospital. She looked at the door at the end of the big room. That is the way they will come, she thought as the pains started. First little stabs, and then a regular and steady pain that forced her to grit her teeth and clench her fists. She knew this would pass. She knew these were the pains of recovery and she had to wait, and in the meantime she needed to pee in the bedpan and she wondered how she would lift herself off the strange device and who would wipe her. The torn and dirty curtain gave her a little privacy, but not much. She wanted to call the nurse, but she had suddenly disappeared, perhaps to talk to the security officer. Only women were around her. Women like her. Older and younger, moaning or silent, all of them speaking a language she didn't understand.

She heard footsteps. Not the nurse in her rubber sandals, not the cleaner in her flip-flops. Vigorous steps that pounded the floor as if it belonged to them, as if it owed them something. Heavy leather boots; steps raising a sound to be reckoned with. This is it, they're coming, she thought, and the idea of pulling out the tubes and trying to escape paralyzed her, she just didn't have the strength. Someone else would have done this, and not waited for them to come and pick him up like an egg laid in the night. A man would have got out through the window, found his way home, picked up his passport, and bolted. And instead of this, there was the option of closing the eyes, to postpone the end, lapsing into helplessness. Despite the pains and the tubes attached to her she tried to sit up and thought of her disheveled hair and lack of makeup and the pajamas, from which repeated washing had failed to remove the ancient stains. And before she had time to pass a hand through her hair he was standing beside her and holding her hand, ignoring the other patients, and the nurse who was pursuing him and intent on ejecting him, because this was the women's ward and there were visiting hours, and all the myriad regulations that every hospital imposes on itself. He leaned over her and touched her lips with his, then moved on to her forehead, and all this time he held her hand in both his strong and warm hands, and she felt cured and ready to fly out of there.

"I came the first moment I could." Not a sentence a screenwriter would have used, and not something he picked up from his counterespionage buddies. "You came when you could," she repeated, and she didn't want anything more. Rashid turned and spoke in a tone of unmistakable severity to the nurse who was standing behind him and still trying to eject him, and then he nonchalantly pulled up a chair and sat down beside her. She had to struggle to move her head and look at him, but he held her hand and that was enough for her. She didn't need anything else, and for one brief moment she was glad she was ill, glad he was sitting beside her, and saying nothing. "I'm a lucky guy," he said after a pause, and explained that he contacted the school to cancel a lesson and Barbara happened to be around and she told him. "I'm lucky too," she whispered, and asked him to close the curtain and bring her a bedpan.

The wound radiated waves of pain and she groaned. Rashid spoke with the nurse again in Arabic. "Soon they'll bring you a phone, you can tell your parents I'll meet them at the airport." And what's she supposed to do now? Tell him about Ehud? Tell him about the mother she invented? Or the father she left so far behind? This isn't the time to tell him her father is ignoring her, he never calls, and he probably wouldn't believe her. Now, after he had come back to her, she didn't want to tell Rashid all the lies that had become second nature to her, and the truth was unbearable. Rachel kept silent and held his hand.

⚜

BY THE TIME EHUD REACHED THIS section of his report, the stay in hospital was already history, another anecdote from the tortuous process of monitoring his operative. He told Joe about the hard times he had back then, and the effort to locate her. The possibility of accident or ill health had of course been raised—among the potential pitfalls discussed in training—but when things really happen and contact is broken, it all looks different.

"Rina saw the way I was mooning around the apartment and bumping into things and she asked me what was happening. I admit I lost my temper with her and with the children too, for no logical reason, and our apartment in Rome was like a prison for them all. My cover story obliged me to go and work for a small company that employed me as a salesman, and because I had nothing to do besides wait for Rachel to make contact, or hope for some intelligence update that would explain her absence, I had no excuse for not turning up at the Office.

"But I didn't go and I stayed at home, sitting beside the phone like an idiot and checking every few minutes that it was working. If she's been caught, I was thinking, the cases of Eli Cohen and Moshe Marzouk would pale in comparison with the catastrophe we'd be facing. A young woman who assassinated one of their top scientists with her own hands. I felt I was going out of my mind just thinking about the torture chambers and the interrogation methods. I remember I lay on my bed and I was close to tears. Rina listened to me and didn't probe too deeply. She sensed, as only a woman can, that my concern wasn't only professional. In the meantime the search for her in Israel was already on. The operations officer who coordinated the search made sure the war room was manned and chaired interminable meetings and updated me in brief cables. Someone suggested sending in one of our locally recruited agents, but this was vetoed; revealing to an Arab civilian, however good an agent he might be, that an Israeli civilian, a woman, was living in his country on a fake passport, was not possible. It would violate all the rules of compartmentalization and need-to-know. Then it was suggested that a veteran operative could be sent to check out her apartment. This was a good idea, but dangerous. The chief security officer opposed it, assuming that if they had caught her, they might catch the veteran too.

"After two days I couldn't restrain myself any longer and I went into the city. I walked the streets, checked no one was following me, and found a public phone. I dialed the number of her apartment. If they asked Rachel who was calling her from Italy, she could talk about her friends who were traveling in Europe, and if they caught me red-handed, I would tell them I was in love with her. Sometimes it pays to tell the truth. No one answered and I didn't leave a message."

⚜

EHUD KNEW THAT TO EXPLAIN WHAT happened in Portugal and what happened afterward he would need to tell Joe everything and hold nothing back. It took him only a moment to decide. His concern for Rachel reminded him of those days, and, as then, he was prepared to pay any price. Personal exposure didn't bother him. On the contrary, he reveled in it; Rina was no longer alive, he had turned sixty-five, and he knew he could rely on Joe's legendary discretion. And there was something else, which he tried to play down. He was enjoying himself. It was pleasurable talking about Rachel and about himself with the freedom that these circumstances allowed. He felt he was putting things in order, describing his relationship in a form of words that would clarify what had hitherto been hazy. He heard a voice in him, telling him to carry on searching his heart for the true sound, that she would answer.

The red phone rang. Joe walked to the kitchen slowly, knowing the caller would wait. He listened calmly to the speaker at the other end, said everything was all right, and put the receiver down. "When did you know she was ill?" he asked, and wanted to know how that episode had been resolved. "She wasn't big on details," Ehud replied, wondering what Joe had been told over the phone. Joe told him to ignore the war room and carry on. Ehud leaned forward and put his hands on his knees. "She didn't make the mistake that a sick and lonely person is liable to make. She didn't give Rashid even one of the phone numbers she had in reserve for occasions like this, and she told me she exercised the right to act dumb. The school didn't do anything either. Nothing happened until she contacted us via the usual channels, with one word: 'appendicitis.' It took us some time to figure out what she meant. Our experts checked the cable again and again and scoured the codebooks, and we came to the conclusion this was the truth, she was in the hospital and she was anesthetized there. Immediately we made sure her aunt would contact her, urging her to come and stay, for a vacation and a rest.

⚜

"'How do you know you didn't give away anything classified and you didn't put yourself in danger?' I was very concerned. She had been gathering information in advance of the mission, and the pressure was immense. I brought the Mossad doctor with me to the hotel in Portugal, to take the stitches out and give an opinion on her readiness to return to active service. He said she was recovering well, and ruled out any connection between the appendicitis and the work she had been doing. But I still had my suspicions. I knew from experience that few coincidences are really coincidental.

"'Because nothing happened. Because everything is okay.' She smiled. I knew she was hiding the pains and the anxieties from me, the kind of things she might have told a good friend. I considered calling in the shrink as well, someone professional and objective who could be trusted with secrets, but the Unit commander vetoed it and reminded me of what I knew only too well—this was all my responsibility. I wanted the operation to go ahead, but I did not want to pressure her. 'You know it's possible to call it a day,' I said, and secretly feared she might agree. There was no way she could be sent back there if she didn't want it. The decision had to be hers. 'Stay here for a long vacation,' I said, 'and then don't go back. You're just a teacher, nothing will happen if you break your contract. And as for us? You've done enough for the people of Israel, and thank God there are peace negotiations going on. And maybe one day there'll be no need for people like us.' That's how naive I was back then. And then I reviewed one more time, as if she didn't remember, all the operations she'd been involved in, and said if she wasn't going to kill that terrorist, we'd find an alternative solution. 'Every dog has his day.'

"She wasn't the same Rachel that I inducted three years before. She was pale, with her hair in a bob, which gave her a matronly appearance. She was thin, and the tight jeans and T-shirt she allowed herself to wear when on vacation with her uncle made her seem even thinner. And there was the look, which couldn't be concealed behind the dark glasses she wore throughout our conversation. The confidence that emanated from her was different. There was a depth to it that told me there was nothing new I could teach her. Something different was happening between us. I give her the job and she does it. That's all. And when I spoke to her I knew she was smiling inside, concealing the smile.

"She picked up the book that was on her lap. The sunshine was pleasant and the shade of the parasol we were sitting under moved slowly with the hours. A young woman convalescing after a serious illness in a smart hotel. Her uncle is looking after her. No one would believe it, no one can prove otherwise, no one cares. We took separate rooms and spent our time together. 'A good book,' she said, and showed me the cover of *The Human Factor*, by Graham Greene. I hadn't read it, and books usually didn't interest me much. People write only what they want you to know. Rachel wiped away a bead of sweat that appeared on her forehead, and there was something childlike about the gesture, the motion of the hand. She was thirty years old, I was fifty and almost a grandfather. I wondered how much she knew about me, and if she cared. More than three years had passed since I met her in Brussels, a young woman who wouldn't hurt a fly, who wouldn't dare smuggle even a single excess bottle through customs.

"She took a sip of juice, licked her upper lip like a contented cat, and leaned back in the cane chair. We were some distance from the other guests, who were older than her and younger than me. With her lacquered toenails and fashionable sandals she looked like a model on vacation. Too thin and too pale. Only her tight lips expressed something else. It was impossible to know what she was thinking, perhaps she really was considering going back to Ramat Gan, earning a pittance as a teacher. Or perhaps she would join us in the department, coming in at nine, leaving at five, standing in the queue for the cafeteria with the other secretaries, other agents, other people who will treat her with respect at first, and then say, behind her back, she doesn't deserve special treatment. At the end of the day she did what she was required to do. We all have our own talents.

"She sat there, and it seemed she was waiting. If I'd known then what I know now, of course I would have acted differently. But she was my operative, and if she were to come home, I'd be heading for a boring desk job too. No more urgent calls from the chief of the Mossad, no more cozy chats with the Prime Minister. So of course I didn't mention the conversation I had with the Unit commander before setting out.

"'It all depends on you,' he told me, as if this were right, as if I were the one out there in the field. 'You're her case officer. You have the authority to bring her home, you have the authority to send her back to her operational duties.' I didn't need more than this. And he didn't need to remind me of the prospect of never seeing Rachel again. Her eyes, her smooth cheeks, her delicately parted lips, and her small breasts, protruding cheekily from under the T-shirt.

"'I want to go back,' she said into the calm void that separated us, 'and what do you want?' The question surprised me. What do I want? Who cares? I'm just the handler; I take my instructions from HQ. I knew what I wanted, besides sleeping with her, that is. I wanted the situation to go on as it was and so I smiled at her. I told her she had made the right decision. Everything would be fine.

"The waiter arrived, and Rachel chose a big steak. 'Doctor's orders,' she said, and smiled at me as she probed the juicy meat with her fork. I watched her eating. Like a princess. Elbows tight to her body, back straight. No drips or spills. The napkin on her knees remained folded and clean throughout. Her light makeup and lipstick remained intact as well. It was a pleasure to see her eating, a pleasure to see her doing the simple things that everyone does. I wondered how she took off her clothes. I imagined her standing opposite a mirror, looking at herself, running her hands over her hips and undressing in one motion. I imagined her bending in to the mirror and examining something that looked to her like a wrinkle and for me was a never-ending source of longing.

"Rachel smiled and her hands touched her lower stomach as if she was checking that everything belonged to her. 'They did a good job,' the doctor said when he came out of the room, and I thought of his hands caressing her abdomen, the sights and the intimacy that he was allowed and I was not. I wanted her to be mine. It crossed my mind to talk to her about forbidden things. I thought perhaps it might be possible to get away for a few minutes from the codes that we imposed on ourselves, from the English language that separated us, from the decision that we talk only about work. I wanted to ask her if she wanted children, if she wanted to marry. What will she do when she grows up, when she returns home.

"This was the moment I knew I was in love with her, that my

feelings for her went far beyond what was permitted. To me she was so beautiful, so vulnerable, so contained in herself and in the world she had out there in a foreign land, and I felt a longing to be with her. Not just to sleep with her, not just to hold her hand. But to be with her. To defend her. To serve her and be her helper."

⚜

EHUD STOPPED AND WAITED FOR JOE to respond. They weren't intimate friends. Joe was his former commander, and Ehud wondered what he thought of him and the secrets he was revealing. Joe didn't share the details of his concealed life with Ehud and he wasn't expected to. This wasn't a friendly conversation. The purpose was different, but Ehud remembered from rumors circulating in the department that Joe too wasn't entirely innocent of mistakes driven by the heart.

Silence reigned, and the two of them listened to the sounds of reality, life on the other side of the fence. Far from there, in the Office, the war room was abuzz, and duty officers worked around the clock searching for a hint of her location. The war room chief had appealed for help from Army Intelligence, and consulates had been alerted. Someone in the higher echelons took the trouble to update colleagues overseas, and Ehud and Joe talked of an old love affair.

"This wasn't a passionate youthful fling. She was around the same age as my eldest son, and a few months later I was already a young grandfather. I loved her with all the tenderness and concern I had to offer. I wanted to hold her in my arms and feel she was mine. Of course I was jealous of Rashid, although I assumed she was sleeping with him only for our benefit. She was leading a double life. In the professional life of Rachel Brooks there was Rashid, and I wanted to be the love of her real life as Rachel Ravid. I wasn't thinking of more than that. I wasn't planning to leave home, I wasn't planning to pull her out of the field and bring her back to me. Nothing like that. I just knew I loved her and I wanted her to love me."

As the evening cooled they moved from the garden to Joe's study and sat on opposite sides of the bare table. There was only one picture on the wall behind Joe's chair. "That was on my watch," said Joe, when he saw Ehud focusing on the portrait of Eli Cohen. "Tell me more, Ehud. I hope after all these years you know you can trust me to decide what has to be passed on and what stays between us."

Ehud listened. Years later, when the pain was still excruciating, he knew why he trusted Joe, why he wanted his attention, the chance of unraveling his story—his and not Rachel's—and earning his understanding and forgiveness, so he could breathe freely again. He wanted Joe not to denounce him for his obvious failings, but to appreciate his restraint and his scale of priorities and thank him for snuffing out his love for the sake of the greater good. As if this were possible. As if it were possible to snuff out a true love, harness it, defer it for another time.

And now? What did he feel about her now? After fifteen years of enforced separation, of mumbled phone conversations once a year, at New Year.

"How are you, Rachel?"

"I'm well. And you?"

"Me too. Life goes on. The children are growing up."

"Well, enjoy the holiday."

"You too."

And so through the years. And even when he retired he didn't tell her he was leaving. When his wife died he didn't say anything to her either. And Rachel didn't tell him what was happening in her life and why she never married, and what about the children she never had. Nothing.

Just, "Enjoy the holiday," and, "You too."

And then he dared to tell Joe how close he became to Rachel on the way to the big operation. And Joe—who had difficulty believing it possible that Ehud, an experienced case officer, the man who had seen it all, was capable of getting himself so embroiled on the way to the enemy country—listened and took notes, which could be sent on to the operations room at a moment's notice.

⚭

CHAPTER TEN

In the Field

"'WE'LL TAKE IT,' I SAID,"—EHUD TOOK up his story again, as Joe listened intently. "I saw the reception clerk smiling at me like a coconspirator and apparently ignoring her. Rachel stood beside me and said nothing. We had already decided between us when she would speak, which hotels would be booked in her name, and how her chosen route to the border might appear to anyone trying to track her movements. So far everything had gone smoothly. We left France in the Audi her aunt gave her and we didn't waste time lingering over a lot of tourist sites on the way. 'This will be a short trip. I'm going to sell the Volvo, which is showing its age, and replace it with something else,' she told the school principal, who wondered where she was disappearing to again, and she promised to be back by the end of the month. I asked her what reasons she gave Rashid, and she said a good cover story is a story that suits everyone who hears it. I felt she was silencing me, and there was nothing I could do about it. She found it hard to explain to Barbara why she was taking this trip. 'It's worth doing,' she told her.

'I'm getting the car virtually free, and the cost of petrol will be about the same as shipping it.'

"'And Rashid?' Barbara asked. 'What's he going to say, now that you're back together?'

"'I think he understands, and besides, he's very busy these days.'

"'So you've taken care of that too?' Not a shred of suspicion in Barbara's voice, just secrets between two women.

"'Yes,' Rachel replied, and she told me she shared her enthusiasm for this adventure with Barbara. 'You want to put a romantic gloss on it? Well, I'm, seizing the opportunity to be alone for a bit. Two weeks on the road is something I've been looking forward to for ages.'

"What was she thinking when she saw there was only one room? Perhaps she was waiting for this as I was, for the chance to figure out just what was happening between us. And perhaps she too was yearning for arms embracing her in the night. I remembered what happened with Stefan, but I wasn't Stefan. Stefan and I had nothing in common, least of all the certainty that it would happen. And she was no longer the same Rachel. Three years in the field is like ten years in Israel. Out there, you're not just earning credits for your pension. And there was Rashid. The Rashid who came into the picture after Oren and after Stefan and after others I didn't know about. And alongside all of them there was me, the old man, with or without quotation marks, the case officer, the driver, the doctor, the listener. I think she knew how I felt about her. I think she was relaxed about the setup, taking from me and giving nothing in return.

"She folded her arms and waited while I paid for the room. The clerk, who seemed to be sure that he knew what was going on, didn't ask for her passport, which was precisely what we wanted. Earlier that afternoon we had stopped at a little seaside parking area. We sat in the car and looked out at the beach and the water, and waited. Then I got out and walked around for a bit, holding a roll of toilet paper in case anyone was interested in what I was doing. When I was sure we were alone, I made a call with the cell phone that had been purchased specially for this assignment, to a number that I had memorized, and said I was enjoying the trip, and a moment later a camper-van with a couple of middle-aged tourists pulled up alongside the Audi. Rachel had opened the hood and was looking at the motor, so they asked if they could help. She explained that the battery was dead and they, with surprising generosity, offered their own spare battery, which apparently every responsible motorist carries in this part of the world. It took them only five minutes and this was no wonder. They had practiced the exchanging of the batteries plenty of times in Marseilles, until it ran like clockwork. The woman brewed coffee while her other half installed the battery and made sure it was working, despite the five kilos of explosives packed into it. We drank their coffee, thanked them, and set off for the hotel—not knowing that thanks to a glitch in the planning, only one room would be available. It had to be this hotel, since it was the only one with an underground parking lot, and we didn't want to leave the Audi outside.

"The clerk didn't offer to help with the luggage. Rachel followed me up the stairs, dragging her suitcase, the wheels bumping on every step. I unlocked the door and went in first. A small room without character: a double bed, a single chair, a little table with an old TV on it. In the bathroom, a small shower, a toilet, a chipped glass shelf. Rachel sat silently on the bed.

"'I'm going down to find a restaurant. Get yourself organized and then we'll go get something to eat,' I said to her, instead of addressing the sleeping arrangements, how we would manage to use the bathroom and the shower, get into bed later and sleep without touching, like strangers to each other, now more than ever.

"Rachel came down wearing the clothes she had arrived in, but she had made the effort to put on a little makeup and had tidied her hair. She gave me a look of appraisal. The short man in the trousers that constantly needed hitching up, with the mustache he liked tending, the glasses he'd recently started wearing, and the shoes with crepe rubber soles. What did she think of me then? What does she think of me now, knowing I'm searching for her? Even then, sixteen years ago, I wasn't handsome, even as a well-preserved man in the prime of life. But I was her case officer, and I loved her. I was the only one she could trust, or so I thought.

"We went to a restaurant.

"We returned after the meal.

"We went out and came back in silence. We both knew what awaited us.

"As we walked back to the hotel, a light rain was falling and my shoes were wet. I needed to piss but I could think of only one thing. And why not? I asked myself. Why shouldn't she want me to hold her? Why shouldn't she want to sleep with me, fortifying herself for the two days awaiting her, a parting gift from heart to heart? There were many days behind us. Many hotels, many separate rooms, meals, long journeys in cars, on planes and trains. There were also handshakes on meeting, a clumsy hug now and then, turning away when she changed her clothes in the car, or in a room, before we set out. But not this. Not one bed, one blanket, and an unforgiving rain in a strange and alien city.

"I called the number I had. 'Everything okay,' I told the duty officer, and added the obligatory code words. I knew the system was starting up, and the monitor in the operations room would be receiving the activation code. Not that we could do anything in the event of a slipup, but we wanted to think we could, and we set up the war room for situations just like this. Sophisticated communications equipment and big maps with the traffic axes marked on them. Arrows and stickers to mark estimated progress, points at which status reports are expected. A sense of security that we wanted to radiate, showing we were in control.

"And I was in control, you see, still functioning even as I was trying to figure out what to do, what was going to happen. Rachel was quiet. Maybe she was thinking about the mission, about the kilometers she had to cover alone, the border crossing awaiting her on the other side of the hill. And I walked beside her in the rain and wondered if she wanted our bodies to touch. More than that I didn't dare think.

"I didn't take a shower. There was no hot water, and in a day I'd be going home. I saw her white nightgown on the side of the bed she had chosen, and for a moment we were like a married couple. I had nothing to prepare. I knew I'd have to sleep in my underwear. I went downstairs again so she could get herself organized in peace and use the bathroom without inhibition. The sidewalk was empty. I inhaled the night air and watched the trucks moving in an endless convoy on the highway. White lights approached and red lights receded.

"I opened the door to our room as quietly as I could, but it creaked. The lamp on my side was on. Rachel lay on her back, covered by the blanket. She opened her eyes, and smiled a thin smile at me, and her lips said, 'Good night,' in English. Then she turned on her side, pulled the blanket over her, but then she freed some up and pushed it over to my side. I took off my pants and shirt, and got into bed in my underwear. The blanket covered us both. I touched her, she touched me, in that confined space it was inevitable. One bed, one blanket, two pillows, two people. I didn't sleep much that night. Perhaps she didn't either. And that's all. When I woke up in the morning she was dressed and ready to go.

"You see? This time they were right, those who say it's impossible to want sex a moment before you need to drive a vehicle laden with explosives through an international border crossing. To think about something else and not about the slow drive to the border, the last bend in the road, the closed barrier with the scruffy sentry standing beside it, checking your papers and waving you on to a building resembling a shed, and beside it the dreaded 'inspection pit.' The operations officer explained to her that if they put her on this, she's in big trouble. 'She's in trouble, all right,' I said. 'Are you going to tell her why?' He explained that if there's anything suspicious they put the car over the pit, wheels on either side, like a woman parting her legs (his expression, not mine!), and they go in underneath and probe around there like gynecologists (his expression), looking for something. 'And sometimes,' he said, 'they seize the opportunity to plant something there, a tracking device or a voice recorder, or something incriminating, a little item that will really fuck you over. And in any case, under no circumstances offer them a bribe. A fine, yes. You can pay a fine, but get a receipt. A bribe can in itself be a trap.' And he carried on in much the same vein, even suggesting she should lean forward for the benefit of the customs officer, with at least one of her blouse buttons undone, but he didn't say a word about the other possibility that became reality out there, which we only learned about after the event, and which for me is connected, for some reason, to that restless night that I spent with her, feeling and not feeling the warmth of her body beside me."

⚜

"SHE PASSED THE BEND AND STOPPED at the side of the road. Just as the operations officer had instructed. I remember that when he was briefing her I sat beside him and watched her, leaning over the map and tracing the route prescribed for her with a fingertip. I had doubts. 'This border crossing is too dangerous,' I said to the ops officer when we went for a smoke break on the balcony. 'Don't worry, remember how she conned her way into the missile base.' He spoke of her with admiration, but I had the feeling his compliments were aimed at persuading me. He knew I wouldn't expose my fears to her. When facing an operative you show a united front and leave the arguments in the Office. I wasn't giving up and I said we had a bad record with this place, not much traffic there, and the customs men check everything. 'She'll be better off going to a big and busy crossing point where she'll be less conspicuous, swallowed up by convoys of trucks and buses,' I said. 'The man's talking a load of crap,' the ops officer told the Unit commander. 'A nice, quiet, relaxed place, that's what's needed. Bored soldiers. Old equipment. No one will suspect, and anyway they'll be too busy dancing around the foreign girl. They'll see her and cream themselves,' that's how he spoke. 'I wouldn't be surprised if one of them takes out his dick and waves it at her'—I can't believe he said that. A vulgar man, but a good ops officer, and that's how it is when only men are sitting at a table. 'But they'll let her pass. They'll be interested in her, in her travel plans, who she is, but they won't suspect.' The Unit commander was convinced, and he said the maximum she could expect would be a pinched bum, but there would be no trouble. The ops officer explained to Rachel that the crossing was small and lacked sophisticated surveillance gear, and that was why we chose it. And we agreed with her that she would stop after the bend, as if checking her position on the map, and wait a few minutes to see if anything would happen. It would always be possible, and she had the option to turn around and go back before she reached the barrier. No shortage of excuses."

❧

"FROM A DISTANCE EVERYTHING LOOKED CALM. No one overtook her on the way, and as far as she could tell she wasn't being followed. The rain had stopped and the sun was shining. She got out of the car and checked that nothing had come loose. There had been no problem before, driving between borders with a battery similar to the one that was now installed in her vehicle. The exercise was important, and the checks at the border crossing between European states were sometimes more rigorous and the technical equipment more sophisticated. Or so we told her, in the hope of boosting her confidence. But I was there waiting for her behind every border crossing, waiting to shake her hand and tell her she was doing great, and the battery was just a battery. And here no one is waiting for her, and in the battery there are five kilos of explosives. She knew what lay ahead, wiped away the droplets of sweat on her upper lip, and moved on to the next stage.

"Getting out of a country is always easy. The cop who stood at the entrance waved goodbye, the customs officer didn't even look at her, and at the border police post they stamped her passport and let her drive on. Rachel stepped on the clutch. The technical team insisted on a car with gears. They said it was easier to repair, and if it wouldn't start, she could always find someone to give her a push. She drove the Audi to the barrier, with its blue and white horizontal bar. A casual-looking soldier was amusing himself raising and lowering the bar. A cigarette dangled from his lips and he reminded her of a prison camp guard in a World War II movie, at the membrane between freedom and captivity, but she was on her way in, not out. She looked at the sentry and smiled.

"'Papers.' She held out her passport and the car documents. He examined them, lifted the barrier up with one hand, and waved her on. There was a demilitarized zone between the borders, the result of agreements that couldn't be agreed on. The road was fenced and there were signs warning, in languages including English, that the sector was mined. She moved along the corridor, and if for a moment the association between barbed-wire fences and concentration camps occurred to her, she didn't tell me. 'Take her to one of the camps,' the Unit commander told me before we sent her to liquidate Strauss. It was hard to explain to him just how absurd and worthless this idea was. 'Rachel knows exactly what a concentration camp is,' I dared to tell him. 'If you read her file, you'd know her whole family was wiped out in the camps. For her, Grunewald railway station isn't just some place.'

"'No-man's-land,' she told me later, 'gave me the chance to think.' She knew that joint patrols were active in the area and she had no reason to stop the car by the roadside, not even for a pee. But the temptation was overwhelming. To take a break, breathe some fresh air, get out of the car for a moment, review the details she has to remember, look at the documents again, and only then move forward. Rachel continued her slow progress. Around the bend she saw a wooden gate covered in barbed wire, blocking the roadway, and an enemy soldier standing and waiting for her." Ehud broke off and took a sip of his whiskey. Joe looked at him, perhaps thinking of his own career, the times he had been caught up in situations like this, and trying to remember what he did and how he reacted. Ehud's glance strayed to the garden, stretching away beyond the glass door, to the life going on beyond the dense vegetation, and he thought of how little he knew of what was happening in the lives of the other people in Rachel's life.

"And Rachel was alone. None of our soldiers stood beside her, none of our officers walked ahead of her. She had no one to talk to and no one to contact. She could still turn the Audi around and retrace her route. Say she changed her mind, she left something behind at the hotel, she'll come back tomorrow. And then she'll contact me and tell me whatever she tells me, and I'll have to believe her, because if I don't believe it I'll be saying goodbye to her. Terminating her contract, in other words. We believe our operatives. We have to trust them even when we know they aren't telling us the whole truth. Even when we hear from them that everything is okay, between ourselves we know everything isn't okay. They're frightened, they're tired, they want to come home. They want to lie down on the sofa and get a big hug.

"In our business everything depends on what the operative says. He creates the reality for us. There's no one else who can submit a different report. No soldier who has seen something different. It's not like *Rashomon*. There's only what he saw, what he felt, what he did. I don't know what she was thinking at that moment, what she thought was likely to happen to her sometime soon. I asked her and she told me that she slowed when she saw the fence and the barbed wire, and then she took a deep breath and moved on.

"The sentry looked at her papers and let her pass. 'Welcome, welcome,' he said, and smiled, exposing nicotine-stained teeth. She smiled back at him as if her whole life depended on this smile. He dragged the barricade aside, took a cigarette from his coat pocket, offered her one, and lit his own. It seemed he'd prefer her to linger and talk for a while, but since the only English words he knew were *hello* and *welcome*, that was it.

"Perhaps you're wondering: Why is he yapping on like this? What's the big deal? Even drug smugglers go through this process, and she isn't the first operative who's done it. But for me she was and always will be the only one. I sat in the hotel and waited for her call. I was the uncle who was left behind. The one who will wander around all alone for a few days before going back to France. The one who gets a migraine and waits until she calls to ask him how he is and confirm that she's reached her hotel.

"I picked up the book I brought with me but I couldn't read it. The words passed me by. I thought of Rachel, who at about that time, at midday, when most people are thinking of the meal that awaits them, would be arriving at the crossing, hoping to exploit their fatigue and their inattentiveness."

⁂

TENSION WAS IN THE AIR. A heavily built man, big mustache, and a thick gold ring on his finger, sat behind an old wooden desk and played with a full ashtray. He moved it from side to side and studied the butts that had piled up in it. The other man, young, thin, and un-shaven, sat beside the desk on the backseat of a car, evidently ripped from a confiscated vehicle, and smoked assiduously, filling his lungs and exhaling perfect smoke rings toward the solitary lightbulb, the only illumination in the semidarkness of the room.

The door was open, or perhaps there was no door. She stood in the entrance and wasn't sure if she'd come to the right place. Both men looked up at her and she asked in basic English if they could give her local number plates. "Yes, yes, maybe," said the young man, still exuding smoke rings. She moved closer to the table and her dress brushed against the knees of the young man. The fat man moved the ashtray and held out his hand without saying a word. She handed him the documents and stood close to the table in the long dress that she wore out of respect for the local culture, topped by a thin sweater and sandals that exposed her red-painted toenails. Rachel tightened the sweater around her shoulders and listened to a muffled racket coming from the corridor. She reckoned this was the generator and inscribed this too in her memory. The ops officer will definitely want to know this. "What's so hard about remembering everything you've seen there?" they always ask.

She waited. The fat man ran a finger over his fleshy lips. He flicked through her passport and the *Carnet de Passages* and checked the certificate of ownership. He opened and closed the *Carnet* as if it were the shutter of a camera, and as she moved closer to the desk the young soldier, sitting on the low seat beside her, was out of her field of vision.

"There's a problem," the fat man said in slow, clear English. "There's a problem," the fat man repeated, and then she felt the hand touching her dress.

A faint rustle. That was all. A touch that pressed the material against her thigh. She wasn't even sure. Perhaps a breath of wind stirred her dress. She didn't move and went on looking at the fat man, who said, "Big problem," like a veteran teacher confronting her in the staff room and calling her to order. The hand that touched her dress touched it again, this time lingering on the back of her thigh, and she had no doubt it was there, the full palm of the hand with all the fingers, working its way up. She could of course have turned around and pushed the young man's hand away; he sat leaning forward with one hand still holding the cigarette and the other groping her. She could also have yelled at him, Stop! or That's enough!, and she knew he would understand, but she also knew the fat man was about to point out the mistake that flashed up now before her eyes, the discrepancy between the car numbers, and exploit the opportunity to tell her again there was a problem, and show her the way out and force her to call Ehud, to explain the mistake that she didn't make. She won't be blamed for anything, but her operation will be killed, stone-dead.

The hand reached the inner thigh. She noticed the narrowing of the fat man's eyes, who saw what was happening behind her, and saw his tongue moistening his thick lips. The hand continued its upward journey, and she froze where she stood and told the fat man that all he needed to do was correct the number manually. This was the mistake of the clerk at the last checkpoint. She felt the hand fumbling between her legs and heard the heavy breathing behind her. The smoke from the cigarette stung her eyes and the fat clerk watched her and waited until he heard his colleague gasp and saw him slump back on the grubby car seat and take a long drag on the cigarette. It was only then he picked up the stamp and stamped her papers, and gave her the crumpled number plates that were on his desk, and said to her, "Welcome home."

Rachel walked down the narrow hallway, keeping a tight grip on the plates, for the sake of which she had stood with legs parted and allowed the young man who had sat behind her to insert his hand in her panties and his finger inside of her. She knew it was by her own choice that she stood and waited until she heard his breathing change. Only then she turned and noticed the stain in the crotch of his pants, still feeling his probing, invasive finger. For the sake of the numbers on the plates, she was thinking, for the sake of the mission, she put up with it, didn't cry out to the officer who sat in the lobby on a rocking chair, looking at her as if he knew what had happened in there. Ahead of her there's another long drive to the hotel, and only then can she strip off her underwear and throw it out, the dress too, and try to forget. But she can't throw out the feeling, or the image of his smile and the dreamy look in his eyes when he leaned back, still holding the burning cigarette.

Rachel said something to the officer and he found some metal wire and helped her put the new license plates over the number plates on her car. The officer waved farewell as she set out on her way, legs shut together tightly. One more checkpoint to pass. The sentry at the gate examined her papers carefully. The passport was stamped, vehicle documentation in order. No one looked under the hood and checked the battery. The barrier was raised and she was finally through.

⚜

"'I WANT YOU TO ASK ME how I'm feeling,' she said to me when she sat down with me two months later, after peering at the press clippings I had saved for her, looking at the ruins of the wrecked garage and reading the report in *Haaretz*: *'A leading terrorist has been killed in a mysterious blast, and a secret office of the PLO has been completely destroyed. The office, masquerading as a garage on the outskirts of a harbor town, served as a center for the planning of terrorist attacks, and a senior source in Jerusalem, who spoke on condition of anonymity and denied any connection with the incident, would only say that the death of this man had thwarted a major attack which had been in the planning stages for some time. Local police investigators suspect that explosives stored in the garage detonated accidentally, while according to one British newspaper this was apparently the result of a turf-war between rival organizations.'*

"And there was also the report we prepared for the Minister of Defense, who wanted to know how we had done it. Of course we omitted Rachel's name and certain other details that even the minister didn't need to know, and only described in brief how she arrived at the garage, having 'found' a fault that had been prearranged, got a new battery installed, and went on her way. No need to explain to the minister that she was acquainted with the garage and the way it worked, having reconnoitered it in advance, and she knew what they did with batteries that had been replaced and where they stored them. Also no need to tell him where she set out from and what she did afterward.

"'I want to know what you think about the operation,' she added, 'the significance of it, the difference it might make.' Her voice trembled and her face was flushed. I could see she was keeping something inside, she was holding herself back from telling me more, and I decided to wait. This was my method—let her choose her moment to speak. And if she doesn't? It's her choice.

"'Have you any idea what happened at the border checkpoint?' she said. 'I know what you wrote in your report. Some clerk mixed up the car number and you had to smile at the fat man and persuade him to turn ignore it. That's what you wrote, isn't it?' And at that moment I didn't suspect anything. I certainly wanted to know more details, but she reported the procedure she had followed in typically laconic style, and I took notes. And anyway, everything was dwarfed by the scale of the operation itself, by the reports in the press and the congratulations we received from the Prime Minister, who wanted to meet her and thank her personally. She told me she felt exploited, and she asked if I was prepared to hear her out, or if I would have a problem with that. Her face hardened and I heard a critical and resentful tone in her voice. What could I do after she gave me the full story, tell her she see should see a doctor? I couldn't do that. The next morning she was due to fly back to her adopted country. God knows why she postponed the conversation to this moment. Perhaps to test me, to see what I would do. I glanced at my watch. I had no choice. In an hour and a half from now I was supposed to be meeting my wife and leaving for a vacation that had been planned long ago. How could I tell Rachel that life goes on, people go to work and come home, they have children, they have their little ways, they have their pleasures?

"'When he put his hand under my dress,' she said, 'I thought of you. I thought of what you would tell me to do, of what you would have done. You would tell me to do nothing. I hated you and I went on smiling at the fat man as if nothing were happening. When his hand was in my panties I wanted to scream, but I didn't. The cigarette smoke was choking me. I didn't move even when his finger went inside me. I remembered you saying something about the terrorist I was going to blow up. I remembered you saying such a thing has never been done before. It took all of two minutes maybe, until I heard his little gasp. I did what you asked of me and I hated you.'

"She began to weep, and I sat there paralyzed and waited. I wasn't the right person to be sitting with her when she is talking about me. The awful story of what I made her do should be told to somebody else, without holding back and without the complications of the relationship between us. I know she felt my devotion to her, she knew I loved her, and that made it harder for me. I tried to be professional, to do my job, but inside it felt like I had been there, in that room, and I had done nothing to help her. Since then we haven't talked about it, and I keep thinking about her visit to the garage with the explosive battery, the mission that she went ahead with despite what she had to endure, despite the trauma to her body and her soul, and all of this was supposed to stay secret.

"And I didn't know, then, if she had told him. If after scrubbing her body and putting on her nightgown, and after hiding her passport and wallet and car keys, and after going over the whole episode minute by minute as she lay on the hotel bed, wondering if anything could have been otherwise, if she was somehow to blame—she contacted him.

"I assume she thought of him and was ashamed. She told me about the guard who raised the barrier and said goodbye to her as if he knew what had happened, as if anyone seeing her would know what had happened. She thought she made it possible. This wouldn't have happened to anyone else.

"She arrived at her apartment in the evening and listened to the news in English. There was no mention of the explosion and the fire, and she had to wait for our clandestine broadcast to hear the plaudits showered on her.

"And today I know that afterwards she called him.

"And she told him, and he listened. And perhaps he had questions, and perhaps he thought of scolding her for traveling alone, but he didn't say anything. I hope he rushed over to see her and took her in his arms and brought her to bed, to prove that he loved her and to earn her everlasting love."

CHAPTER ELEVEN

⚬

Exit

"And what did you do then?" Joe yawned, and Ehud tried to hide his disappointment. The stack of files on the small cart beside them hadn't shrunk at all, and the security personnel assigned by the department to guard the classified documents were working around the clock. Joe reflected sadly that he was too old for all this, and in his day things were done differently. True, he knew how to use a computer and a cell phone, and like all of them he too admired the work of the surveillance teams, and the satellites that the Intelligence Corps had launched into orbit, but he still believed there was no substitute for dialogue and for the human factor when dealing with people and their innermost thoughts. He didn't think Ehud was lying, or deliberately withholding vital information. Ehud was searching for something deep inside him, and he had no way of getting to it without talking and talking and unraveling whatever was in his heart in the simple and familiar way—word by word, date by date, event by event.

When Ehud took a short break for a nap, Joe had a talk with the

Unit commander. The red phone allowed him to speak freely and he asked the commander to be patient: "Ehud is the key to this lock. He was her case officer, and he was the one she contacted. She told him her father was dead as if this is a password that he'd forgotten."

The commander had learned a thing or two about Joe, and he let him continue.

"Ehud too wants to know where she is. It's been fifteen years since they parted company. In the meantime his wife has died and his children have grown up, and I think he's still in love with her."

"Are you sure he's telling you the truth?" The commander reminded Joe that all they had was what Ehud was telling them, including the call he received.

"Even if he is lying and even if he's hiding things, he's not the type who would be helped to confess by the interrogation room and the cold water treatment. He's too experienced to be intimidated by that."

The commander mumbled something, and Joe had no doubt that the idea of a third-degree interrogation had occurred to him.

"The problem is that Ehud doesn't know what to do either. He doesn't know her anymore, and now he's afraid that even then he didn't know what she was thinking and where her loyalties lay. She had a lover out there, did you know that?"

The commander didn't know, and he sent Yaniv, their liaison man, to go and scour the files. Joe waited on the line and listened to the commander giving Yaniv his instructions, and he knew this was pointless. All that Yaniv would find, if he found anything, would be a handful of dry, laconic reports, nothing that would be helpful.

There was one more important point to be raised, and he wanted the commander to grasp precisely what he meant. "Ehud is not one of us," he said, and he heard the sharp intake of breath at the other end of the line. "Ehud is on her side. He wants to protect and rescue her.

If we back him into a corner, he'll choose to defend her interests rather than ours."

"I'm not sure I understand," said the commander.

"*We* are looking for her to make sure that she doesn't divulge the secrets she knows. *He* is looking for her because he loves her. These are two completely different things, and we have a classic conflict of interests." He paused to let this sink in and continued: "We need to treat him like a target, the same as Rachel. We need his help and his knowledge and we have to exploit the fact that she turned to him and not to her regular contact. This shows there is something between them. She could have been missing for weeks and months without anyone noticing her absence, and that's why I need him here in my house, and not in the war room or the archive."

"Okay, so what are you doing?" The commander wasn't the impatient type and he was a good listener. This was part of the reason that put him in the big leather chair.

"I'm talking to him, that's what I'm doing, I'm listening and letting him tell the whole story in his own way, until he himself leads us somewhere. It's obviously connected with her past, and obviously connected with what they shared. Otherwise she would have contacted someone else, or no one at all."

The commander murmured his agreement.

"But where is she now? In Canada, where her cover story is based? In Europe, in one of the places she stayed for months before she went out to the operational zone? Or none of these places? I don't know, but I think we're making progress. Don't bother us, that's all I'm asking for."

The commander agreed. He added that they were working on all the leads they had—the phone card that she bought, the brochures they found in her father's house, her British and Israeli passports. "We sent teams to all the possible places, spoke to all the intelligence agencies that we cooperate with, and right now we're waiting."

Joe asked the Unit commander to check a few things for him, and after speaking again to young Yaniv and telling him which of the old files to go through, he woke Ehud and asked him to continue.

♪

"AFTER SHE TOLD ME ALL THE details of what happened at the border crossing, I told HQ I was postponing her return to active service and sending her to Israel for a break. Deep silence prevailed over the preparations for what should have been a vacation and most of the time she spent in her room. Before the journey I gave her a makeup set and a wig that we had prepared for her at home, and she took them from me as if she really did want to change her identity. I could barely recognize her when we set out, and her whole demeanor had changed too. The restrained young woman I knew had turned into a noisy flapper, in keeping with the blond wig and the heavy makeup. At first I thought she was being the consummate professional, going deep into the image assigned to her and making it unlikely that anyone flying with us would recognize her as Rachel Brooks. But when I watched her then from a distance of three rows away on the plane it seemed to me she was allowing herself the relief that only a change of identity could give her.

"We went to the Prime Minister's residence as soon as we landed. She went into the bathroom and got rid of the wig, removed the makeup, took out the contact lenses, and was once again the woman we knew. The Prime Minister welcomed her to his inner sanctum, and although all of this had been laid on in her honor, I thought she felt uncomfortable being the center of attention of four men. When he asked her how she succeeded in smuggling the explosives across the border, I was afraid she was going to tell him. It was a bit strange. On one side there were the four of us—the head of the Mossad, the Unit commander, Rachel, and me—who knew what had happened, and on the other side the Prime Minister, who was asking her how she did what she did. She answered briefly and politely, and when he stood to award her the certificate of meritorious conduct I saw she was on the verge of tears. After this I took her to a hotel in Tel Aviv, left her some cash, and I took the certificate back to the Office. To this day she hasn't been allowed to keep it at home. Security comes first, doesn't it? Actually, she probably felt more isolated in Tel Aviv than in her apartment out there. She had nowhere to go, no home, no partner, and a father she had no intention of contacting. Before we parted in the hotel she stood with her back to me and stared at the dark horizon, and if there had been a single ray of light out there, I doubt she would have seen it.

"We had to decide what to do with her. Opinions were divided. The chief security officer wanted to bring her home. The trauma she had suffered could undermine her judgment and there was the risk that she would put too much emotion into her work. I wanted her to carry on and I relied on what she had told me, that she would get over it and she had no complaints about the way we had treated her.

"'You should understand,' I told them, 'besides us she has nothing. Now she's a highly esteemed operative making an honorable contribution to the success of our early-warning systems. At least, that is what she feels. If we bring her back, all she will have left is a sense of failure. She'll pack her bags, tell the school she's leaving, and be off. And what will she do here? Go back to teaching? Join the department as a junior bureaucrat? I agree we need to plan for the termination of her service there, but we should do this calmly and construct a routine for her. That's the only way she'll recover and be ready for more operations.' The Unit commander suspended the discussion and called in the operations officer. I hadn't agreed he should be told what happened to Rachel at the border crossing. I didn't want the story to go any further than it already had, especially if there was a prospect that a few weeks from now she might be applying to our department for a more conventional job.

"'What do you say?' the Unit commander asked. The ops officer was unequivocal. He insisted she be kept in place until we could find a replacement. 'We can't afford to give up such a valuable asset. The intelligence branch would kill us.' 'Don't exaggerate,' said the Unit commander. 'If anything happens that puts her in danger, I'll have her out of there at a moment's notice.' But even he couldn't foresee what was going to happen. Even he underestimated the power of chance.'"

⚜

"THE CALL CAME THROUGH AT TWO in the morning. The Unit commander was on the line. 'Congratulations are in order. We got the big project.' I thanked him and didn't ask any questions. We didn't know if anyone was listening in on our conversation, and we always worked on that assumption. We agreed to talk again in the morning and I put the receiver down. I confess, my hand was shaking. It had come. I didn't need to consult any list of projects to know what he was talking about. Rina asked me what had happened and when she saw my face in the light of the bedside lamp she said she would take the children to school in the morning and then wait for me at home.

"It took me ten minutes to get to the Rome railway station. I made sure no one was following me. I knew how to do that, and at two in the morning it's easy. When I decided I was clean, I used one of the twenty vacant phone booths and called HQ. The Unit commander was in the Office and in the background I heard other familiar voices. It was clear there was a state of emergency. 'Take the first available flight. Everything will be explained when you are here. But before anything else, call Rachel and tell her to start moving at once. We've made all the arrangements we can here.' I repeated his words so we would both be sure we were referring to the same thing, and hung up.

"I moved to another booth and phoned her. The conversation was short and polite. I introduced myself as a good friend of her father's, and the news was that the old man was dying. There was no risk of misunderstanding on her part. I was her regular contact and she recognized my voice. I gave the code word we had agreed on. That was all. In the original briefing she asked me what would happen if her father really did die suddenly. I said we would find someone else to contact her. And then she asked what would happen if on the day we needed to tell her to leave everything and get out at once I was ill, or couldn't be contacted, and we agreed on code words that my stand-in would need to use, so she would get a clear and unmistakable message and know she was leaving.

"I returned to the apartment to pack before leaving for the airport. I knew the flight schedules by heart and I had time to say goodbye to Rina and kiss the children, who were still asleep. I didn't know what had happened, and I didn't indulge in any speculations. There were so many things to do, the most important being to think about Rachel. At this moment she was supposed to be following the instructions she had been given. She needed to be sure this was it, there would be no going back. I knew what was going to happen. We had practiced this scores of times. The phone conversation. The knowledge that someone might be listing in, that the Mukhabarat had already put her under tight surveillance. She knew what she had to do.

"But an exercise bears no resemblance to the real thing. To the churning of the stomach, the irresistible urge to go to the bathroom, the dry mouth, the thought that won't go away—what will happen now, will she have time to get out before they come for her? How do you cope with pressure and danger and maintain an unruffled exterior? With the feeling that an entire life is about to be left behind? Like refugees, like soldiers fleeing from the battlefield. I remember this. I saw Egyptian soldiers in headlong flight in the Yom Kippur War, and we were chasing them. And Rachel? For her it must be different. She has to act calmly, discreetly. Do everything slowly, in an orderly way, not arousing any suspicion at the last moment, not giving them a reason to lay a hand on her shoulder."

⚜

RACHEL NEVER TOLD EHUD WHAT HE so much wanted to know. She didn't think he was worthy of it. She won't be going back there, and there's no reason why he should know more than he needs to know and what she wants to tell him about her life there. She confined herself to dry information and only tried to include every technical detail that would enable the security section to assess the damage done to the Mossad and be better prepared when the next operative was sent out into the field. Ehud hoped in vain that she would settle in the small and depressing apartment that they gave her in Tel Aviv and tell him what she felt as she was leaving behind everything that she had been.

She didn't tell him because something in her was broken. Because from the moment she boarded the plane and left the airspace of her adopted country she knew there would be no more dreams, no more dwelling in two worlds, no more Rachel Brooks living in a pleasant apartment in a foreign and exotic capital city, and loving Rashid. There's just Rachel Ravid, Israeli citizen returning home after a long stint in Europe and needing to rebuild her life.

IMMEDIATELY AFTER PUTTING THE PHONE DOWN, Ehud's urgent voice still reverberating in her head, she thinks of Rashid and she's glad he isn't there beside her, forcing her to lie to his face. In her imagination she sees him in his bed in his parents' apartment, covered by the blanket she bought him for his birthday. "It's sad needing to buy two blankets," she told him, and cajoled him into promising her this was temporary, and now she's folding the blanket they won't be using again. There's no room in the small suitcase she's taking, and no room for a blanket in the cover story she intends to sell to anyone who asks her where she's rushing off to. She's shocked when she realizes she's already thinking about him in the past tense, and remembers how she used to lie beside him, her hand on his body, waiting till he's asleep before she allows herself to drift off until he wakes up and tells her in a sleepy voice that he loves her. I didn't have time to tell him, she thinks as she scours the flat and checks that everything is in place, I didn't have the chance to tell him again and again how much I love him, I want to live with him but I can only die with him. Rachel puts into her purse the cuff link that Rashid left on the shelf in the shower, and knows she hasn't the time to look for its twin, which was lost in their frantic haste of undressing a few hours ago. She won't give him back what he has lost, and he can't ask her what happened. She's leaving him and everything that was between them. She's burning her bridges. Whatever happens she will not be . . . She's not coming back here, never, never, never.

She doesn't remember the instructions by heart, and there's no need. "It's just the essentials you need to know," the chief security officer said, and he explained that if she gets the evacuation order, "which would never happen," she has to leave everything and think only of herself. Not think of anything else. She's not to worry about the communications equipment, not worry about the connections she's formed, not worry about her past. "Rachel Brooks will no longer exist, and the reason why isn't important."

She looks around her. The cat that she took into her home to be a companion for the dog is curled up asleep on the sofa. She didn't tell Ehud about him. There were other things she didn't tell him about, and afterward, when he asked her why, she said she wasn't a little girl and he didn't need to know everything about her. She was coming up with the goods, and that should be enough. The cat didn't seem perturbed by the unusual activity at three in the morning. Mango will be all right, she knows how to fend for herself. And the plants? They're going to die, obviously. And Rashid? He will be history too. He'll look for her for a while, he'll want to know where his lover has disappeared to, and then things will return to normal.

Rachel waters the plants and imagines Rashid when the interrogators come calling, answering their questions and thinking about the woman who has abandoned him. How long have you known her? they'll ask, and he'll tell them about the first time he visited the school office with his driver, and saw her coming in. He'll tell them about the school, her frequent leaves, the supper he suggested, the trip they took together, her eagerness to see more and more, their trip to the coastal town—and suddenly he'll understand.

And she imagines him falling silent, the way he does when they're together and there's something he doesn't like, something he needs to think about. He glances attentively at the man who sits facing him with the open file on his lap and thinks of the ways she has deceived him. Pieces of the puzzle start fitting together and he remembers her answers, the nights she lay awake beside him, the tension in her muscles when they discussed politics, the look in her eyes when they passed a military base. And if he's angry, he manages to hide it. And if he's offended, he'll let no one see it.

There's no haste in her actions, because she's in a hurry, and when you're in a hurry you need to work slowly and methodically. She finishes packing, drinks a glass of water, and makes a last circuit of the apartment. The music room is in a mess, as it should be, and the equipment looks tired and out-of-date. She will take from here only what she can, and that's very little. The fridge is full of yesterday's shopping, and the roasting tray, with the relics of the last supper she ate with him, cuts her to the heart. The wardrobe is arranged the way she likes it, and she tries not to think of the hands that will be rummaging through her drawers sometime soon. She wonders what to do with the sack of laundry that she prepared for tomorrow and finally kicks it into the corner of the bathroom, and decides not to throw anything in the bin. The next person in here needs to think she has just gone out for a while. What goes through the mind of someone checking her home for the last time, her fortress, her apartment, before leaving it forever? This wasn't her apartment. She leased it, by arrangement with her superiors, who agreed to the exorbitant rent. But it was her home. These were her flowers, the carpets she bought, the souvenirs she collected, her bedding, and the memory of Rashid's body, a precious and tangible memory, the toothbrush she kept for him, his favorite coffee, the semen stains on a sheet not yet laundered.

And then she does something that is strictly forbidden, a contravention of the most basic rules. She takes a piece of paper.

⚜

"MY LOVE," SHE WRITES, AND THE pen scratches the surface of the wooden table that he bought her as a present; she placed it by the window, as far as possible from the music room, just in case the table had some kind of listening device. Do not accept gifts—that's another rule she's broken.

"When you read this letter I will be far away from you, as far as the living are from the dead. We will never meet again. I will never again see you watching me, feel your hand caressing my body, and you won't feel the thrill that passes through me. I will never hear your voice again. I will never again smell your beloved fragrance, as a mother inhales the scent of her baby in her arms.

"I'm leaving you. I will always remember the look in your eyes when you stood in the doorway, after you had already said goodbye, after you kissed me again and again, after you said you wished you could stay. A long look that infused and sustained me.

"The secret won. A transparent yet impenetrable secret. Since the first day it has been a barrier between us. I thought it would disappear, I was wrong, and I'm to blame. I'm to blame for making you love me, for falling in love with you, for keeping the secret inside me and letting it poison me. I fought it until it defeated me."

⚜

SHE WANTS TO CARRY ON. SHE wants to tell him everything, explain it to him, as if that were possible. She knows there is no chance, but deep down she is still hoping. She crumples the letter, drops it in the garbage disposal, and turns it on.

⚜

GRACIE HAS FOUND A COMFORTABLE PLACE to rest on the carpet, and now she raises her head and looks at Rachel, who goes over to the dog, kneels beside her, and then stretches out alongside her and hugs her. She caresses the warm and hairy belly and remembers the vet who told her to have the bitch spayed. "She's a stray," he said with his guttural local accent, and Rachel felt he was criticizing her, Rachel, personally. "Why cause more problems? She's been vaccinated, let's stop the bloodline here." He was right, and she brought her in on the appointed day, and stood beside her and cried while the dog was sedated. "You can leave now," said the vet, and he laid out the surgical instruments on the table beside him. Rachel felt that she was the one who was about to be cut and she stiffened her stomach muscles to resist the knife. She went, and the feeling that she had betrayed the dog, the dog who had trusted her, would never leave her.

And here is another betrayal, worse than the first. She looks at her watch. She needs to get to the airport and board the plane—this is no time for sentiment. It was the same in training, when her cover was threatened. But then she knew it was an exercise. And then she didn't have houseplants, goldfish, a dog, a cat. And a lover.

She puts extra food in the aquarium. The cat arches her back before settling down, seemingly unperturbed about being put in the hallway. The dog looks at her. They will all die, she knows, Rashid and Gracie too. She's going to kill them off in her heart just as she must kill off the identity she had in the past. It's all over.

As she went out she turned around. Gracie stood by the door and wagged her tail. She wasn't bothered by the early hour. Anytime is right for a walk. Anytime is good for a stroll up to the top of the hill, looking down on the Presidential Palace and the gates of the Defense Ministry.

Perhaps she could leave her with Barbara, call her and tell her she has to go, and the dog needs looking after. Impossible, she knew it was out of the question. Not because of the danger they knew about, because of the danger they didn't know about. Who could say what Barbara would do? So just go, as in the exercises, as in the reality she's confronting now.

The dog climbed into the Audi, sat down beside Rachel, poked her head out, and breathed the cool night air. When she reached the second intersection, she opened the door on the dog's side and knew what would happen. Gracie leapt down and waited for Rachel to emerge from her side. Instead, Rachel stepped on the gas. In the mirror she saw the dog, confused and considering her next move, and then starting to run after her. Rachel clutched the wheel with both hands and made no attempt to wipe away the tears. It seems she's still hoping, she thought, and accelerated, turning at the next intersection and onto the expressway leading to the airport. A final glance in the mirror revealed the abandoned Gracie receding, as she reached the intersection and stopped at the roadside, waiting for Rachel to come back and take her in her arms again, like the day she picked her up and took her home.

She sat on one of the tattered seats by the departure gate and waited. The plane wasn't there yet, and her flight was going to be delayed. She was thinking only of what she had left behind, and the details of her cover story. She'll have time yet to think about the future, just so long as she passes the final test. Rachel held on tight to the life she had created for herself and knew she must not weaken under any circumstances. Every man in uniform, every single mustachioed man who passed by her and looked at her, could be the one who would ask her to accompany him. But why? she will say, and hold out her passport. Rachel Brooks is catching the first flight to Europe to reach her father, who is gravely ill. Here's a phone number they can call. And here's the number and the address of her aunt. And here are the numbers of Barbara, and the school, and her apartment, and there's even the parking ticket for her car, which is in the airport parking lot. And only Rashid's name will be omitted, as if he doesn't exist. As if his eyes never looked at her. She remembered his phone number. She remembered his eyes, also the eyes of the German scientist, who looked up at her the very moment he kissed the poisoned glove.

⚜

"How could I convince her that this was an unwanted end for me as well?" Ehud wrapped up the story and sighed. "We took her out of the life she was leading at a stroke, and gave her nothing in return.

"I think I can imagine what the flight was like for her. The sigh of relief that she stifled when the plane took off, the leaning back in the seat and attempting to ignore the view below, mountains and roads she would never see again. It's hard to run away when you don't know what you're running from, harder still to leave behind the things you loved. I know she relied on us and she had no doubt the danger was real, but the moment the plane left the airspace of what we define as an enemy country, which for her was home, she began to weep. And when she told me about the tears that streamed down her face, I didn't know if they were tears of sorrow or of joy.

"No one was waiting for her when she arrived at the airport in Rome, and she wasn't expecting anyone to be there. Perhaps she didn't want to meet anyone, and perhaps she was secretly hoping that after she had checked into a hotel and called the number she knew by heart, I would tell her everything had been sorted out and after a short vacation she could go back there. That didn't happen. Things like that rarely do. I wanted to be the first to meet her when she abandoned the persona of Rachel Brooks. But even this didn't work out because at the time I was on my way to Israel to join in the efforts of damage control and prepare for her arrival. Someone met her in a café, gave her a new passport and took away the old one, and that was that. The next day I met her at Ben Gurion and drove her to Tel Aviv. She wasn't in disguise. There was no need for that. To this day I curse myself for not inspecting the apartment that the management team had prepared for her. I'm sure they meant no harm, and it wasn't only the minuscule budget that hampered them. They were busy, they had no conception of who Rachel was and where she was coming from, and from their point of view a single bed with an iron frame, a bundle of overstarched sheets, and a woolen blanket from the quartermaster's store were more than adequate. On the wall there was still a poster someone, probably a young trainee, had left behind, and the fridge contained a bottle of cola and a packet of biscuits evidently put there to protect them from the ants.

"I opened the door for her and saw her scouring the empty rooms, the walls that hadn't been whitewashed for years, and the metal grilles over the windows. That's the way it is with ground-floor apartments in Tel Aviv. On the little table there was a telephone, and in the corner an ancient television set supplied by the army welfare fund. Rachel put her case down and leaned against the wall with arms folded, a defensive posture.

"'Are you planning to lock me in here?' she asked, and pointed to the grilles and the bundle of keys I was holding.

"'Don't be absurd.' It was the only response I could think of. 'You've come home, and this is just a temporary arrangement until the inquiries have been finished.'

"We could of course have put her up in a hotel. When she was an operative on duty and came to Europe for briefings, we made sure she got five-star hotels and everything she needed. A doctor had come from Israel when needed, and we even paid her hairdresser's bills. All that was over. She was like all the others and the head of personnel said there was no reason to treat her as a special case. She did a good job and now she's finished it. End of story.

"She looked tired. Her hair was a mess, and it seemed she hadn't changed her clothes since leaving the apartment in her adopted country. 'Would you like to go out?'

"She said no.

"'You're not hungry? There are plenty of good restaurants out there. The city has changed since you were here last.' I listened to myself, and I knew how hollow this sounded. I could no longer tell her what to do, say we're going out, we need to talk. That was behind us. She and I were equal, two Mossad employees whose professional relationship had kept them close together for four years, making them one entity, and now it was over. She turned the offer down, her lips in a frown, and lines that I had not seen before appeared along her face.

"It was only then I could tell her the real reason for her abrupt exit. The German paper *Der Spiegel* had launched its own investigation into the death of Strauss. They suspected poisoning and linked this to the Mossad. They checked all the nearby hotels and knew that Strauss and Rachel Brooks had been in the city at the same time. That was it, no more and no less. But she couldn't be expected to resist enhanced interrogation techniques on the part of the Mukhabarat, and who knows how Rashid would react if he was told she might be linked to the death of his personal friend? She listened to me, and the look in her eyes told me she possibly believed me, or possibly not. She asked to see the text of the article that we obtained from our source at the paper. The English translation had been done in haste and was full of errors, and she commented on this and even started penciling in her own corrections. For a moment I saw her as she was, an English teacher.

"The rest you know. There was an appeal through secret channels to the German police and they made sure the investigation was spiked. Things like that happen all the time. Strauss was a lowlife by any standards, but if the story broke, Germany stood to lose as well. National interest, they call it, and they understand this too. Of course, we couldn't ignore the risk that someone in the police department, out of misplaced zeal or a longing for publicity, might leak the story to the press, along with her picture."

"And what became of her?" Joe asked, although he knew the answer. She was no different from the others. The combatant comes home. They do the debriefing and close the files. The personnel department sends someone to explain pension arrangements and employment options. The Unit commander calls to say goodbye. And that's it. No more access to the Prime Minister's residence by the back door, no more cozy chats with the Mossad chief, no more intimate suppers with Ehud, telling her the world revolves around her. Rachel will be confronting life like any other mortal, no one paying her bills, no one looking after her apartment when she's away. Many former combatants go for work at the Mossad HQ. Rachel tried this for a while, and hence the sensitive and important secrets she had access to, secrets that must not fall into enemy hands. Like others, Rachel couldn't stick with it. It's hard coming to work every morning in a place that sent you far away, and protected you as the one and only, and suddenly you're one of many. And there are people around who say you're not the genius you were described as when you were in the field, and they remember your mistakes and don't hesitate to remind you of them.

"And so it ended. Suddenly she found herself back home, unprepared, and unable to disengage and bid farewell properly, as if that were possible in her life. The reality that she grew accustomed to, that was second nature to her, that she loved, had become history that couldn't even be talked about. It was very hard for her. You could see this in how she looked. She put on weight and neglected her appearance, and our relationship cooled. She was no longer my operative, but someone who was in urgent need of reconstruction. That's a job for shrinks, social workers, and human resources, not my job. They gave her a lot of that and tried to do what they could, but there was no love there, and that's what she missed.

"I had problems too. I had to return to Israel, as there was no point in staying abroad. Rina didn't want to come back, and she never stopped complaining. Try explaining to her that's the way the Mossad works. Our eldest son was studying in Rome and we saw the grandson at least once a week. The younger children were in the middle of their schooling, and it was obvious that if we came back here, they couldn't just slot into the education system. The department wasn't interested; they don't concern themselves with such trifles. I flew to Rome to pack up our lives and return to the measly salary they were offering me here. I was deflated too, and I hoped Rachel would change her mind about me, and I might get the chance to tell her that now, as equals and both working for the Office, there's nothing to stop us meeting. I didn't need to look in the mirror to know this was impossible; at best she would smile silently, and at worst laugh in my face and perhaps say something she had been holding in all this time, something that would spoil the small things we had achieved.

"I don't know why they were so quick to place her in a special department and put her to work on ways of foiling the development of biological weapons. Apparently it was because someone who used to be an operative deserves special treatment at first, and she was a respected operative. A decorated hero who knew how to get things done.

"I saw her from time to time when she was working in the department, and she was always the first to say hello and to ask after my wife, as if marking the border between us in the clearest way possible. I would tell her we were okay and ask her how she was. There was no point asking about Oren, or if she had a boyfriend. Rachel knew how to avoid answering unwanted questions. She'd been trained for years in the art of leaving you satisfied but without an answer."

☙

CHAPTER TWELVE

Tel Aviv

THE CONFERENCE ROOM FELL SILENT WHEN Ehud entered, and he knew that what was being discussed was not meant for his ears. It seemed it had already been a long session. Joe sat next to the Unit commander, showing him a piece of paper that he was careful to shield with his hand. Ehud was unshaven and hadn't changed his clothes. It was only at three in the morning that the long-awaited call finally came through, and he'd barely had time to get home and collapse on his bed. Joe, who had given Ehud a rare hug as he left the garden a few hours before dawn, was wearing a suit and was clean-shaven, fragrant, and positively radiant. He had good reason to smile. He was the one who had sat down with Ehud and unearthed the background story, while in the war room they were engaged in a frantic and futile search for the missing Rachel. He was the one who asked, after hours of patient listening, where and what Rachel wanted to get back to. He was the one who told the exhausted Ehud that Rachel didn't really run away. Joe assumed Rachel had nothing to hide, and the little life she constructed for herself in Rehovot wasn't a cover for anything furtive—it was only a little life of unremitting isolation and despair. "She could kill herself here," said Joe, and Ehud's blood ran cold. "No one would care, and I'm sure some people in the department would breathe a sigh of relief if that happened. One less pensioned former combatant to worry about." He leafed through his notes. "I think that, having checked with Oren and Stefan and her friends from the school, we can rule out the possibility of a romantic entanglement."

"So what are you trying to tell me?" Ehud was confused, and Joe's whiskey wasn't helping his concentration.

"I think she wants to go back to the last place she was happy. She's trying, in some way only she knows, to start the whole process again. I don't think she's crazy. A small screw has come loose, maybe, but there's still time to tighten it up. She has something to give and something to get, and we need to bring her home before it's too late, before she sells what she knows in exchange for a new life."

"Where are you going with this? Are you saying she's a traitor? She's gone over to the other side? What does she stand to gain by giving secrets to the enemy? Rachel has no interest in money. We've seen what that flat of hers looks like, and she has no children, so what's it for?"

"For Rashid," said Joe. "It's to get him back. To live with the man she loves, the man she loved, who was prepared to take risks for her."

"But she left him . . ."

"She's sorry about that. She thinks it was a mistake, and now she wants to turn the clock back."

"And you think she's going back to him just like that, after fifteen years? How will she explain it to him?"

"Don't underestimate the power of love," Joe replied, patient as ever.

"I don't believe it," said Ehud, but he knew it was all too possible. Things like that have always happened and always will. People cross the line for love more readily than for money or ideology. I would cross the line too, he reflected. I'd cross the line for her.

"You don't need to believe it," said Joe, his voice firm and authoritative. "Just one detail to be checked, and then we'll be sure." He called the operations room on the secure line and spoke for a few minutes to the duty officer, paying no attention to Ehud, who felt the last of his strength draining away. "I don't care what the time is in Europe. Wake them up, or find someone in South America or Japan. I want this conversation now." He covered the mouthpiece and asked Ehud the name of the hotel where she stayed on arriving for the first time in the capital city, before it all began. Ehud couldn't remember, and Joe sent Yaniv, who was on hand in the operations room, to search the files. "All she needs to do is contact the hotel, yes, a woman should make the call, it will sound more convincing, and ask for Rachel Goldschmitt. When they transfer the call to the room she must hang up. That's all."

⚜

THE UNIT COMMANDER BRIEFED EHUD. HE's to use a French passport. He'll explain that he's Moroccan and has lived for some years in a small village in France. "And besides that, no one will ask. You've worked under this cover before, and I hope you haven't lost your old talents. So make all your arrangements today, fly to Europe this afternoon, and tomorrow you're booked on a flight from Paris to the operational zone. I'm sure you can find her and persuade her to come back."

Ehud nodded. He wanted them to trust him.

"Your support team will fly out with you. Of course, you'll give no indication that you know any of them. If things go well, you and she will be on the first available flight out of there, end of story. If she shows the slightest sign of unwillingness to cooperate, hand over the baton . . ."

Joe gave him an encouraging smile and told him everything depended on him and he was the only one who could carry out the mission. Ehud wanted to ask what would happen if she refused, if he couldn't find her, but he knew their answers—and already he included Joe among those on the other side of the table—would be as good as his. He has to find her. He has to look her in the eyes and explain to her why staying there will be suicide. That the damage to the Mossad and state secrets will be devastating. No one will forgive her. There's no other option, she has to come home.

"I want to see the letter," he said. The commander took a piece of paper from the file and handed it to Ehud. It was a document from the Prime Minister's office. The terms were clear—she must return, be interrogated, take a polygraph test, and if it is concluded that she has disclosed no sensitive information, she may resume her former life. Even her pension will not be affected. Ehud had laid down these conditions, and they had been accepted.

On the way out he and Joe passed by the operations room. On the door was a sign: ENTRY FOR AUTHORIZED PERSONNEL ONLY. Ehud was no longer in that category. Now he's on a mission. There are things he needs to know, and things that he doesn't. He told the commander he remembers some secrets too, and the commander replied as he closed the files, "Her secrets are more important. They go beyond the range of our normal activities. We can only regret that they decided to employ her then without thorough vetting and a proper psychological assessment. But I'm not criticizing my predecessor in this post; the past is the past. We're relying on you, Ehud, and we're sure that if the worst should happen to you, you'll know how to use what we're giving you. One strong bite, and you'll be the best-dressed guy in the morgue." He wasn't smiling.

⌒⋏⌒

CHAPTER THIRTEEN

The Capital City, Two Days Earlier

THE PLANE DESCENDED, DIPPING BELOW THE thin layer of cloud. She gazed down at the city, reflexively looking for the Presidential Palace and the large buildings of the Defense Ministry. Rachel remembered the first time Rashid took her for a drive on the switchback road, and their desperate search for a secluded spot. "Stop here," she said, and couldn't help thinking that their budding romance would provide a good excuse for coming back here with a camera—and getting shots of the fences and the perimeter walls. Rashid slowed and stopped the car by the roadside. A thin dust cloud rose behind them, and the lights of passing cars cast a murky radiance and left them in darkness. He cut the engine and doused the lights, and she knew this was unprofessional; at any moment a police patrol car might pull up alongside, or another vehicle could run into them. But she repressed these thoughts, sat with her hands between her knees, and waited for him to make the first move. She knew perfectly well this was against the rules, this wasn't what Ehud meant when he talked about cultivating friendly relations with the locals, but a moment later she wasn't thinking, because Rashid was leaning toward her, holding her head and giving her a long kiss, and she closed her eyes and let him unfasten the buttons of her blouse.

The pilot told the cabin crew to take their seats for landing, and she fingered her passport, which she made a point of keeping in the front pocket of the denim skirt. Rachel glanced at her picture; it seemed to her she was looking at someone else. She knew she had beautiful eyes. Suitors often told her this but still lost the battle since Rashid whispered to her, after the first time, that he could see her heart through them. The eyes in the passport photograph smiled at her and kept a secret. And her eyes now? She took the miniature makeup kit from her handbag and looked at them in the mirror—sad and tired.

Long live old habits and hurrah for convention, she thought as she fixed her makeup and filled in her landing card. This time it was all true, and there was no need to remember what her name was supposed to be on this assignment. Rachel Goldschmitt, born in London, April 10, 1965. Mother's name: Eva. Father's name: Michael. Profession: Teacher. Nationality: British. So far it was all correct. She came to the box marked purpose of visit, and wrote: Expedition. If they don't understand, she'll explain it. And while writing slowly and in big letters, she told herself she had come to restore something that had been lost. And then came marital status: Single. That was true too. What could I have done differently? she was thinking as the wheels hit the runway with a loud thump. Did I not know what to expect when I abandoned Oren, my safe haven? "I'm like one of those offshore oil rigs," he said. "Big and stable, and people can tie their boats up to it and land their helicopters on it. But in a few years from now I'll be moving on. Like the oil rig. I won't be here forever."

"Old soldiers never die, they just fade away," someone or other said, and she thought of Rachel Brooks, Canadian citizen born in England, who one day disappeared without a trace. Where is that Rachel, and what about the scars she left on the woman who took on her identity and did her duty until it was time for her to fade away? There are those who believe that the soul leaves the dead body and moves to a different place, but what about someone forced to leave behind a living personality, a woman who had a name and work and friends, even a lover, and one day she faded away but didn't die? I was like a snake, she thought, I shed my old skin and moved on.

The plane came to a stop and she stood and retrieved her luggage from the overhead compartment. One small case, as always, that's all she needs. Anyway, she isn't staying here long. How much time does it take to check into a hotel, wash her face, which had aged with the passage of time, pick up the phone, and tell him she's back? Rashid speaking, he'll say, and she'll want to erase the years, the lie—that unbearable weight—and tell him she still loves him.

Rachel handed her passport to the immigration officer sitting in his cubicle and smiled at him, the way she had been trained and her standard technique whenever she needed to cross a border or smuggle illicit goods. All about gaining trust. He smiled back at her and focused on the passport in front of him. No chance of anyone remembering her. Eighteen years ago she was someone else.

A moment passed. The official looked again at the passport and at her face, and she felt her heart beating steadily, as if she had nothing to reveal, as if she had nothing to hide.

"First time here?"

"Yes, and I hope it won't be the last," she said, and it occurred to her she was actually telling the truth. Rachel Goldschmitt, British subject, is visiting this place for the first time. And that other woman?

Rachel Brooks? She doesn't know her. "Welcome home," the official said, and she forgave his mistake.

From the start she knew she would be going to that hotel, she would try to travel step by step the way she had traveled before, and when she reaches the intersection this time, perhaps she'll choose another option. "If you lose your way," Ehud told her once, when she had trouble finding him in the streets of Rome, "always go back to the point where we separated."

The Arabic she remembered was enough for her to charm the driver, and he was sure that at long last a tourist had arrived who understood him, and he talked incessantly. She didn't understand what he was saying, but to her his nonstop patter was like fresh water cascading over rocks, a cataract of meaningless words in a language she had learned to love. Now and then she picked up a word she remembered, and she had no doubt he was talking about politics, the economic situation, and other things that taxi drivers the world over talk about when they're taking tourists to their hotels, and she agreed with him, saying, "Naam, naam"—yes, yes—so he wouldn't stop.

The scenery on the way to the city had changed little; it was just the trees that were taller, and the neon advertising signs were more prolific than before. She leaned back in the seat and looked up at the cloudy sky. In training they had taught her how to land a helicopter, how to check the cloud cover and the air temperature, how to choose the landing site, measure the wind speed, and ignore anything not germane to the mission. "A course in the destruction of romance," she wrote once on the blackboard in the lecture room, and when the bewildered lecturer asked her what she meant, she said you would need to be a woman to understand. And now, she reflected, it was impossible to see the sky and the clouds without thinking of helicopters, just as it was impossible to sit on a beach without estimating the height of the waves, and deciding whether rubber dinghies could come ashore. You even look at people differently, listen to them in another way, assessing every word and inflection. This is the punishment of the liar—the one who lies habitually can't trust anyone.

⚜

THE BELLBOY PUT THE SUITCASE DOWN on a worn divan, insisted on explaining how the air-conditioning worked, and pointed to the view from the window and seemed quite willing to carry on and on until she gave him the dollar he was expecting and sent him on his way. Rachel slumped on the bed, stared at the ceiling, remembered the fear she felt the first time she came here, and wondered how much of it remained—just a vague apprehension that everything would be as it was, a new lie replacing the old one, and she would be unable to tell the truth.

Through the closed window she heard the familiar noises of the street. She had grown accustomed to listening to the muffled clamor of the teeming city, the rustling from the room next door, footsteps in the corridor. Old habits die hard, and she was a veteran and experienced combatant, once described by the head of the Mossad as a sophisticated war machine. Rachel listened, searching for the exceptional sounds, the siren of a police car, heavy footsteps outside her door, and especially the silence. The ominous silence that falls after a black car has squealed to a stop at the entrance to the hotel and men in suits have emerged. The sound of the silence in the lobby as they go up in the lift or take the stairs, and then the waiting for the knock on the door. Because even today, when she's probably a tourist like all the rest of them, she still has something to hide. A secret has an odd quality. It doesn't grow old. It doesn't lose its value. It just becomes harder—harder to reveal, harder to confess, harder to receive absolution for it.

And suddenly something that has been on her mind for a long time becomes clearer to her. What is the difference between this time and previous times? What thought has been with her from the moment she boarded the plane in Brussels? This time she's on her own. No one sent her, Ehud isn't waiting for her call, and the command center, with all its clever gadgetry, isn't tracking her movements on a computer-generated map and checking her contact codes. Who cares that she took the train from London to Brussels so the British wouldn't know which way their citizen was heading? Who wants to know that she got a visa from the consulate in a few hours? Who will know that she spent the night in a transit hotel where they don't check the names of guests?

She felt the isolation touching her and spreading through her limbs, and she resisted the silly urge to say something in Hebrew into the void of the room. Nobody knows I'm here, she was thinking, no one can listen to me, tell me I'm valuable to them. Rachel stood up and sighed. Her joints ached, a migraine was threatening to kick in, and she calculated the number of pills she had brought with her. She stripped slowly, put the clothes on the bed, and again the first time came to mind. The fear of hidden cameras, microphones, feeling exposed. And what has changed since then? Perhaps the confidence that age and experience bring, or perhaps it's down to fatigue, or the fact that now she's here to reveal, not to hide.

The stream of hot water washes over her, and she closes her eyes and wonders who she will see when she stands in front of the mirror. Who will promise her that everything will be okay? Ehud said nothing good just comes on its own, good things have to be made to happen. And she's ready for anything, but nothing will happen until she begins to act. Thoughts don't move anything. She has wrapped herself in a towel before going into the cool of the bedroom, even though the curtains are closed. Modesty? Perhaps. Habit? Definitely. But she has no one to hide her body from. She lets the towel fall to the floor. There are women more beautiful than she is, there always were, but her body is long and lithe and her skin soft to the touch, and her breasts, which never suckled a child, are still as firm as they were then, when she waited for Rashid.

The lobby was empty. Late afternoon is always dead time, the right time to talk to the concierge, to survey the place at leisure and understand that the differences are in the heart, not in the structure. Not much has changed. They've made some improvements, added an outdoor pool, but they haven't succeeded in getting rid of the smell, or wiping the bored expressions from the faces of the hotel employees.

⚜

A YOUNG WOMAN IN TRADITIONAL GARB sat at the desk and busied herself with the endless sorting of invisible paperwork. Rachel sat down facing her and waited. The girl looked at her with gloomy eyes. A faint mustache adorned her upper lip, and she fiddled affectedly with the thick wedding ring on her finger. "What can I do for you?" she asked in heavily accented English. "Anything that's interesting," Rachel said, and asked if there was a list of recommended tours. The girl pulled out a few brochures and Rachel picked out one of the guided tours. A short day, not too tiring, suitable for a tourist like her. "There are some nice churches here," said the receptionist, and she asked, with the courtesy typical of hotel workers, how long she was staying.

"A week," said Rachel, and she wasn't sure. "Do you happen to have a phone directory of the city?" The girl looked surprised, and Rachel knew she had made a mistake. She was getting rusty. She should have given the receptionist a reason to offer her the directory. Occasional tourists don't make such requests. She is not in Europe and even an innocent question can arouse suspicion. She didn't know what the security officer had said to the woman sitting opposite her, or if someone came to the hotel from time to time to ask if there was anything unusual and how the foreigners were behaving.

The clerk pulled out a tattered phone book from a drawer in her desk and asked what she was looking for. This time she had an answer ready, and she wouldn't make the same mistake twice. And why not tell her she's looking for Rashid? Why not let her into this little secret? she's thinking as she and the clerk are going through the phone numbers of English language schools. "I don't want to bother you anymore," she said to the clerk with a smile, and was secretly grateful to the French tourist couple who stood behind her, waiting patiently for their turn. "Give me the book, and I'll take it over there and return it when I've finished." The clerk handed her the book, the tourists smiled at her, and she felt she was back in business, she could still cut it.

When she knew no one was paying attention to her, she took a tourist guidebook from her handbag, along with the conversion chart from the Latin to the Arabic alphabet, and turned to the Arabic directory. Her heart was beating faster, and a wave of anxiety threatened to swamp her. Rashid Kanafi, or Kanafani, or Raashid, God only knows how they spell this, and perhaps his name doesn't appear in the book and his number is unlisted. She jotted down some likely looking numbers, disguised with a simple code, and went out into the street. Years of training and experience had taught her not to call from hotel rooms, and not to use the cell phone she bought at the airport in Brussels.

The old, dirty, shabby street was now a thoroughfare paved with artificial stone, and instead of the little shops where corpulent traders swathed in broad sashes used to sit in the doorways, there were now department stores, all display windows and illuminated signs. Everything had changed, but everything looked familiar. And the smell remained. It was a smell that was hard to define and impossible to ignore. That thing that you could swallow with every step, with every breath. It was born aloft on the thick air. Smoke and dust. A mixture of the two, far from the desert and close to it, everywhere, like the smell of garlic in Korea, like the London fog, like the faint vapor of drains in Tokyo, and the stench of the canals in Amsterdam. Dust and smoke carried the smell of this city, the city that was hers.

She walked slowly down the street, and the flat soles of her shoes slapped the paving stones. She had no clear idea of where she was going, besides the knowledge that she wants to see, wants to smell, wants the city to give her what is missing, the strength she needs to summon. She wants it to lead her to him, as it did before. Because then everything was clear. She's come for the experience, and to save some money, so she can start living a life without her father in it, far from the love she left behind her.

And why did you come here, Rachel?

To work.

And how long will you stay here, Rachel?

That depends.

Depends on what, Rachel?

On what I find here and how much money I can save.

That's all. Simple questions, simple answers. One clear line that has a reason behind it, which has a beginning, a middle, and an end. A life that can and must stand up to daily examination. A life that has a reason, a logic that has no time for the mania of loneliness, or the mania of love.

⚜

ON THE WAY TO THE MAIN bazaar she passed by what had been the school. It was gone, replaced by an office building. She remembered the little classrooms, the lessons, and the achievements of her students. She loved teaching, and she was a good teacher despite all the other things she had to do. Rachel tried to remember names, but could remember only his name, and she was searching only for him among the passersby when she entered the square, which was surprisingly clean. The carpet-seller, a short, squat man, looked at her curiously, as if assessing his chances, and she was comfortable with that. So it was and so it will be. He's a man and she's a woman. She went inside his shop. Obviously he wanted a sale, but there was always something else and she could use it. Rachel let these thoughts go, accepted the cup of tea that he offered, sat down in a wicker armchair, and modestly arranged her skirt. She was silent, and he talked incessantly. "What are you looking for, madam? Here, take a look, at this," and he unrolled a carpet from the end of the pile on the floor and passed a flashlight over it to illuminate the intricate weave. "Not this one, of course," he said to her as she shook her head, and asked her where she was from. She was ready with her answer. "Can't you tell?" she asked him, and he said she was from London and she didn't deny it, and she knew that although she couldn't remember all the prices in the supermarket or who won a football match last week, she was still adept at dodging much harder questions.

"From England?" he said. "That's good. I love England and Manchester United," and then launched into a lengthy discourse in limping English about his family and friends in London. "And what does madam have to say about this carpet?" Out of the corner of her eye she noticed two men in long coats coming into the shop. Security men? Relatives of the shopkeeper? Random customers? It makes no difference now, she reminded herself, and sipped the tea. Those days are gone. The two men disappeared behind a door hidden from her view, and all was quiet in the shop.

A sense of freedom loosened her limbs and she relaxed in the chair.

In her former life she lived in two dimensions, always able to see two pictures of reality. She was like someone who keeps both eyes open but presses on one to watch the situation from another side. No more.

She didn't have to hide her intentions from the rug merchant. She intended to buy the small carpet that he showed her and to talk freely about her apartment, without telling him it just happened to be in Israel. She didn't need to reconsider whether the carpet was appropriate for a teacher's salary and would Ehud approve the expenditure. She sketched the apartment house on a scrap of paper, explained to him where the light came from, and realized she actually loved that house. The thought of giving up this whole idea occurred to her, and she regretted that it was impossible to make all her wishes come true, to make a mosaic of them all.

She left the shop after paying for the rug. The man promised to send it to the hotel and she believed him. Nice to trust somebody, for a change. I'll put it in the entrance hall, she reflected, so I can think of him when I go out and come in. So I'll be reminded of an opportunity I didn't take. The opportunity I have now. Then she considered the possibility that he won't remember her. She'll sit facing him and look into his eyes and see nothing. Rachel sat down on a dirty bench without bothering to gather up her skirt. The traffic swirled around her. People came and went. Strangers, all of them. Women covered by voluminous dresses, young girls daring to expose a bit of bare skin. Men in suits and in traditional garb. Tourists. All of them going about their business. And she has business that makes her sit and wait.

☙

THE CALL OF THE MUEZZIN AND a car revving put an end to the stillness of the early dawn. She called him after a sleepless night. Hard to know if this was a call for help, or a protest about something she wanted to discuss. Even Ehud, days later, would be unable to explain what happened. And he knew her better than any of them. The Unit commander's main concern was the possibility of a trap, and he said the situation was unclear and he hoped one day there would be the chance to talk to Rachel and ask her why, after running away and acting in contravention of all the rules and conventions, she picked up her mobile phone and keyed in the dialing code that would reach him. And having reached him, why didn't she say more, why did she want only to hear his voice and tell him her father was dead, again? Then someone in that meeting expressed an opinion and dared to suggest that perhaps she wanted to stretch an imaginary line between what she is today and the past, like a cable thrown into the deep ocean with an anchor on the end of it. Maybe what she wanted, so he said (perhaps he was a poet), was to have that anchor reach the seabed, and hold fast to it.

꩜

CHAPTER FOURTEEN

Rashid

THE MOSQUE HE USED TO ATTEND was located on a hill in the outskirts of the city.

"In our tradition anyone can pray anywhere, and that is why this mosque was built some distance away. It works like a filter, meaning we can associate with people like ourselves."

"I'd like to come with you sometime."

"Why would you want to do that?" he asked, caressing her.

"I want to see that you also kneel to pray," she replied, and knew immediately this was a mistake, that she was straying into a minefield; when she had finished asking her questions and Rashid had answered them all, he would ask how things were in her culture, to whom did she pray, and which customs did she uphold. And at that moment, while hugging him and nipping his earlobe and putting her leg over him in a ploy to distract him from the question he wanted to ask, she remembered the festive holiday meals in the bosom of Oren's extended family, the lavishly laden table, and the succulent, aromatic dishes that one could smell at the door of the house, and Grandpa, who looked like someone out of a story, sitting at the head of the table wearing a white *kittel* and keeping order with a wave of his hand. Rashid caressed her head and didn't feel the salty tear falling on his shoulder. "I'm surprised you haven't bothered to find a church here that would suit you," he said, before turning to more carnal pursuits. Lovers have gods of their own.

All this happened in another time, an age she can't return to, and has no prospect of reliving. Graying hair can be dyed, makeup can conceal wrinkles, and she also knows how to cover the veins in her thighs. She still wears the same size, but she knows that being thin isn't necessarily a sign of health. She knows Rashid is also bound to have changed. He's grown older; perhaps he's put on weight, perhaps he is ill and doesn't keep up his old habits, like going to the mosque for Friday prayers. She suppresses another thought that occurs to her: In fifteen years she's not heard anything about him, is it possible he is gone?

It was no problem finding out the times of prayers in the mosque. Any tourist can take an interest in the rituals and customs of the local population. That's why tourists come, to see what other people do. The reception clerk was happy to help her. "Prayers, madam, you're interested in prayers? How nice." She couldn't remember the name of the mosque and didn't want him to know where she was going, so she showed him a map and asked him to point out the most important mosques in the city and repeat the names to her until she found the one she was looking for. The clerk, impressed by his enterprising tourist, stressed the need to dress modestly and offered to take her there himself, Friday being his day off. She politely declined. It was hard dispensing with his services, but she knew how to do that too.

She wasn't happy to find she was still capable of exacting information and shrugging off unwanted company. Her old talents hadn't been lost, but they moved her further away from the mundane life she aspired to. They didn't allow her to make mistakes, or lose her temper; they denied her the privileges enjoyed by normal people. Normal people ask questions, get angry, laugh if they feel like it, but she needs to think everything out in advance and calculate all her moves, and never losing sight of her objective. Like a partner in an affair, like a criminal. Rachel looked at the reception clerk. She didn't owe him anything. Some tourists like to be taken around from place to place like parcels. Some not. Some tourists bother to explain all their actions. Some not. She couldn't behave like any of them, not even this time. She was no ordinary tourist. She was using a British passport, but her Israeli passport was waiting in a luggage locker at a station in London. She had something to hide, rather a lot, in fact, and the nice man sitting facing her mustn't know where she was going and who she was looking for.

THE FILE OF MEN MOVED SLOWLY toward the entrance to the mosque. Rachel stood in the shadow of a wall and watched them as they approached and made a point of taking an interest in the impressive architecture as well as the assembling worshippers. Any other day she might have complained about the smells wafting from the shoes left behind at the door, even expressed her opinion on the socks she saw, but she was interested in the faces, not in the feet. Old faces, young faces, most of them gloomy. Mustaches and more mustaches. Taciturn men walking into the capacious mosque and exchanging barely a word. Her heart was beating fast. She didn't even have a picture. All that stuff had been buried in the archives, in the deep cellars of Mossad, places she had no access to, not after she slammed the door behind her and went back to being just a civilian. She had no time now to regret not taking at least one photograph for herself, something to remind her brain of what the heart knew—what did he look like.

How will she pick him out, if he comes here at all, among all the people streaming inside? After all these years will she recognize his short and powerful body, his eyes that enchanted her, his smile? Men and more men passed by her. For a moment she thought every one of them was him, and for a moment she was sure that even if he passes by and looks at her, she won't know it. And in fact she hoped he would see her, hoped that he too was looking for her and expecting that one day she would be waiting for him at the corner of the street, in the doorway of a mosque, or in the café they used to sneak off to.

And suddenly she was sure it was this one, approaching the doorway. He wasn't staring down at the ground like most of the others, and on his face was the tight-lipped smile that she so much loved. The sculpted nose, the expressive eyes, the light steps, as if about to break into a dance at any moment, all of these once belonged to Rashid. He came closer and looked at her with curiosity, and she knew it was only her imagination that saw him, and if she calculated correctly the years that had passed, the days and nights without him, it could just as well be his eldest son she was seeing. She should take a look at the old man walking behind him—now he might be the object of her dreams and her quest.

And at the end of the line she saw him. Her body shook and her legs trembled, and she wanted to take the few paces separating them and tell him she's come back. Rachel leaned against the high wall and clenched her hands against her chest. His hair had thinned and his leanness surprised her. But it was him. The same gait, the same confidence and poise, and the same big hands—as always, clutching his prayer beads and the promise to caress her.

Rachel tightened the scarf on her head and hoped the dark sunglasses would do their job, but there was no need for them. He seemed preoccupied, his face forward in only one direction, and he strode into the mosque as if it were his whole world. Could it be? She always knew he was committed to his religion, and he often talked to her about his beliefs and his determination to live one day according to Sharia law. And she would laugh and ask where she fit into this scheme of things and he had no answer other than a confession accompanied by a kiss—even he, Rashid, wasn't perfect.

She sat on a concrete bench and watched the empty space. No one was left of the crowd that had streamed inside. A bored guard stood at the other end, by the reserved parking spaces, chatting to the chauffeurs who had been left outside with the cars. Shoes had been left at the entrance to the mosque, and she wondered if she could get to the place where Rashid left his and identify them. For a moment she toyed with the idea of taking his shoes and waiting for him, while he's standing there in his socks and looking for a way out of the predicament she's forced on him, until she walks toward him slowly, takes off the dark glasses, and asks if he remembers their vacation on the beach, when someone pinched their flip-flops while they were swimming in the sea, and how he carried her in his arms to the car so she wouldn't have to walk on the blazing sand.

And what can he say to her as he waits for her to hand over the shoes? That he remembers her? That he remembers the drive to the secluded beach, the tent they put up, the campfire in the evening, the two days they spent there, flip-flops or no flip-flops? How he stood and touched her shoulder while she photographed the sunset, and the beach, and the army camp behind it, in the minutest of detail, according to the instructions of the ops officer? Or he'll apologize to his friends, who came to pray with him, and wonder with them who she is, this crazy woman who's stolen his shoes, and he'll thank her and go on his way. And then and only then, will he look back and hope to see her shadowing him?

She stood up, straightened her skirt, and pulled out the cheap camera she bought at the airport. A few pictures of the mosque, and a close-up of some interesting architectural features, provided the reason for her visit to the holy place. From a distance she saw the guard watching her and pointing to her. She was used to such looks. If they ask her, she'll show them the list the reception clerk gave her and the little tourist guide she got from the car rental service. There are things you don't forget, that are inscribed deep in the soul, and it's hard to uproot them, and hard to plant genuine feelings among them. I loved him, she was thinking as she walked back to the rented car. And I exploited him for those surveillance trips. I used him when I photographed forbidden places. I copied the picture of Strauss from him. But I loved him. I really loved him, although I lied to him and left him without saying goodbye.

She turned on the air-conditioning in the car and alternately looked at her map and the people leaving the mosque. When Rashid reached his car, she saw with a twinge of sorrow that he had fallen on harder times. He no longer has a driver-bodyguard waiting beside a polished Mercedes, but a battered Toyota parked on the open dusty ground. She followed him and remembered the driver who used to stay in the car while he was in her apartment and in her arms. "I've no doubt he's told somebody about you," he said. "They have to know everything. Nothing happens here without their knowledge." She asked if there was any chance of them telling his parents. "Why would they do that?" He was genuinely surprised. "It's between us, it's our brotherhood."

❧

RASHID SET OUT AND SHE WAS close behind him. Stalking him was simple enough because she was not trying to be surreptitious. In her heart the little devil was dancing, demanding that Rashid would stop his car and come out to her, and she will lower the window and look at him, and he'll recognize her at once and ask, Rachel? And she'll say, Yes, and that will be the truth. And he'll ask, Have you come back? And she'll say, Yes, and that will be true as well. Then she'll need to lie to him but that will be later, after he's touched her lips with his finger and bent down to kiss her.

Rashid drove slowly and blended into the traffic and she kept a distance of two cars between them and assumed he was going home. Once she knew where his parents lived. She told Ehud and that's how they found out about the private compound where all the dignitaries lived. And she visited the area too, although Ehud warned her of the dangers and vetoed the trip. One Sabbath day she felt she couldn't restrain herself any longer. She missed him and wanted to see him, if only for a moment. The drive to the gate of the compound took only a few minutes. She smiled at the guard, who spoke no English, and gave him a spiel, inserting a few names that he recognized. He didn't want to obstruct someone who knew all these important people, and besides that, she was young and beautiful and she shook his hand and palmed him a ten-dollar note. Rachel drove her Volvo down the narrow street between well-tended gardens, and when she saw Rashid sitting in a deck chair on the lawn and talking to an elegant young woman she was glad his back was turned and could not see her and her tears.

When he came to the intersection he turned right and stopped opposite an apartment building badly in need of painting. Fifteen years had passed since she left the city, and him, and it occurred to her that someone in the department had leaked information to their security services, warning them that Rashid Kanafani was no longer to be trusted, and should be kept away from centers of activity. All in the interests of protecting her, Rachel; without the means of locating her and without the freedom to leave the country at will. Just like her, he was of no further use to them. She overtook him and when she saw him getting out of the car and walking slowly to the door she went on driving at a crawling speed, stopped for a moment, and gave a display of reading the map and the tourist guide, to explain to any professional followers that she was just a confused tourist, and she'd soon be heading back to her hotel.

What could be simpler, she thought, than to park the car, check her makeup in the rearview mirror while verifying that she wasn't being followed, then climb the five steps to the door, ring the bell, and wait for him to open the door? She estimated how long it would take him to get to the elevator and up to his apartment, and when a light appeared on the sixth floor she knew he was alone; if not, the lights would have already been on. An irresistible urge pulled her to do this. To be ready to pay the price. Danger against chance. This is what they taught her, and she wanted to hear his voice and see him standing before her, and say . . . whether he says one thing or says the opposite, she'll know what the future holds in store for them and what has happened to him in all the years she's wasted without him.

A police car pulled up beside her and put an end to her daydream. The cop certainly wanted to help, but he had some difficulty locating himself on the English language map, so he suggested she follow him out of the neighborhood, and Rachel had no choice but to accept his help.

She didn't put the light on when she returned to her room. The last rays of the sun grazed the window and burst inside. She lay on the bed and looked at the pictures she'd taken and couldn't but be impressed by the new digital technology. Here's Rashid coming out of the mosque, and here's a short video that she shot when he was putting his shoes on after the prayers, and here he is going to his car and in the background, as if by chance, the might and grandeur of the mosque. Rachel touched the screen and her finger covered his face. She longed for him and wanted him beside her, as it was before Rachel Brooks disappeared, and with her all that she used to have.

⟡

AND AGAIN SHE WAS STALKING HIM, and she knew it wasn't right. It's no way to act with the people you love. I should have approached him yesterday, he'll be angry if he knows I followed him like a hunter, and observed him while I was deciding what to do. If he asks, I'll have to tell him I found him and I was waiting for the right moment—if there is such a moment, when two hearts beat as one and the clocks show the same time and the same desire. The morning traffic was sparse, and she kept some distance behind the Toyota until the car was swallowed up in the dark parking space of a gray office building. A smile and five dollars were enough to persuade the security guard to disclose that the effendi wanted his car brought out to the main entrance at four in the afternoon.

Rashid came out to the car that was waiting for him at the door and she wiped the sweat from her brow and stopped drumming on the wheel. He merged into the slow traffic and she latched on to him, following him until he stopped at the front of an old, timeworn café. Rachel overtook the Toyota, stopped around the corner, and hid her face with a scarf. She wandered back and forth for a few moments, and entered only when she saw him sitting alone at an inner table. She sat in the corner and watched as he drank his coffee. Drops of sweat streamed down her back, ignoring the ceiling fans that were working on full power, and she wiped her hands on the fringes of the tablecloth and waited. There was something familiar about this, unpleasantly so. She's been in situations like this one before. This is not the first time she has taken a seat close to a target and planned her next move. She remembers all the stages, knows how to lead him toward the trap that's waiting for him. Outside, hidden from her eyes and very real, other combatants once lay in ambush and waited for their prey. Not this time, she whispered to herself, the hunting season is over.

She removed the scarf, took a mirror from her handbag, and adjusted her makeup. Old habits weren't forgotten, and she used the mirror to check out the sparse clientele of the café and the few pedestrians outside. Rashid sat with his back to her, and if she were to get up at this point and leave, he could simply carry on with his life as before.

Rachel can't carry on living as before. That's why she's here. She has to get to the bottom of the well she is falling into since the day she left the city on a morning flight. Something inside tells her that only with Rashid can she climb from the depths and reach for the sky again. She knows that in all the things she has done and in all the years that have passed, Rashid has had a place all his own, and now there's a chance to reach out to him, the barriers are down and the way is open. She feels she has the strength to stand before him now, fill in for him what's missing, and help him find the way back to her.

He's still reading the newspaper when she approaches and stands beside him. From above he looks even shorter and there's a round bald patch on his head. This eternity lasts for only a moment, but she still has time to turn around and leave. Eventually he looks up, as if ready to pay, and his eyes go first to her slim ankles, the fringes of her dress, climbing up to the neckline and the face. He can't be expected to recognize her at once. She sees surprise, the hesitation, the question.

"It's me," she says. He says nothing and she takes the chair opposite his, sits and waits. The thin gold ring on his finger is the only thing she sees. This is a pointless exercise, she thinks, and she's about to go, and then he says, "Hello, Rachel," and smiles a thin smile, a smile of triumph.

"Hello, Rashid," she says, her eyes still fixed on the ring.

"Yes, that happened too," he said.

"And is she good for you?"

"As good as she can be."

"And are you happy?"

"As happy as I can be."

They fall silent. What else is there to say? She sees his eyes wandering over her face, dropping to her ringless finger, and she wants to tell him this doesn't matter. She doesn't consider the possibility that what burns in her has burnt out in him long ago, because after the distance she has traveled to reach him it all seems to her bright and transparent, as if there's only one way and it's clear what its end will be. She is sure that he is preserving the seed of their love within a hard shell, waiting for water and light that she is bringing with her. This won't be easy, she knows. It's not certain that he's happy to see her. Not right now. He's angry with her for appearing so suddenly, without giving him time to prepare. But all of that will fade away when she tells him what's ready on her tongue and what's been buried in her for so many years. He'll understand that she had no choice, and although she betrayed him she didn't betray her feelings, and he'll forgive her. Not in a moment, not before he hears her out, but he will forgive her, and they will start again.

In the café too there is silence, and she feels they have turned into actors on a stage, trying to play the roles they took on, and reciting the texts they're supposed to remember. There are moments when it seems everything depends on one definitive statement that has been chosen and rehearsed endlessly, practiced in front of the mirror until it can't be improved. It's hard to invent statements like these, harder still to infuse them with the right color and tone, the weight that might make a difference. And she wonders if her journey has come to an end. Suddenly it all seems to her strange and surreal, as if she's looking at herself from another place, from a distant vantage point, and examining what she sees. Who is this strange woman who sits down uninvited at the table of a man who is accustomed to drinking his evening coffee here, alone? Who and what has she left behind to turn up again in the heart of a hostile Arab capital? What does she expect to gain? What is she running away from?

The lightbulb that was hanging on a long lead above him stirred gently in the artificial breeze generated by the fans, and the shadow on his face moved as if scanning him. She knew he was thinking of the journey she had traveled to get to him. God knows how hard it was. God knows how easy it was. That's the way it has to be, the one who abandons is the one who must return.

"I love you," she said, "and I want you to take me away from here."

"Where to?"

"To the hill."

"Like before?"

"Like before."

⚘

"Your English has improved," she told him as he started the motor.

"Especially when I'm quiet," he replied, and drew a smile from her.

Rashid drove with confidence and she was glad for the silence between them. When they came to a red light that refused to let them through, he turned to her and smiled. She smiled back at him and sneaked a look at his lap. The car reeked of cigarettes, and even the scented stick hanging from the mirror couldn't hide the smell. Rashid took a pack of cigarettes from his pocket and, without offering it to her, lit one for himself and threw the match out of the window. "I've acquired some bad habits," he said when he saw her look. She put her hand on his and said this was the least of her worries. The wind through the window blew on her face and messed her hair. She gathered it up into a ponytail. "That looks suits you," he said, and she blushed.

He parked the car at the side of the road. The lights of the city and the antennaes on the summit winked at them as if greeting old friends. "Those are the antennaes you were so eager to see, and this is the road that takes you all the way to the army camp. And if you look carefully," he said, pointing to the Presidential Palace, which was brightly illuminated, "you can see who's going in and who's coming out." She didn't respond and clasped her hands together to stop them from shaking. Her heart was beating hard, and she knew her face had turned white in the dark.

"What are you called these days?" he asked, and added, "As if it makes any difference." She turned to face him. "Rachel, I've always been Rachel . . ." she said, and wanted to add something, but he cut her off. "Later," he said. "Allow me to speak first. When you didn't turn up for school that morning, I asked the school secretary to contact you, but there was no reply. I thought you'd gone out with the dog and been held up, or you'd disappeared on one of your little adventures. In the evening I went to your apartment. I had to wait a long time before one of the residents let me in, and I cursed you for not giving me a key. Later, I understood why. And I knew something was wrong when I saw the cat curled up on the outdoor mat and I remembered you never used to let him out, because he didn't have the life skills he needed to survive, and you were always telling the story of how you rescued him from the jaws of a dog on the street. He whined and wailed as if he knew me, and stood beside me while I knocked on the door, desperate to return home. I knocked again and called your name, till the neighbor opposite came out and said your car had gone too. I was furious. Whatever had happened to you—I was the one being dumped. The cat touched me with his paw and I did something I never meant to do. I took him with me.

"A few days later they told me at the school that your father had died and you weren't coming back. Barbara wanted to contact you and offer condolences, and she tried the numbers you left, but of course they were no good. She told me she figured you'd run away. She suspected drugs, though she wouldn't have believed it of you, but whatever it was, in the end she realized that you weren't such an innocent after all. 'She fooled you too?' she asked me.

"I carried on studying and I took lessons from Barbara too, so I knew the day your flat was being cleared and I joined her. Barbara presented the letter that you sent the landlord. Apparently you trusted her stupid innocence so you hoped that she wouldn't figure anything out. The landlord opened the door. I thought you were still in there, in a box. All kinds of ideas go through your head at times like these. Maybe for a moment I wanted this to be what happened—at least I'd know you hadn't abandoned me. I hoped perhaps you had left me a letter, and I wanted to pick up my toothbrush before Barbara inspected the bathroom.

"We packed up your possessions, and I even found one cuff link.

I remember you buying the pair. I threw it away, one of those things that only works in pairs. When we finished up Barbara asked me if I wanted to take the amplifier. 'You play a bit, don't you?' she asked me, and though I didn't need an amplifier, I thought I might as well take it. I also took your album of dried flowers, which gave you the excuse to go to places all over our country. It surprised me that you left that behind but took your electric guitar with you to your father's funeral—"

She interrupted him: "My father died last week. I buried him in London and came back to you." He said he was sorry to hear this, and she suspected he didn't believe her.

"On your birthday I tried to play something that would remind me of you. The amplifier wasn't working and I dismantled it to see if I could fix it. Something about it looked strange to me and I compared it with the small amp that I have at home. Even today it's hard to imagine your technical staff making mistakes like that, but the fact is they did. One of the unfamiliar components was marked with the logo of Israel Aeronautical Industries. And then I understood it all. The extra weight. The fact that you never really enjoyed playing and hardly knew anything about music. I took out the component and smashed it.

"I hated you. I felt you'd betrayed me and made a fool of me. And at the same time I believed you loved me, some element inside you was doing that messy and inefficient thing called loving somebody.

"Of course, I could have taken everything I found and handed it over to my friends. I knew what would happen to me. No one would believe you succeeded in duping me. I'd be sitting in jail now, a kind of slow execution. I tried to forget all about it, and in the meantime my father died, and with him our connections with the powers that be. That's the way it is with us. Connections are what it's all about. If you don't have them, nothing will help you. The business is all right, I'm not complaining, but it isn't what it once was."

Rachel urgently wanted to explain to him in detail that it was possible to deceive your heart's love and also love him, to use him and lead him astray and yet want what is best for him. That's too complicated. It's impossible to convince him now, not when everything is so new to us. There will be time for this afterward, one day, when he sits in the kitchen as I slice the vegetables with my back to him and watch our son playing in the garden. Then I'll tell him everything, and he'll forgive me. He'll understand I had no choice.

"I never asked myself why you were doing this," he continued, his face turned away from her, "but I wondered where you were. Now and then I even searched for 'Rachel' on the Internet. Millions of possibilities. I don't know you, Rachel. I thought I knew you then, but I didn't realize there were two of you. Two Rachels talking to each other and nourishing each other. And one of them isn't on my side. Don't ask me what would have happened if you'd told me who you are."

"And now, when you know?"

He went on looking straight ahead, not at her. Her hand reached out for his hand, but he pulled it away.

"You deceived me," he said.

"I didn't deceive you in the most important thing of all," she said. "I loved you. I love you."

How is it possible to believe someone who has deceived you once? How can you be sure this time it's the truth? Only if you want to believe. That's the only way, and it's your responsibility. They sat in silence and they both knew that if they didn't touch at that moment, they would part forever.

"Come to me," she whispered. "Come to me now."

Rashid folded his arms on his chest.

"What are you afraid of? They'll see us? Let them. They'll arrest us? Let them. I want you."

"I don't want you, Rachel." His style of English suddenly sounded stilted, strange, and repellent, perhaps because she sensed what he was about to say. "It won't work. You're beautiful and free and you came here because it was what you wanted. But you forgot me. You never gave me a moment's thought. You do whatever you feel like doing. You never contacted me and asked me if this arrangement suited me. You didn't want to know how I was and what I was doing. You didn't even ask about my children. You're so sure that I'll fall in love with you again, that I'll leave everything behind just to be with you. That isn't the way it goes."

She wanted to say something, but he continued. "I've built myself another life. Not as good as I'd like it to be, but it's life. I have a family, Rachel. You want me to go to the village, sit my wife and children down, and tell them? What shall I tell them? I once had a love affair with a foreign woman, and she dumped me, and by the way, she was a spy?"

"But you have a new opportunity," she said, and her voice sounded hollow.

"I don't need any new opportunities. The time for that has gone. I didn't come to you. I'm not the one who's jumping back in time, to return to what used to be. I haven't forgotten anything, Rachel. I haven't forgotten, but I'm over it. And I want to carry on with my life. Fifteen years have passed. It's only in your mind that time has stopped moving. Before you arrived at the café I was thinking about a delivery that needs to clear customs, and about next year's school curriculum. I was living a normal life, Rachel, and that's fine by me. Sometimes I remember you. Angry with you, loving you, but it's all in the past.

And you turn up here and you want to take me to a place that doesn't exist anymore. A place I came out of, that I extinguished, buried, and turned into memory."

"And what's to become of me?" she asked. "Are you going to turn me in? Celebrate your exoneration? Get a medal for unmasking a spy? So they give you back your special rights?"

"No, Rachel. None of those things is going to happen. But for me this is over. It was over long ago."

She wanted to touch him. She thought if she touched him now as she had in the past, and he felt the warmth of her body, it would all come back to him. But he was so far away from her, although they were sitting side by side.

"And if we go to bed?" she asked.

"And if we go to bed?" he repeated her words, and there was no way of knowing what he was thinking. "Like a first love. Do you think that if we make love everything will be resolved?"

"So why did you bring me here with you?"

"Because I wanted to prove to myself that I'm capable of standing up to you," he replied, and she heard the triumphant tone in his voice. "Now I feel our account is settled. I hope I've been cured, and this is behind me."

"I know what I want," she said when the silence threatened to engulf her.

"I'm listening," he said.

"I want you to give us both another chance."

He didn't respond.

"Let's get out of here, Rashid. I'll go back to my hotel and you go back to your apartment, and I'll wait for you." She took the hotel's card from her handbag and pushed it into his hand, feeling his cold fingers. Her mind was racing ahead. The words didn't come out the way she intended. She knew she wanted to preserve these moments a little longer before it was too late, because the way back is always short and violent. These were just words, she knew, and she only had the power of words to persuade him, and the fact that she is sitting beside him, that he remembers her, that he told her he loved her once.

"I must get back," he said, and turned on the ignition and looked at her. In that fleeting moment it seemed to her that if she found the right thing to say or leaned her head toward him, the clock could still be turned back, but the moment passed and his body language was eloquent. Both hands clamped on the wheel, and eyes looking straight ahead. She didn't respond, and he put the car in gear and accelerated, leaving behind them a light dusty cloud.

CHAPTER FIFTEEN

∽

Out There

SHE WAS BUSY PACKING HER SUITCASE and did not hear the light knock on the door. Ehud knocked again, this time louder. He knew she was in there, and he only entered the building after the spotters had seen her car driving past the entrance of the hotel and parking down the road, at which point she walked up the hill and checked that none of the pedestrians or drivers heading her way was hiding his face from her. "She's still the professional she always was," the team commander whispered to Ehud before ordering him out of the van. Ehud tucked the earpiece in place, and asked the team commander if he hears him. "Don't worry," said the commander. "It's a brilliant system, the kind of thing television correspondents use. We hear everything that's said in the room, and we can relay instructions to you via a separate channel." He went through the operating instructions again and concluded: "Talk to her as if you're alone. We won't interfere, but if you need us, if something isn't right and you want us to go into emergency mode, say something about your father. And try not to forget to use the other codes."

Ehud nodded. He didn't remember all the details, but the principles hadn't changed. They were so clear it was painful: He goes into the room and talks to her. If she agrees to return with him the team will keep its distance and continue monitoring. If she refuses, she will be the responsibility of the team, leaving Ehud with nothing more to do than sit quietly and hope. Stefan was sitting behind him, and Ehud knew why they had picked two old-timers like them to send on this mission.

Joe wanted Stefan. The Unit commander told him times had changed, and there was a special team for this kind of assignment. "He's old, he doesn't even ride horses anymore." Joe insisted. His gut feeling was that the veteran Stefan was the best man for the job. "There's no choice," said Joe. "If Ehud doesn't succeed, she won't let anyone else get close to her. And if we need a quiet operation leaving no traces behind, something in her hotel room that will look like suicide, or a sexually motivated murder, or a robbery—only Stefan can do that. She knows him, she remembers him, he's cold and steady, and he'll succeed." So the summons went out to the kibbutz. It wasn't hard to locate him; even cowboys have cell phones these days.

"She's one of ours, Joe," said Stefan when the two of them were waiting for the Mossad chief, and with this he was saying it all. That it's inconceivable, that we don't kill one of our own. He stood up and went to stand by the window. Below, the city seethed, but the double-glazing shut out the sounds. Joe wanted the meeting to take place in the office of the Mossad chief and not in the training facility. "It will make the right impression on him."

The Mossad chief came in when Joe pressed a hidden button. Stefan stiffly stood at attention and blushed. He was a veteran, deco-rated combatant, but it had been a long time since he saw the Mossad chief. The chief was once a cadet in one of the courses he used to give and Stefan was never impressed by him.

"A loose cannon," said Joe. "She has to be stopped before it's too late." Then they brought in lunch, served on little trays from the local, and stringently vetted, Japanese takeout. The Mossad chief asked Stefan about his kids and the latest developments in kibbutz politics.

"So, I understand we have to do this," said Stefan. The Mossad chief just nodded. They carried on eating, the chopsticks disappearing in Stefan's large hands. The chief looked at his watch and Joe and Stefan went out into the blazing sunlight. The plants that the gardeners placed opposite the door so it could remain ajar were wilting, testifying that the saving of water was democratically assigned. The parking lot was almost empty. They crossed the broad open space and arrived at the armory. Stefan chose an automatic pistol with a silencer and signed for a box of bullets. From there they went to the range and Joe put on ear protectors and was amazed once again by the speed and accuracy of Stefan's target shooting.

"You know I slept with her once?" Stefan said to Joe as he methodically cleaned and reassembled his weapon.

"And . . . ?" asked Joe.

Stefan stared down at his boots and inspected his toe caps, as if about to kick a recalcitrant calf. "Nothing. That's all it was," he muttered, as if spitting out watermelon seeds. "Strange. I never thought anything like this would happen to me. But there is no choice, right?" He turned to Joe, who saw a look of entreaty in his eyes.

"No choice," said Joe, trying to sound confident.

⚘

RACHEL FASTENED HER DRESSING GOWN AND went to the door. "Oh, it's you," she said, and let Ehud in. "I wasn't expecting you, but now it's obvious you were going to turn up here." Ehud sat down heavily and she went back to sorting through her clothes, which were piled up on the bed. Through the gap between the curtains he could see the van and the command vehicle, out there in the dark. "I've come to talk to you," he said, "just to talk."

"About what, Ehud, about what? What do you want from me?" He said nothing and she carried on packing her case with her back turned to him. Her legs were more lovely than ever, and Ehud imagined the other contours of her body under the thick fabric. The commander whispered to him through the earphone, telling him to get moving. "There's no time for a heart-to-heart," he pressed him. "The morning flight leaves in a few hours, and there are other arrangements to be made."

Ehud assumed that Joe would have handled things differently. Joe would tell her to shape up and to stop acting like a crybaby, she's still a combatant and that's something you never get away from. There's no meaning to all the years that have passed, the sterile isolation that reality forced on you, love that went wrong. That's all garbage, he would say. You did what you had to do, you served the state, you didn't betray your friends, you did your job like we all did, and now it's time to come home. Carry on with your life without him. But he isn't Joe, and they sent him on this mission, as if he's the father of a wayward daughter and all he needs to do to bring her home is turn up in person and tell her he loves her.

And there was another thing. Of course there was. In this profession, and in the heart of the Arab capital, nothing could be left to chance. He knew her paths were blocked, and the other option of leaving her here was the worst of all. They had no problem locating Rashid and getting his address from his office. They would happily help anyone who wants to send him flowers. The two combatants who waited for him on the steps looked like any other Arab youths, loitering idly around the town. They saw him parking his car, and followed him into the elevator for the ride up to his apartment. "Make sure it looks like a botched robbery," the commander told them in the preliminary briefing, and they practiced both their knife skills and the art of ransacking a flat while leaving no trace. Rashid was trapped between them. They pinioned his arms and told him to stay quiet. Five minutes later they left the building by the stairs and crossed the street to the getaway car that awaited them. Ehud didn't know all the details. The commander, who was supervising both operations simultaneously, simply informed him that the secondary target had been neutralized, and it was up to him to decide whether to use this information.

"I came to ask you to come back with me. It isn't too late," said Ehud briefly, as if wrapping up the conversation, and she, without turning to him, said, "No," and went on folding her clothes together in the suitcase. "You know I can't allow you to stay here. It's impossible. It just isn't going to happen."

"What do you want?" she seethed. "That I just finish packing and come with you to the airport? And once again fly off on a little excursion, me and my uncle, and then we get to Israel and talk to whoever we need to talk to and I promise to be a good girl, is that it? Then I'll go back to my apartment and wait for the end that refuses to come, and forever know that it could have been different?" She turned her back to him again and considered the other possibilities. On the closet beside the bed there was a heavy ashtray. She examined it. She's forty-five, and Ehud twenty years older. She's stronger than he is, there's nothing he can do to stop her from escaping. "I'm not a businesswoman," she said, and to Ehud it seemed she was trying to stall for time, "but this doesn't look like a good deal to me. Think of something else, Ehud, something matching your talents." They were now on opposite sides of the barricade, and Ehud remembered the cuff link he had brought with him from the flat in Rehovot, and knew there was nothing to be gained by showing it to her now, and explaining to her it wasn't only the shirt that no longer existed.

In the war room they were getting impatient, and the team commander ordered Ehud to tell her about Rashid. He knew this wouldn't help, and Rachel would lose whatever faith in him she still had, realizing she had nothing left to bargain with, and so he remained silent. The war room was concerned about the silence and the team commander sent one of the combatants to the hotel lobby, to stand by and await developments that were getting more complicated due to the delay.

Ehud heard the change of plan in his earpiece, and had to struggle to control his reaction. He didn't know if Rachel noticed the clenching of his jaws. Back at the WR it was agreed there was now no prospect of Rachel returning willingly, and the commander told Ehud to go downstairs with her, and they would take care of the rest. "Get her outside, that's all you need to do. Suggest a walk, a breath of fresh air, anything; from the moment we have visual contact, it is our operation."

Rachel didn't say anything; neither did he. He wanted the voices prompting him to shut up, he wanted to tell Rachel things irrelevant to the war room, things that had built up in him over the years. He took out the earpiece. Rachel saw it. He threw it on the floor and crushed it with his heel. In the war room they knew something had happened and decided to wait a little longer before sending in Stefan and the team.

"Now it's just us." He tried to smile at her. "Just us?" she said, and reminded him of the team waiting downstairs, with their weapons, poised for a final showdown. She made no attempt to hide her bitterness. "We don't have much time," Ehud retorted, "you know the procedure as well as I do. There are some things that don't change over the years; it's just the technology that's more sophisticated. In a few minutes they'll be moving in, and there'll be no time for talking then." The urgency in his voice was genuine. Rachel, standing there facing him, she was genuine too. A few flecks of gray in her hair, a few more wrinkles on her cheeks, and weariness in her eyes, but it was still the same Rachel, the Rachel he had always loved. She gave him an appraising look too. He had aged and his back was stooped a bit, the bald patch had strengthened its hold, and the suit he picked from his closet for the operation was too small for him. But he was the same Ehud, the one she knew, the one who wanted what was best for her, on his own terms and according to the instructions he received. As always, a loyal soldier serving the state. She knew he couldn't give in to her. He could talk about his love, about things he'd kept hidden from her for years, but his loyalty was not to her. "I love you," he said into the silence that had widened between them. "Since the very beginning."

"But you lied to me," she said.

"Only when I had to."

"You all destroyed my life."

"Anything that can be destroyed can be rebuilt."

"Really?" She gave him a critical look, as if assessing him for the last time. "You're going to bring my father back to me? Give me the words I never said to him?"

"No," said Ehud.

"I found the letters," she said.

Ehud said nothing.

"I found other things too." Rachel was speaking in a low voice, in Hebrew, and Ehud could barely hear her. "He knew everything. I don't know how, but he knew everything. I found press clippings about our operations, even interviews with the chief of the Mossad, the Strauss investigation, and the leaks. You wrote to him and you didn't tell me."

"I wanted to protect you."

"Protect me? Who from? From my father? You wrote to him and told him the truth, and you told me to lie. You forced me to lie to my father, and you forced him to pretend he didn't know anything."

"You don't understand."

"I understand perfectly. You exploited me, and you made him turn his back on me and think he was doing me a favor. He knew I wasn't teaching English somewhere in Africa, and I was so angry with him all the time. He was looking out for me, and all those years I thought he wanted nothing to do with me."

"All this was before." Ehud was sure that if he let her carry on, he might yet succeed in changing her mind, as before. "So I came here for what is still possible, for what still remains."

She adjusted her robe and picked up the clothes she had prepared. "Give me a moment," she said, and turned toward the bathroom, with a sidelong glance at the ancient key, still there in the hotel door lock.

SHE WAS QUICKER AND MORE DETERMINED than him, that was all. When she came out, in baggy pants and a soft buttoned blouse, he was watching her and not her left hand. She whipped the key from the lock and before he had time to move from his chair, she was out of the door and locking it from the outside, leaving him trapped inside.

What was she planning? Where was she going? The questions were overshadowed by the urgent practical need to get out of there, at once. He moved to the window, discovered it was impossible to open, and was panicked to see the lights of the parked vehicles switching on, and the middle-aged couple hurriedly leaving the balcony of the adjacent hotel. Again he tried to open the door, without success. He pulled out his phone, and when the team commander answered, told him there was no choice and they must take the next step.

He phoned the concierge, promised him money if he came immediately, and had to wait two precious minutes before the door was opened from outside. The concierge took his twenty dollars and disappeared. Ehud didn't wait for the elevator but raced down the stairs from the third floor, gasping for breath.

He didn't hear the commander giving the final order, nor did he see the doctor in the backseat preparing the injection that would incapacitate Rachel. "An overdose, I'm afraid," the doctor will say when he stands with Rachel at the airport check-in, and the local authorities will be glad to have this problem off their hands and will let them board. A few hours later she'll be in Europe, and from there to home, for interrogation and whatever else awaits her.

The hour was late and the street almost empty. Rachel walked briskly. Even when it was all over Ehud didn't know what she was thinking. Perhaps she'd decided to go to Rashid's apartment, perhaps she just wanted to get away from Ehud and from any more conversation with him, or transfer to another hotel and cover her traces, or perhaps she had something completely different in mind. The team commander, ordering his driver to hit the road, wasn't interested in the possibilities. The phone conversation with Ehud was enough for him, and in front of him was a moving target who needed to be overtaken, grabbed quickly before she had time to react, bundled into the car, overpowered with the help of the combatant sitting in the backseat—and then the doctor could do his job. One injection, and she's theirs.

He knew it was too late to drive slowly to approach her, and it would be dangerous to get out and pursue her on foot. She's on the run, and if she spots them she could dodge into one of the hotels on the avenue, and there will be nothing they can do about it. All that's left is the fast and aggressive option. He unfastened his seat belt, as did the combatant behind him. The driver engaged a lower gear and picked up speed to catch up with Rachel, then stopped with full brakes to startle her so that the commander and the combatant could get out and overpower her.

The driver said later, in the course of the inquiry, he saw Rachel turn back toward them, as if she heard the sound of the engine. He also said that although his attention was focused on the road and the light traffic and the single vehicle he needed to overtake, he saw her quickening her pace, and then for some obscure reason she went off the sidewalk and into the street and broke into a run. The team commander said the same thing. As for the other details, there was no difference of opinion.

The driver accelerated, passed the vehicle that was holding him up, and bore down on Rachel at speed, engine roaring under the strain, as she ran down the road with a lightness they all remembered. She didn't stop, and someone said she even ran faster. When she suddenly veered into the middle of the road and started crossing to the other side, it was too late to stop. The heavy Toyota Land Cruiser hit Rachel and tossed her to the side of the road like a rag doll (in the words of the driver, subsequently cleared of any blame), and her head struck a lamppost. They stopped beside her only for a moment, as they did in exercises back home, just long enough for the doctor to put two fingers to her carotid artery and return to the car without a word. They weren't allowed any association with bodies, and there was no point anyway. Corpses can't talk. The car roared off.

Another hit-and-run. Who cares if a tourist gets killed crossing a dangerous road?

Ehud arrived too late. The text that he received was unequivocal: Get out at once. He didn't do this, and he refused to explain his motives when he was back at home, after making arrangements—breaking every rule in the book—to have Rachel flown to Europe and buried beside her mother, in London.

All this came later.

Now he was just in time to see the vehicle receding as per the operational instructions and the backup car doing a U-turn. They signaled to him to climb aboard and he waved them on. Knowing the chain of command and knowing they weren't allowed to wait around, they drove away.

Ehud stopped running; there was no need to hurry now, Rachel lay inert in the road like a knife whose blade is almost returned to its place. A small crowd began to gather and he heard the sound of an ambulance approaching.

He knelt down beside Rachel and took her body in his arms. He looked into her face and into her eyes, green and wide open. Suddenly she moved (later they told him this was a common phenomenon) and the expression on her face changed, as if she were waiting for something. And he saw a smile, or perhaps he only imagined it.